Praise for
Stewart's Incredible Machine

"One of the best books I've ever read!"
— Cam, 14

"I liked this book so much, I've read it three times! When will there be a sequel?"
— Cal, 12

"A very enjoyable book!"
— Kathy, mother of three

STEWART'S INCREDIBLE MACHINE

Upcoming Book

Stewart's Unbelievable Adventure

STEWART'S INCREDIBLE MACHINE

Richard Sotiros

Stewart's Incredible Machine
Copyright © 2020 by Richard Sotiros

Published by

3 WOMBATS
PUBLISHING

Lakewood, Colorado
www.3WombatsPublishing.com

Book cover design by Elena V Miller
Book interior layout by YellowStudios

ISBN: 978-1-7328456-0-2
Library of Congress Control Number: 2018913776

First Edition

Printed in the United States of America

*This book is dedicated to those who have
suffered at the hands of bullies. The power to overcome
the pain and find joy in life is within you. Always believe
in yourself and never give up.*

Acknowledgements

Many thanks to Lauren Harvey and Blake Christiansen for your valuable editing contributions. Thank you to my family for their input after reading various drafts of the story as well as their continuous encouragement. To my childhood teachers, words cannot fully express my appreciation for all that you did for me. A big shout-out to Tim Dyer whose effort in writing *Wavemaker* inspired me to finally sit down and write this story. And thank you to my wonderful wife Polly, and children Haley and Christopher, for all of the joy you bring to my life.

Contents

01. RADIO SILENCE   1

02. LUNCH MONEY   17

03. ROPE CLIMBING   31

04. THE TEST   45

05. RECOVERY   61

06. NEIGHBORS   75

07. TO THE RESCUE   92

08. HALLOWEEN   106

09. THE MAKING OF A MACHINE   126

10. EXPERIMENTS   137

11. IMAGES   153

12. DISCOVERY   170

13. SAY CHEESE   185

14. REVENGE   200

15. THE DANCE   214

16. REDEMPTION   231

17. ACTIONS AND CONSEQUENCES   248

EPILOGUE   266

ABOUT THE AUTHOR   269

01

RADIO SILENCE

SEATED AT THE DESK in his bedroom, thirteen-year-old Stewart Camby's fingers darted over the keyboard with the staccato precision of an expert tap dancer. From the moment he received his first computer as a present from his parents on his fifth birthday, Stewart had spent countless hours playing games, and typing on a keyboard was as second nature to him as tying his shoe. The brightly-colored images on the monitor mesmerized him at first, and the increasing complexity of the games appealed to his keen mind. As he became more and more proficient with the games, he also learned how computers operated and how to repair them. Word of his talent spread among his classmates and he found their mothers were more than happy to pay him to fix their children's various hardware and software problems. This extra income came in handy, as he was always buying new parts to update his computer and keep up with the constant changes in technology.

Beside his desk was a cabinet containing shortwave radio equipment, given to him by Grandpa Frank, his maternal grandfather. Grandpa Frank wanted to share his passion for shortwave radio with his grandson and taught him how to use it when Stewart visited during summer vacations. Although shortwave radio wasn't as popular as when his grandfather was a boy, there were still enough people operating the equipment and willing to communicate. Stewart's favorite memories of summer were the days he spent with Grandpa Frank on the radio and talking to people around the country and in other parts of the world. With his grandfather's encouragement, Stewart studied and passed all of the licensing exams required to make legal transmissions and became one of the youngest people ever to receive a license at the highest level.

As fun as it was to talk to other people, he realized most everyone he spoke to was a lot older and didn't have much in common with him. One night while looking at the stars, so numerous that clusters of them took on the appearance of twinkling clouds, he wondered about other life forms in the universe. With his love for outer space, he decided to put all of his efforts from then on into seeing if he could contact aliens.

Stewart reached over to the dial on his radio and adjusted the setting. His hands shifted to the keyboard and he typed in the new frequency. Peering at his monitor, he glanced at the log of dates, times, and frequencies filling the screen. He adjusted his headset and cleared his throat. "This is Starhawk Ranger of Mother Earth. Does anyone read me?" A minute went by. Silence. "This is Starhawk Ranger of Mother Earth. Does anyone read me?" Stewart ran his fingers through his light-brown hair. Another minute passed. "This is Starhawk Ranger of Mother Earth. Does anyone read me?" A crackling noise came over his headset. Stewart pressed the headset over his ear. More crackling noise. Stewart felt his heart beating faster. "Hello! Is anyone out there?" The crackling grew louder and louder. The crackling stopped.

"Alaska Twenty-Two do you read me?" uttered a faint voice.

"No!" Stewart yelled as he threw off his headset and covered his head as he slumped in his chair.

"Honey, breakfast is ready!" a pleasant, female voice shouted from just outside his partially closed door.

Startled, he jumped out of his chair. "Mom!" blurted Stewart. "Don't do that!"

"Do what?" asked his mother, Nora, as she leaned into the room. "Please eat before your food gets cold."

"Okay." Stewart pushed back his chair and followed his mom down the stairs. His nose caught a whiff of something wonderful. Fresh and sweet, just like a bakery.

Stewart looked at Nora with a large smile. "Cinnamon rolls? Yes!" Nora smiled back at him, pleased with his reaction. Stewart dashed past Nora and into the kitchen. He saw a batch sitting on a cooling tray and went right over to them. Leaning over the tray, he closed his eyes, and slowly inhaled, the magical aroma of freshly baked cinnamon rolls causing his senses to tingle with joy.

"I could smell this forever!" proclaimed Stewart.

Nora immediately handed a plate to him as he reached for a roll. "Take this and please sit down," she ordered. "I'll get the rest of your breakfast."

Stewart made his way to the table, happily enjoying every bite of his mother's culinary masterpiece. He glanced at the empty chair at the head of the table.

"Is Dad ever going to be here for breakfast?" Stewart mumbled between bites. Nora turned from the stove with a plate filled with an omelet, bacon, and hash browns.

"He's very busy right now, Honey." She set the plate in front of Stewart, who grabbed the salt and pepper and shook them vigorously over his omelet.

"He's always busy," Stewart responded dejectedly.

Nora sighed. "I know."

While Stewart devoured the omelet, she noticed his pants were getting tight and his stomach hung over his belt, a sign to most people that he had reached the pudgy category. She liked to tell herself he was only carrying a little baby fat and that he would grow out of it, so not to worry. Although she wouldn't admit it, she had eaten a few too many of her delicious baked goodies and the pounds were adding up with her as well. Every time she began thinking about her physical shape, her thoughts quickly turned to her next baking mission. A perfect day to make chocolate chip cookies she thought to herself, which should occupy the afternoon and make one boy very, very happy.

- - - -

Nora and Stewart climbed into their new sedan, a white, luxury model. Stewart dropped his backpack full of textbooks on the floor and fastened the seat belt. Nora started the car and backed down the long driveway past the flowers, nicely pruned bushes, and lights that illuminated the driveway at night. The Cambys lived in a neighborhood of large homes with beautifully landscaped yards and numerous trees. This was the only house where Stewart had ever lived and he couldn't imagine living anywhere else.

Across the street and down one house was a beautiful two-story brick home that had a "For Sale" sign in the front yard. An older, well-dressed lady with perfectly coiffed hair, and a couple around Nora's age, stepped out of a black car parked in the driveway and headed towards the house. The older lady took out her keys and opened the door. In a grand sweeping motion, she gestured for the couple to enter the house and followed them inside.

"It sure would be nice if the Rogers' house sold soon," said Nora, as she slightly accelerated the car. "I hope whoever buys the house has children. Don't you?"

"I guess so," was all Stewart could say. He really didn't care if the new neighbors had any children. He already had friends at school and the kid living closest to him was a fourth-grade brat named Zack, who always seemed to be riding his bicycle. Every time he saw Stewart walking down the street, Zack would pedal just close enough to remain at a safe distance, and taunt Stewart by calling him various names such as "Fatso," "Blubber Boy," or "Chubmeister." No, Stewart didn't really care if any more kids moved into the neighborhood.

Slowing down as they approached the school on this sunny morning in mid-October, Nora pulled into the turn lane and waited in a small line of cars. The school was a fairly new brick building with stylish metal trim. It was surrounded by a green lawn and contained small, young trees planted in clusters at the ends of the yard. The sign in front of the school next to the flagpole located in the center of the property read "Thomas Jefferson Middle School." Finally, at the front of the line, Nora turned into the school parking lot and stopped. Stewart reached down for his backpack and instrument case.

Nora ran her hand through Stewart's hair and tried to push a few stubborn clumps to the side where they belonged. Stewart gently pulled his head away from the comb of mom fingers and opened the door.

"Have a nice day, sweetie," she said.

"You, too," replied Stewart, as he got out of the car and headed for the entrance. Nora watched him take a few steps, then drove out of the parking lot.

Stewart walked a little further down the sidewalk toward the front entrance and stopped dead in his tracks. The hair on his arms stood up straight as if he had walked right into a freezer. Leaning against the wall by the door stood Raymond Burns and his two henchmen, Damon and Willie. Raymond happened to be the biggest and baddest boy in the school, with a large muscular frame, piercing eyes that could take on the look of a wild, crazed person in an instant, and an unruly mop of dark-brown hair that appeared to have never been combed. Damon and Willie were the second and third biggest and baddest boys in the school, with equally messy hair. To Stewart, Damon seemed to have far too many teeth in his head and they were always visible, as he constantly laughed at anything Raymond said to him. Willie had begun sprouting hair in patches on the lower half of his face and either didn't notice them or had sworn an oath to avoid a razor at all costs. Stewart was convinced they had all been held back at least two grades and were lying about their age. How else could they be so much larger than everyone else? Based on his always unpleasant interactions with them, he was certain they weren't very bright, supporting his theory that they were held back. He liked to think they were the human version of dinosaurs – large bodies with tiny brains. Stewart wanted to ask them if their brains were larger than a walnut or even larger than half a peanut and decided it wouldn't be a good idea if he wanted to avoid having his underwear yanked over his head. His last atomic wedgie at the hands of Raymond was enough to last a lifetime.

Going through the main entrance would be foolish with Raymond, Damon, and Willie forming a blockade through which all students had to pass. They stuck out their legs as various boys walked by and managed to make them stumble as they entered the building. Raymond kicked one poor boy in his rear end as he tried to crawl past them after falling to the ground, causing Damon and Willie to burst into laughter. When a cute girl went by, they instantly transformed themselves into gentlemen, opening the door and bowing as the girl entered the school. They closed the doors behind her and resumed their places, ready to harass the next male student.

With little time to get to class before the bell rang, Stewart swung his head around, looking for alternative entrances. He glanced at the doors on the side of the building and walked toward them. All students were supposed to enter through the front doors, but he did not want to deal with Raymond and his gang of thugs. Getting in trouble for going through the side doors would be worth it.

Stewart reached for the door and pulled. It was locked. He headed for the other door further down the side of the building and pulled on the handle. It was also locked. Time was getting short, and Stewart realized he would have to go back to the front of the building and face Raymond. Just as he turned to go, the door opened and a janitor emerged, his arms full of boxes. Stewart instinctively grabbed the opened door and held it for the janitor.

"Thanks," said the janitor, making his way to the dumpster.

"You're welcome," replied Stewart, as he slipped inside the building, the door closing firmly behind him.

Stewart rushed down the hallway as the door closed shut. He weaved through the students heading towards him as they filed into the classrooms lining the hall. Unfortunately for him, the door he used to enter the building was on the opposite side of the building from where his first class was located. He made his way through the crowd, hoping there would be enough time to get to his math class. The school had a policy of calling the parents for every absence and tardy, and he didn't want his mother to have to deal with such a call. He was proud he was a good student, which to him meant getting good grades and not being late or missing class, unless there was a good reason.

Realizing he had quite a way to go, he started walking as fast as he could. Suddenly, after a couple of steps, Stewart started sliding, feeling as if he had walked onto a floor covered with banana peels. Losing control, he flailed his arms faster than a pinwheel with exploding pop bottle rockets attached to the tips, his legs sliding every which way. Falling to his knees, he looked at the other kids, who were walking without any problems. What was going on here? Didn't this only happen to cartoon characters? He ran his hand over the floor and felt the slick surface. The janitor sure does a good job of waxing the floor, he observed. From now on, he was going to wear tennis shoes, not these darn loafers his mom thought made him look fashionable. Carefully standing on both feet, Stewart slowly began to shuffle forward at the speed of an inmate with shackles on his legs. Shuffling seemed to work and he ignored the looks from the other kids as he made steady progress. He reached the end of the hallway, turned, and entered the main hall. Reaching another hall, he turned and headed down the corridor that would take him to his class at the far end of that section of the building.

He looked ahead and screeched to a halt, not believing his eyes. Raymond, Damon, and Willie stood in front of the door to his class and were talking to Sofie Lindstrom. With her long, blonde hair and elegant grace, Stewart believed she was the most beautiful girl to ever exist since the dawn of man. Hoping Sofie would distract Raymond, Stewart concentrated on becoming invisible so he could stroll past them undetected.

Stewart had only taken a couple of steps when, much to his horror, Sofie waved goodbye and stepped into the classroom. Raymond, Damon, and Willie turned and headed towards Stewart, who frantically tried to think of an escape. There was nowhere to go and nowhere to hide. Stewart decided his only chance would be to lower his head and avoid making eye contact as he passed by.

Spotting Stewart, Raymond walked straight towards him, while grinning slyly at Damon and Willie. Raymond pretended to stumble as he approached Stewart and slammed him forcefully into the lockers.

"Hey, watch where you're going you fat pig!" sneered Raymond. He stepped on Stewart as he walked over him and continued down the hall. Damon and Willie also stepped on Stewart and laughed at him as he lay in a crumpled heap on the floor.

Stewart gasped for air, the wind knocked out of him. He climbed to his knees and sunk back on his heels, his ribs aching as he struggled to breathe. The bell rang loudly, indicating the start of class. With a determined effort, Stewart rolled to his knees and forced himself to slowly stand on his feet. Hunched over, he made his way into his classroom while taking short, painful breaths.

Going to his assigned desk directly behind Sofie, Stewart took off his backpack and tenderly sat down. Though his chest throbbed, he was relieved that his breathing was returning to normal. He was also relieved to see that his teacher, Mr. Leiker, was busy looking at the textbook and didn't seem to notice he was slightly late to class. Stewart's friends around the room looked at him with puzzled expressions on their faces, wondering what was going on with him.

In the front row to the left was Dino Petropoulos. Dino wasn't very tall, but what he lacked in physical stature, he more than made up for with a surprising amount of confidence. His full name was Constandinos Eleftherios Petropoulos and he was immensely proud of his Spartan heritage. As early as kindergarten, Dino stubbornly refused to let teachers or anyone else mangle his first and last names. Despite the shortened version of his first name, he couldn't believe anyone could mispronounce 'Dino' and resigned himself when meeting someone new, to saying his name slowly as "Dee-no."

Behind Dino was Ethan Jenkins, who carefully wiped his glasses on his shirt. Ethan stood just a few inches below six feet and may have weighed a little over one hundred pounds after a huge dinner. He was constantly teased for being skinny, and his height only enhanced his appearance of being skinny. Having once read that stripes could alter a person's appearance, he insisted on wearing shirts with horizontal stripes, convinced it made him look shorter and thicker. His identical twin Nathan, also wearing a shirt with horizontal stripes, sat diagonally across the room in the last seat.

Mr. Leiker, like the other teachers, believed it wasn't a good idea to have the twins sit near each other for fear they had developed a superior method of communicating and would cheat, even if unintentionally. The school had three levels for certain classes, and Stewart, Dino, and the twins were in the top level of these classes, with the twins always placed on the opposite sides of every class. Ethan and Nathan were unique in that their fingerprints were almost perfectly identical, unheard of even among identical twins. Only a top fingerprint expert could detect a difference in their fingerprints. This was a true genetic feat that had been published in medical journals and all of the teachers were aware of this fact.

Stewart unzipped his backpack and removed a textbook and spiral notebook. He placed the backpack under his seat and as he reached for his textbook, Sofie ran her hand through her hair and knocked a hair clip loose, causing it to fall onto Stewart's desk. He stared at it as if a diamond had fallen from the sky. Sofie turned around and picked up the hair clip.

"Sorry about that," she said with a smile so gorgeous, Stewart expected the room to become instantly filled with sparkling light.

Stewart opened his mouth to speak and was unable to utter a sound. Instantly, the blood in his temples pounded his head and he broke out into a small sweat. Managing a small nod, he opened his textbook and pretended to read as Sofie turned back around. Within moments, Stewart saw that his book was upside down and promptly turned it right-side up. He buried his head in the pages, hoping no one was paying attention to him.

Mr. Leiker, a thin man who wore a clip-on tie with a vest every day, stood up from his desk and cleared his throat as he looked at the class. "Open your books to chapter three." Everyone in the class followed his instructions and as Stewart thumbed through the pages, Sofie reached back, pulled her hair, and tossed it behind the seat, barely touching the edge of Stewart's desk. He stared at her blonde locks cascading over her shoulders and immediately became unaware of everything else around him. Mr. Leiker's voice sounded like he was talking underwater and frankly, Stewart didn't care what he was talking about. All he could think about was Sofie's hair. And Helen of Troy. Did Helen have long, golden hair like Sofie? And blue eyes? She must have, or how else could her face have launched a thousand ships? If Helen's face could launch a thousand ships, how many could Sofie's face launch? One thousand? One thousand five-hundred? This was a great question, he reasoned, because Sofie was Scandinavian and the Vikings had been just as fierce as the ancient Greeks. The Vikings definitely would have sent at least a thousand ships.

Stewart stood in a line with other boys, wearing the standard school gym shirt and shorts. The boys were lined up in alphabetical order based on last names, making it easier for the teacher to take attendance. What made it horrible for him was that Raymond, who he was still angry with for slamming him into the lockers, was right next to him near the front of the line. Why couldn't Raymond's last name have been Zyzinski? He would then be standing at the end of the line, far away from Stewart, who always had to be ready for Raymond and his sneaky elbow to the ribs or finger flick to the back of the ears when the teacher wasn't looking.

Not only did he have Raymond standing next to him, P.E. was the class he dreaded most. He was not athletic and knew that no matter how hard he tried, he would not get an A. His parents understood that P.E. would be the only time when he didn't get the highest grades and wanted him to try his best and certainly not fail. Last year, Mr. Pike, the P.E. teacher, told him he couldn't believe someone could be so nonathletic and that the best grade he would ever get in his class would be a C. Minus.

Mr. Pike strolled out of the locker room holding a clipboard and carrying a bag of footballs. His hair was cut in a version of a modern mullet, short on the sides and longer in the back. The gold chain he wore around his neck stood out due to his perpetual tan. His shirt was tight and barely contained his thick barrel chest and arms bulging with muscles. Mr. Pike was definitely proud of his looks as he strutted towards the boys. When he reached them, he stopped, set down the bag, and began reading last names from the clipboard. Each boy answered "Here," as his name was read. Stewart always felt like Mr. Pike's inflection changed when his name was read, almost like spitting out the word "Camby" or turning it into two words like "Cam Bee." Mr. Pike finished taking attendance and gestured to the door. "Everybody outside! Two laps, then go to the middle of the football field." The boys sprinted for the door with Stewart behind the group. Picking up the bag of balls, Mr. Pike glanced at his watch as he followed them outside.

With Raymond leading the way, the boys eagerly ran to the track surrounding the football field. Following the boys, Mr. Pike looked over at the teacher's parking lot just outside of the gym door. He stopped to admire his brand new, gleaming red truck. To avoid anyone parking close to him, Mr. Pike always parked in the middle of two spaces furthest away from the other cars. Nothing made him angrier than someone parking too close and hitting his vehicle when they opened their doors.

Mr. Pike arrived at the track and stepped onto it as a group of boys approached, forcing them to swerve to avoid hitting him. He could have waited for the group to pass by, but this way, he could show them all he was clearly in charge. What was amazing is that he did this all the time without really thinking about it, as if constantly putting people in uncomfortable situations was normal behavior. He stepped onto the football field inside of the track oval, dropped the bag of balls, and watched the boys run around the track. Raymond was in a group of six boys leading the way. The usual six boys, observed Mr. Pike. Those boys were leaner with better natural endurance and he knew the hulking Raymond would not be able to stay with them on the last lap despite Raymond's fighting spirit that made him hate losing anything to anybody. He loved Raymond's competitive spirit, which Mr. Pike believed would come in handy when Raymond went to high school the next year. He considered Raymond to be a beast at linebacker, the same position he played in college. Raymond would get the best coaching, because he, Tony Pike, was the linebacker's coach at West Lakewood high school. He was going to see to it that Raymond would go further than he did, barring any injuries.

In Mr. Pike's first game of his senior season in college, he burst through a gap in the line and grabbed the running back behind the line of scrimmage for a large loss, only to have a group of linemen fall back on his leg. He heard popping all around his knee as his leg twisted awkwardly beneath him and felt an unfamiliar wave of intense pain. The team doctors hovered over him and while they assessed his injury, all he could think of was that his career was over. Despite working like a man possessed while rehabbing his knee, he never regained his speed and agility, and wasn't able to return to a level that might have resulted in an invitation to try out for a professional team. With his dreams of playing professional football crushed, he finished getting his degree in physical education and got the job at this middle school. It's a start he decided and after a few years, he would look for an opening at a high school, preferably West Lakewood, which had a very good football program and whose coaches he had already worked with for a couple of seasons. Yes, a high school position would be a step up not only in pay, he would be teaching kids that signed up for the course because they wanted to, not because they had to, such as in middle school.

The school district insisted that physical education was mandatory through eighth grade. Mr. Pike's conclusion about this policy was that the school district must not care if the student's health deteriorated after eighth grade. In a way, the policy was all right with him. He didn't want to teach nonathletic kids, especially the kind like that worthless Stewart Camby who might be the only student in the school without a fiber of athleticism in his body. Even those dopey, skinny Jenkins twins in the next class could at least run in the middle of the pack. Not Stewart Camby. As the boys finished their laps and gathered around him, he ordered them to stretch while he waited for Stewart to finish, one more lap to go. Seeing Stewart chug around the track always made him irritable. Mr. Pike hated being at the mercy of waiting for Stewart and he didn't want to give Stewart a break by making him run one lap less than the others. Why couldn't this kid lay off of the doughnuts and pizza?

"Listen up. Put on the flags," shouted Mr. Pike as he dumped footballs out of the bag. "Same teams as last class." Each boy fastened a belt of two red flags around their waists and headed towards various ends of the field. With large classes, Mr. Pike had to divide the boys into four teams and play sideways on half of the field. He wanted to get the boys moving because once they started standing around, they became more restless by the second and harder to control. Mr. Pike glanced at his watch as Stewart, his face bright red and gasping for breath, finally approached the finish line.

"Camby, people in a coma run faster than you!" barked Mr. Pike, pointing at his watch. "Put on your flag and find your team. Hurry up, the class is half over." Stewart quickly put on his flag and jogged to the closest team. As he joined the huddle, he realized it was the wrong team. He looked around the field, saw his team and headed over to them. Mr. Pike put his hand on his forehead as he watched Stewart run around the field. High school has got to be better than this.

- - - -

Mr. Pike reclined in his chair in his office. He watched the last of the boys file out of the locker room after getting dressed. Stepping out of his office, he quickly strolled past the bay of lockers. All of the boys had left the locker room. Hustling back to his office, he closed the door and pulled a cell phone out of his pocket as he sat down. He punched in a number and waited as the phone rang. A raspy voice answered.

"Yeah?" said the voice.

"It's T-Rex," said Mr. Pike.

"Who do you got?" said the voice.

"I'll take Denver, New York, Dallas, and San Francisco," replied Mr. Pike. "No change," Mr. Pike continued and ended the call, slipping his cell phone back in his pocket. He felt good about his picks, for he was on quite a roll this football season. He was on such a roll in fact, that he no longer felt nervous about the amount of his bet for each game. Who knew football like he did? His recent streak was so good that it bought him that shiny red truck in the parking lot. If he kept this up, he figured he might not have to worry about getting a job at the high school. He would be able to support himself betting on games. A couple thousand dollars a week during football season would be a good living, especially if it meant not having to yell at soft kids like Stewart Camby.

02

LUNCH MONEY

CARRYING A PICNIC BASKET, Nora entered the upscale lobby of the modern skyscraper in downtown Denver where her husband Byron had an office on the 51st floor. She pushed the button and admired the painting on the wall while she waited. The elevator door opened and as the people stepped out, Nora moved to the side. Two other elevators, also full of people, reached the lobby and opened their doors. Nora was instantly engulfed in a swarm of humanity, all eager to get out of the building and begin their lunch hour. She reminded herself to pay better attention to the clock at home and leave five minutes earlier to avoid the crowds. Stepping into the now empty elevator, the doors closed behind her.

The elevator reached the 51st floor and Nora walked to a suite with a sign that read: Williams and Camby, P.C., Certified Public Accountants. She entered the office and walked over to Bernice "Bernie" Shaw, who served as the efficient receptionist and office manager. Bernie had just put on her sweater and picked up her purse.

"Hello, Bernie. How are you doing?" asked Nora.

"Doing well, thanks. Off to run errands," answered Bernie as she headed for the door. "Have a nice lunch, you two."

"Thank you," Nora replied as she moved past the reception area and to the hall. She walked down the short hallway and entered Byron's office.

Byron peered at the image on the screen of his computer monitor, picked up a pen, and wrote down a few notes on a yellow legal pad. He was in the middle of analyzing a tax case involving corporate mergers to see how the ruling in that case may benefit his client's situation. Byron was a Certified Public Accountant with a Master's degree in Taxation and had earned a reputation as one of the top tax strategists in the country. He had a gift for remembering everything he read and could instantly recall information that applied to the immediate issue.

His office was spacious with a beautiful view of the Rocky Mountains. Behind his desk stood a credenza stacked with files of paperwork. A framed picture of Byron, Nora, and Stewart as a toddler faced sideways, stuck between two files, a victim of limited space. There wasn't room anywhere else in his office for this picture because every surface was covered with file folders and tax research books.

Glancing up from the screen, Byron smiled at Nora. "Hello, dear."

"Hi, Honey," she responded, walking to the coffee table. Setting down the picnic basket, she carefully moved the files, placing them on the floor in their exact order. She opened the picnic basket, took out a small white cloth and spread it over the coffee table. Removing plates, silverware, and containers of

Byron's favorite food from the basket, Nora arranged everything in perfect order.

While Nora set up the table, Byron finished making notes, satisfied with reaching a good stopping point. He stood up from his desk and sat in the chair across from Nora. She handed him a large cloth napkin and he tucked it into his collar so it covered his shirt. Byron felt like he was wearing a bib but after spilling food a few too many times on his nice silk ties and shirts, Nora put her foot down and insisted he cover himself with a napkin.

They cherished their frequent lunches, for this was their best opportunity to spend time during the day together. As word got around of Byron's talent, more and more people requested his services and being the workaholic that he was, Byron increased the amount of time spent at the office to accommodate their needs. It was easy for him to become so focused on a project, he would lose track of time and forget to eat. By coming to the office, Nora made sure he ate at least one decent meal.

The cafeteria at lunchtime was full of students excitedly chatting while enjoying their temporary freedom. Stewart emerged from the food line holding his tray and headed over to a table near the corner. Everyone had their usual spot to eat and the table near the corner was the spot for Stewart and his friends. This particular table was chosen by Stewart, because it was next to the table where Sofie and her friends, Linh Tran and Debbie Sanders, ate their lunch. Stewart slid into the seat next to Dino, making sure he sat facing Sofie, though she usually had her back to their table. He didn't mind gazing at the back of her head, because facing her might mean making eye contact and would immediately lead to the sensation of the numbing drug procaine being injected into his face. This feeling wasn't welcome as it became nearly impossible to chew and swallow any kind of food.

Stewart turned his attention to Dino, who was in a heated discussion with Ethan and Nathan.

"What are you guys arguing about?" asked Stewart, picking up his fork.

Frustrated, Dino threw up his hands. "They think a Romatron is the GREATEST game character EVER."

"No question about it," said Ethan trying to conceal a smile. Stewart sighed as he glanced at Nathan who had the exact same expression on his face. He knew the twins loved to bait Dino into these nonsensical arguments. If Dino didn't agree with something, he would argue it to the death, his voice rising with every sentence, and certain words taking on greater importance. This was a major source of amusement for the twins.

"Okay," said Dino triumphantly. "The next time we play Age of Romans, YOU take a Romatron. I'll go with the CENTURION!"

"Good," Ethan confidently replied. "You won't stand a chance." Dino felt his blood boiling and instead of yelling at them, chose to take a vicious bite of his apple and stare at the twins, while shaking his head.

Stewart heard a loud giggle a couple of tables away and turned his head to the source. Brittany Robertson, Shelby Daniels, and Courtney Sanford, wearing trendy, fashionable clothes and sporting similar hairstyles, were having a conversation about Sofie, Linh, and Debbie. He watched Brittany lean towards Shelby and Courtney, and whisper to them. Giggling, the girls would turn in their seats, and shoot glances over at Sofie and her friends. Brittany, in the boys' informal rankings, was the most attractive girl in the school after Sofie, with Shelby and Courtney coming in at numbers three and four. Stewart refused to include them in the rankings, as he thought Brittany and her friends were mean girls who enjoyed nothing more than making fun of others, especially Sofie. He knew that Brittany possessed a world-class sharp tongue and woe to the person she decided to use it against. This was a lesson he had learned as a victim of her wrath on a number of occasions through the years. If Brittany's tongue were a blade, he was positive she would be able to use it to cut through ten feet of steel surrounding a bank vault. Brittany, Shelby, and Courtney came from well-to-do families and they all lived in the same part of town as Stewart. He started kindergarten with all three of them and had endured their behavior for far too long.

Sofie heard one of their outbursts of laughter and glanced towards them. Shelby and Courtney quickly looked away from Sofie while Brittany held her glance for a moment, then looked away. Sofie looked over at Linh and Debbie, shrugged her shoulders, and resumed talking to them. She is a truly special human being, marveled Stewart, observing Sofie interact with her friends. Was she bulletproof from mean comments, Stewart wondered, or was she unaware that the Princesses of Pain, or the POP Sisters, as Stewart liked to call them, made her the butt of their jokes? No matter what, her radiant glow never seemed to waver under any circumstances, a feat Stewart compared to the wonders of the aurora borealis.

Dino jumped to his feet with his tray and motioned to the clock. "You guys ready?" As they stood up, the bell rang and the rest of the students headed for the trash cans and tray racks. They had ten minutes to get to the next class and wanted to get out of there before the next wave of students made their way to the cafeteria. Depositing their trays on the racks and milk cartons in the trash, they walked through the doors just as Raymond, Damon, and Willie approached.

Panic crossed the faces of Stewart and his friends. He glanced around and saw that there weren't any teachers in this area of the hall. They braced themselves as Raymond, Damon, and Willie stood shoulder to shoulder and herded them behind a row of lockers just off of the hallway.

"Hey, it's the geek club," smirked Raymond. On cue, Damon and Willie laughed as Stewart quickly estimated at least 50 teeth in Damon's mouth. Raymond's face hardened as he put out his hand and stared at Stewart, then Dino, then the twins. "Hand it over," he sternly ordered. Stewart pulled out a couple of wrinkled dollar bills and a handful of change from his pocket. The twins also retrieved a few handfuls of change and handed it over to Raymond. He moved over to Dino and stuck out his hand. Dino didn't move a muscle. Stewart felt his knees growing weak. Though Dino was a head shorter and fifty pounds lighter, Stewart knew that he would not back down from Raymond. Even with the heart of a lion, Dino could never win this confrontation. Stewart glanced towards the hall, hoping he could step out from the lockers and flag down a teacher, students, anybody. He quickly realized he wasn't going anywhere with Damon and Willie blocking the opening to the hall.

Dino stood straight and looked up at Raymond. "I don't have any money," Dino admitted. Raymond's eyes narrowed.

"Pull out your pockets," commanded Raymond. Dino grudgingly pulled out his front pockets to show they were empty. "Turn around." Dino obeyed and Raymond thrust his hands in his back pockets and pulled them out, empty-handed. Dino turned back to face Raymond.

Raymond poked a finger in his chest. "Next time you better have something for me." He motioned at Damon and Willie, and as they began to leave, Raymond stepped sideways and threw his shoulder into Nathan, slamming him into the lockers. Laughing, Raymond, Damon, and Willie disappeared around the corner.

Ethan turned to Nathan, grimacing as he painfully rubbed his shoulder. "You okay?" he asked expectantly.

Nathan moved his left arm in circles while he rubbed his shoulder with his right hand. "I'm fine," he said through clenched teeth.

"Those guys are the biggest JERKS in the world," declared Dino. "Someday, they're going to get it." He stormed down the hall with Ethan and Nathan following in his wake.

Trudging behind them, Stewart felt badly for Dino. Dino's family didn't seem to have extra money, just enough to get by each month. His parents emigrated from Greece before Dino was born and settled in this country, barely able to speak English. For a decade, his parents worked long, hard days, and saved every penny. A few years ago, they opened their own little Greek restaurant. Their food was wonderful and their reputation was growing though they still had a way to go before they would be comfortable financially. Dino, his younger brothers Nick and George, and his baby sister Maria always helped in the restaurant when they weren't in school.

Dino as well as Sofie, Linh, and Debbie lived on the other side of Lakewood Boulevard, a busy, wide street lined with businesses, that served as a divider between the area where Stewart and the twins lived, and Dino's neighborhood, made up of homes ranging from modest and well-tended, to houses badly needing repair and with broken down cars parked in the front yard. The kids in those homes had attended Grant elementary school, while Stewart had attended Lincoln elementary school. At the beginning of seventh grade, Stewart noticed that the kids from Grant elementary school were far tougher and rougher than any of the kids from his school. Raymond, Damon, and Willie also came from Dino's school, and from the day they first walked into Thomas Jefferson Middle School, were happy to have a new group of kids to terrorize on a daily basis.

As tough as Raymond and his friends were, Sofie and her friends were the opposite of them, undoubtedly the sweetest girls in the school. Stewart pondered this enigma last year and was never really sure of the reason. His best theory was that the girls had sweet moms and the boys had jerks for dads. After meeting Sofie and her friends, he often found himself wishing they had gone to his elementary school instead of the POP Sisters.

Nora set down the magazine she was reading and looked over at Byron, seated at his desk, deep in concentration. She had already packed the basket and carefully placed the files back on the coffee table exactly where they had been before their lunch. Turning away from Byron, she noticed the family picture wedged between the files. Carefully moving a few files aside, she found enough room to move the picture to the front of the credenza. Leaning over, she kissed Byron on the cheek. "I'm going home now," said Nora, heading for the picnic basket. It took a few seconds for her words to penetrate his concentration. He looked her way as she was close to the door.

"Oh, goodbye, see you tonight," said a distracted Byron.

"Will you be home for dinner?" asked Nora.

"It depends on the afternoon. I'll give you a call," Byron replied as he turned back to his work.

Nora stepped out of Byron's office and as she passed Bernie's desk, Charlie Williams, a very warm, likeable man and

Byron's partner in the firm, opened the outer door and entered the office suite. He smiled broadly as he gave her a quick hug.

"Well, Nora, a pleasure to see you today."

"It's nice to see you. How is everything going here?" Nora wondered.

"We're busier than a soccer mom with ten kids and two flat tires," replied Charlie.

Nora laughed as she knew she could always count on Charlie to keep the mood light. Waving goodbye, she left the office. She truly appreciated Charlie and everything he did for Byron. While Charlie was a sharp accountant, Byron was the tax wizard of the firm. Charlie, though, was the smooth communicator who explained to the clients all of the intricacies of Byron's tax planning. This was his important contribution to the firm because Byron was virtually incapable of speaking with clients.

Byron learned early in life that any time he was put on the spot, something happened to him that changed him from an extremely intelligent person into a bumbling mess. He never forgot his first day in school when the teacher asked every child to stand and say their name. Climbing slowly to his feet, Byron began shaking and to his dismay, found a strange mass of mucus forming in the back of his throat. As he tried to speak, the mass seemed to block his vocal chords and he could barely utter a sound. He kept trying to spit his name out and it began sounding like a stutter. The harder he tried, the worse it got. All of the other kids began laughing and he felt light-headed. He sunk his head to his chest, sat back in his seat and didn't look up the rest of the class.

The teacher asked the kids to stop laughing and moved on to the next kid, who was able to execute the horrific task of standing and stating his name without any difficulty. After class was over, the teacher went over to Byron who remained in his chair with his head cradled on his arms on his desk. No matter how much she tried, Byron could not be consoled.

This incident would repeat itself in every instance and Byron could not overcome it. He would stand in front of the mirror and practice saying his name, over and over and over. It worked great at home, but once he got in front of a group of people, the shaking and lump in his throat rose up to throttle him, just like that first day of kindergarten.

Upon graduating from college, Byron was courted by all of the major accounting firms and chose one of the most prestigious international companies in the world. While his work was exemplary, his inability to speak with bosses and clients left them wondering what to do with him. Climbing the ladder to a top position in the firm seemed out of the question for Byron. Fortunately for him, Charlie came to the rescue. Charlie had been his college roommate and they formed a solid friendship. He understood Byron's plight, for he had a brother that stuttered terribly and knew how incredibly difficult life could be for him. The difference from his brother, he discovered, was that when Byron was comfortable with people, he could speak very well. It helped tremendously that Charlie and Byron went to the same firm together and after a few years of working long hours, Charlie could see that Byron did not have a bright future at the company. Charlie also didn't want to spend the next decade working hard and hoping to be promoted to a partner, so one day he approached Byron about starting a firm together. Just the two of them and a secretary would be all they would need to go into business. Byron jumped at the chance and after a slow start, they found they had more work than they could handle. Despite the workload, they would not hire any more people in order to spare Byron the stress of having to get comfortable with new employees. When it came to meeting with clients, Byron would attend and Charlie would do all of the talking.

English class just did not appeal to Stewart. He didn't really care about writing essays or poetry or learning anything about famous authors. Even though his mom told him it would be one of the most important classes he would ever have, he didn't believe her. He loved math and science and felt those subjects would lead to his getting a job someday, whatever that would be. If he were to become a computer programmer for example, he didn't think it would matter to a company if he were able to describe the syllabic patterns of a Japanese haiku. However, no matter how much he disliked a subject, he promised his parents he would always try his best and maintain an "A" average. Except for P.E., of course.

The students in Stewart's advanced English class were the same students in his math class. With friends in the class, it helped make English tolerable for him. And seated squarely in the front row was Sofie. No matter how long Mrs. O'Brien prattled on and on about a book he absolutely did not care about, there was Sofie to save him from this insufferable boredom.

Mrs. O'Brien, a life-long teacher nearing retirement, loved teaching English and especially loved the writings of Mark Twain. She spent the first part of the class discussing "Huckleberry Finn" and asking whether the class felt this story satirized society in any way. Stewart felt his eyes growing heavier by the second. Gazing at Sofie's golden locks didn't seem to help. The room was warm. He felt himself growing sleepy. His mind was drifting…drifting to outer space….

Captain Stewart Camby of the First Inter-Galactic Space Division expertly navigated his starcraft through the meteor shower. His fuel was dangerously low thanks to a meteor fragment that punctured one of his fuel tanks. If he could just fly in a straight line to planet Herculon, he would have enough fuel to land safely. Despite a furious meteor shower causing him to constantly swerve and waste time and precious fuel, he was determined to get through this predicament and arrive on Herculon in time to rescue Queen Sofie from the dungeon of the evil Raymond the Terrible. Once he made the rescue, his starcraft would not be operable and he would need one of his wingmen to swoop down to Herculon for them. Hopefully, First Lieutenants Dino, Ethan, and Nathan survived the meteor shower and had radio reception. A female voice came on over his headset. What happened to his wingmen? Don't tell me they didn't make it safely through the meteors! What was this annoying voice babbling about? Why would she be talking about Huckleberry Finn? Then, it sounded like she said....

"Stewart? Stewart Camby?" asked Mrs. O'Brien patiently looking directly at Stewart, as he was jolted back to reality. "Excuse me?" Stewart weakly muttered with everyone in the class staring straight at him. "Stewart," repeated Mrs. O'Brien. "Have you read the assigned chapter?" Stewart nodded his head. "Yes ma'am."

"Good. Please share your thoughts concerning Mark Twain's use of metaphors in this chapter." Mrs. O'Brien clasped her hands behind her back as Stewart gathered his thoughts. How long was he in outer space? Had he fallen asleep? Did he have drool running down his face? He put a hand to his cheek to make sure it was dry and looked at the clock out of the corner of his eye, noticing the bell would ring any second. Taking a deep breath, he opened his mouth to speak. The bell rang.

"We will continue this subject tomorrow," announced Mrs. O'Brien. "Class dismissed." Grateful for the bell, Stewart grabbed his backpack and followed the students out of the room.

Band was one of Stewart's favorite periods. He enjoyed music and his class sounded really, really good. Jonathan Stimple, the band teacher, dressed impeccably, as if he were ready to direct an orchestra in a grand concert hall at any moment. He was demanding with the students and this resulted in everyone playing with the precision of a high school band. Stewart didn't mind Mr. Stimple's teaching methods, he just didn't agree with his selection of music. He rolled his eyes every time the sheet music for a new song was passed out to them. Frankly, including last year in seventh grade, he had enough with songs by masters who had been dead for three hundred years. Why couldn't they play modern songs heard on the radio?

Stewart wasn't crazy about his instrument, either, not that he had any say in the matter. During the summer after fourth grade, his dad came home from work with a songbook and a clarinet. Having never seen one before, Stewart wondered what was going on as Byron opened the case and stuck a reed in his mouth as he began putting the pieces together. Sucking on the reed moistened it his dad explained, which was necessary for producing beautiful sounds. When the clarinet was assembled, Byron proudly held it out, as if displaying a royal scepter. He held it in place, wiggled his fingers, smiled at Stewart, and blew into the mouthpiece.

The ghastly blaring noise drove Stewart backwards as he covered his ears. Had someone shot a goose at close range? Puzzled, Byron stopped blowing. "Uh, I'm a little rusty. It's been a few years." Byron tried again, with the same ear-splitting result. "Looks like I'm going to have to practice." He handed the clarinet to Stewart. "They offer band class this coming school year, so start playing and you'll have a head start." With that, Byron left the room. Stewart just sat there, bewildered, wondering why anyone would play such an awful instrument.

Over the next few years, Stewart became quite good, though he never was really in love with it. His dad hoped to inspire Stewart by telling him stories about great players such as Benny Goodman and Peanuts Hucko. Though they were swing band and jazz legends, he learned, Stewart didn't want to play their style of music. He wanted to play an instrument of his own choosing, one that seemed more masculine to him, not one chosen for him because his dad had played it. What if Byron had played the kazoo? Or, a saw and nail in a country band? Would he have been stuck with either one of those devices? Why hadn't his dad played the trumpet, an exciting instrument used during medieval times to announce the arrival of kings? He felt pangs of jealousy watching Dino play the saxophone; Ethan, the French horn; and Nathan, the trombone, instruments they very much enjoyed.

Every grievance Stewart had about the class was once again lessened by the presence of Sofie, who with Linh and Debbie formed the core of the flute section. At times, Stewart wished he played the flute, though he wasn't sure he would be able to play a note if he sat next to Sofie. He probably would have sounded like Byron making those dreadful noises years ago. Despite his numerous objections with the instrument that was forced upon him, everything was forgiven as the clarinet players sat next to the flutists in the woodwind section, placing him very close to Sofie. All things considered, he liked band class just fine.

03

ROPE CLIMBING

RED LIGHTS FLASHING, THE school bus rolled to a halt near Stewart's neighborhood. His stop was the last one of the day. The doors opened and the remaining handful of students hopped down the steps with Stewart being the last to get off the bus. Ethan and Nathan were on a chess team and had practice after school, so he was used to riding the bus without his friends who lived nearby. Stewart didn't mind the bus ride home in the afternoons as long as the weather was good, which Nora appreciated, as it gave her a chance to run errands and not deal with the traffic around the school. She didn't mind driving Stewart in the morning because it gave him an extra half hour to sleep, something she felt was very important to a young person.

Stewart only had to walk a couple of blocks to his house from the bus stop on this warm, fall day. He noticed the leaves on many of the trees were turning yellow, with a few oranges and reds scattered through the neighborhood. Soon, all of the trees would be changing color and the neighborhood would look like a giant yellow Van Gogh painting.

He turned onto his street and admired the large ash tree on the corner with leaves of maroon and gold. This is my favorite tree, thought Stewart as he passed by. As he gazed at the tree, an apple bounced off his head. Stewart dropped to his knees and covered his head. What was that? He looked around and didn't see anybody. He thought about where he was standing and the angle the apple hit his head and spun around.

A group of juniper bushes stood forty to fifty feet away. Stewart squinted to see if someone was behind the bushes. Sure enough, he heard stifled laughter, and the neighborhood brat Zack Anderson rushed to the street with his fancy green bicycle from behind the bushes. Zack jumped onto the seat and pedaled away from Stewart. After riding a safe distance away, Zack circled back towards him.

"Gotcha fatso!" yelled Zack, careful to keep enough distance from Stewart. "You're an idiot!" bellowed Stewart. "I'm going get you one of these days and you'll be sorry you ever messed with me!" Zack laughed hysterically at Stewart's anger. "You'll never get me fat boy! Never!" taunted Zack, as he turned and pedaled up the street towards his home, laughing the entire way.

Stewart picked up his clarinet case and backpack and continued up the street. He rubbed the back of his head and felt a small knot where the apple had struck. At least it didn't hurt that much. This is the last time Zack gets me like this, fumed Stewart.

The wonderful aroma of chocolate chip cookies baking in the oven greeted Stewart as he entered the house. He walked into the kitchen and found a batch of them already on the warming racks. With the dough soft and the chocolate gooey from just being taken out of the oven, Stewart appreciated his good timing in not missing this important phase of cookie making. With surprising speed, he raced to the cookies, grabbed one, and took a bite while sliding to a stop. "Wow, this is so good!" Stewart loudly exclaimed.

Carrying a laundry basket, Nora passed through the kitchen. "Glad you like it," said Nora.

"Of course, I like it! Next to cinnamon rolls, these are the best!" Stewart grabbed another one and stuffed it in his mouth.

Nora pointed at the timer ticking on the counter. "Please let me know when it dings."

"Will do, mom," replied Stewart, somehow able to speak, despite his mouth stuffed full.

"Don't eat too many and save some for the twins," gently chided Nora.

"Mmpf," mumbled Stewart as he chewed vigorously.

After the timer sounded, Stewart alerted his mom, and ran up the stairs to his room. Setting down his backpack and clarinet case, he turned on his computer and sat at his desk. He wanted to send messages to outer space before the twins came over to hang out after their dental appointment. Stewart thought they might not be up for chocolate chip cookies after a teeth cleaning. The last time he went in for a cleaning, the hygienist flossed his teeth so vigorously, his gums hurt for days. He expected to see her chasing kids in the next horror movie, waving a roll of dental floss and wearing a hockey goalie mask.

Over the next hour, Stewart repeated his routine of sending messages over the radio and making notes of his transmissions. As before, his transmissions went unanswered. Leaning back in his chair, he gazed at the fleet of model spaceships he put together over the years on the shelf before him. Wouldn't it be great if he were to someday be on one of those spaceships? He believed there had to be intelligent life somewhere out there in the universe and wanted to be the first from earth to meet them.

Two heads leaned over Stewart as he stared at the spaceships. "Boo!" yelled Ethan and Nathan in unison. Startled, Stewart leaped to his feet, but his headset, which he was still wearing, acted like a leash and yanked him back down to his chair. Furious, he ripped off the headset and turned to see the laughing faces of the twins.

"When you're sleeping tonight, I'm going to give you both tard-ectomies!" yelled Stewart. This made the twins laugh even harder and soon, Stewart laughed with them.

"You should have..." Ethan began, "seen your face," continued Nathan. "Your eyes almost popped out of your head."

"Fred," said Ethan.

"Ed," chimed Nathan.

"Shmed," chirped Ethan.

"Stop!" ordered Stewart. He hated it when the twins started the rhyming routine, especially because they knew how much it bothered him. "You got me," admitted Stewart. The twins flopped on the bed as Stewart spun his chair around and put his legs on the bed.

"What have you been doing?" asked Ethan.

"Sending messages to space," replied Stewart without much enthusiasm.

"No luck, huh?" Nathan asked, as he bit into a chocolate chip cookie.

Stewart shook his head. "I haven't heard anything."

Ethan thought about this for a moment. "So, all you're doing is speaking into the headset and hoping for an answer?" Stewart nodded. Nathan finished his cookie and looked at Stewart. "What if they," asked Ethan, "don't speak English?" finished Nathan. Stewart's eyes widened at this question.

"I never thought of that," said Stewart, thinking of the possibilities. He jumped to his feet and began pacing the room. "Aliens might speak German...Spanish...French...Italian. It could be anything."

"Pig Latin!" joked Ethan. Stewart rolled his eyes.

"It could be, we don't know," Nathan said in defense of his brother.

"Well, it could be, but I doubt it," countered Stewart. He reached for a cookie off of the plate Nathan was holding. "So, what do I do?" asked Stewart as he took a large bite, leaving a chocolate chip stuck to his upper lip. All of them pondered this question while devouring the remaining cookies.

"I've got it!" yelled Stewart, chunks of cookie flying out of his mouth. "I'll get a translation of messages in every language over the internet, record it on the computer, and send them out. It will all be automated!"

"Great idea," said Ethan.

"How long do you think it will take to record the translations?" asked Nathan.

Stewart thought about it for a moment. "I don't know, days I guess. We have a lot of languages on this planet. Let's get started right now!" he shouted, as he jumped back on his chair and started typing rapidly on the computer with the twins peering over his shoulder.

Nora brought a plate filled with chicken, steamed broccoli, and a salad to the table in the breakfast nook of the kitchen where Stewart had just taken his seat. Returning to the kitchen counter, she picked up her plate and basket with bread, and made her way back to the table.

"Did you make the bread?" asked Stewart as he reached for a slice.

"I did," replied Nora.

"Thought so." Stewart ate the slice and reached for another one. "When is dad going to be home?"

"In an hour," Nora responded. "He said to go ahead and eat, as it may be later."

Stewart knew that "it may be later" meant it would be later by far more than an hour. Late enough so that he would be going to bed when Byron came home. He rested his head on his hand as he slowly moved the fork from his plate to his mouth. "Does he have to work so much? We hardly see him."

Nora took a deep breath as Stewart spoke. She felt the same way though she understood Byron's drive to be successful in his career and to provide a comfortable life for them. It was easy for her to understand, not so easy for a thirteen-year old boy.

"Honey, many people rely on your dad for help with complicated situations and he is very, very good at helping them," explained Nora.

"Why can't someone help him so he doesn't have to work so much?" countered Stewart.

"Well...." said Nora trying to come up with a good answer. "I guess there are very few people who can do what he does, so it isn't easy to find someone who can help him."

Stewart thought about her answer while he ate but wasn't convinced. Suddenly, his mood brightened.

"Mom, guess how many languages there are in the world?"

"I have no idea. How many?" replied Nora.

"Seven THOUSAND!" said Stewart.

"That many?" Nora was truly surprised.

"Yes, and 90% of those languages are spoken by less than 15% of the total number of people in the world. That means 85% of the people speak something like seven hundred languages. Amazing, right?"

"It is amazing," confirmed Nora, delighted in seeing Stewart explore a new subject. She enjoyed the various topics Stewart would bring to her attention and believed her encouragement would help strengthen his thirst for knowledge, a trait she felt would help him go a long way in this world.

- - - -

Nora peeked in Stewart's room and found him with his head down on his desk, sound asleep. She went over to him and gently shook his shoulder.

"Stewart, wake up." Stewart continued to sleep. "Honey, wake up." Stewart barely opened his eyes as Nora helped him to his feet. "Let's go and brush your teeth." She led him down the hallway and to the bathroom. He went to the sink and began to brush his teeth in slow motion, still half asleep.

The front door opened and Byron entered. He headed to the kitchen and seeing no one, went to the family room. Finding it empty, he headed for the stairs.

Byron reached the top of the stairs and went to Nora, still standing by the bathroom door. He gave her a hug.

"Sorry I'm home so late. I lost track of time."

"It's okay. We know you're busy," Nora whispered. Stewart came out of the bathroom, went to Byron and gave him a big hug. "You're home," he said. Byron patted Stewart on the back and led him to his room.

"It's past your bedtime. I'll see you tomorrow," Byron said as he reached for Stewart's door.

"Goodnight dad. Goodnight mom," mumbled Stewart.

"Sweet dreams," said Nora as Byron closed the door. Nora looked up at Byron.

"How are you doing?" asked Nora.

"Tired. I've been preparing for a meeting tomorrow with someone who has many companies and who just relocated to Denver. It could be a very big client for us." Byron yawned as he and Nora walked down the hallway to their bedroom.

Nora sat at the table in the breakfast nook and read the paper, while she drank a cup of coffee. Stewart ran into the room and poured cereal into a bowl. He was in such a hurry, he haphazardly dumped most of the cereal out of the box, sending it flying all over the counter. He grabbed a handful and stuffed it back into the box. With the other hand, he swept the remaining cereal on the counter into the box.

"Honey, what are you doing?" asked Nora, not too pleased.

"I need to get to school early," Stewart managed to say while eating as fast as he could.

"That's not an excuse. Slow down, please."

Stewart paused and began eating at a normal pace.

"Why do you need to get to school early?"

"I have to do my math homework. I forgot to do it yesterday."

Nora crossed her arms. "Why can't you do it here?"

"Uh, I need to ask the teacher a question," Stewart responded somewhat unconvincingly.

Something seemed odd about Stewart though Nora didn't want to press the matter. Besides, getting him to school early meant missing the crowd of people dropping off their kids, so she really didn't mind. What Nora didn't realize was that Stewart wanted to get to school early to avoid Raymond and his friends.

Stewart enjoyed science class more than math and thought Nathan was the perfect lab partner. While he loved the constant challenge of solving problems in math class, it was hard to beat the project that lay ahead of them that day – dissecting a frog. Stewart had been looking forward to this for quite a while and he was eager to cut into the frog and see exactly what was inside of that green skin. Best of all, he had a great practical joke ready for this project. It was actually Nathan's idea, who had read that adding salt to fresh frog legs caused them to twitch. Because these frogs weren't freshly dead, he wasn't sure if salt would work and asked Stewart, the electronic whiz of his friends, to figure out another alternative.

Stewart thought the solution was simple; attach an electrode to a small battery and an on/off button. Then, he would attach the other end of the electrode to the spine of the frog. When the button was pushed, the electrical charge would cause the muscles in the frog's legs to spasm. He just had to do a good job of hiding the wire running from the electrode to the battery and placing the button in a good spot. His front pocket would work just fine.

Mrs. Murphy, their serious science teacher, instructed the students to get their frogs and begin the dissection based on the notes they had taken from the previous class. Stewart and Nathan situated the frog on the tray and glanced at Mrs. Murphy, who was helping other students on the other side of the room. Near Mrs. Murphy were lab partners Ethan and Dino, who were looking their way. They were aware of what Stewart and Nathan were up to and wanted to see how this joke would play out. Stewart quickly pulled the electrode out of his pocket and attached it to the frog. He placed paper towels on the table and over the wire, which was barely visible from Stewart's pocket.

Who would fall prey to their scheme, Stewart wondered? Tingling with excitement, he imagined that this was how a diabolical genius must feel. He surveyed the class and his eyes immediately rested on the lab partners in front of him – Brittany and Shelby, the two top members of the dreaded POP Sisters. He was staring at a golden opportunity. As if on cue, Brittany and Shelby turned around and Brittany looked at Stewart with the demanding demeanor of someone used to a lifetime of getting her way.

"Hey, you," Brittany directed at Stewart. "I left my notes at home. What are we supposed to do?" Though Stewart felt like running for the hills whenever she looked his way, he forced himself to stay calm.

"Well, look real close and see how I open the chest," instructed Stewart, trying to speak without his voice quavering. The girls leaned closely over the frog. Stewart could almost feel their breath as he too, leaned close to the frog. "Then...." Stewart reached into his pocket and pushed the button and the frog's legs twitched violently.

"AAAAAHHHHHHHHHHHHHHH!!!" screamed Brittany and Shelby as they leapt from their chairs and began jumping up and down. Their ear-splitting screaming was so startling, the rest of the girls in the class started screaming with them.

Boys covered their ears and near panic ensued. Mrs. Murphy rushed over to them, her eyes bulging with confusion.

"What is going on here?" she demanded. Near tears, Brittany pointed at Stewart's frog.

"It moved!" she cried.

"Nonsense," said Mrs. Murphy. "It's dead. Now you girls sit down and get to work." Brittany and Shelby reluctantly returned to their chairs and sat down. Mrs. Murphy looked around the room, clearly unhappy with this outburst. "Everyone, get back to work right now."

While Mrs. Murphy looked around the room, Stewart quickly pulled the electrode from the frog and fumbled with the wire, stuffing it back in his pocket just as Mrs. Murphy turned towards them. She eyed them sharply as Stewart stood nonchalantly with his hands in his pockets. A long-time teacher, she sensed there was something going on, but couldn't see what it was and after a moment, decided to let it go.

"Back to work you two," she finally said and walked over to a student who was waving at her for help. Their ears still ringing from the bloodcurdling screaming, Stewart and Nathan sat down and tried not to look at each other for fear they would burst out laughing. They looked over at Ethan and Dino, who were smiling broadly and giving them a subtle thumbs-up. Though Stewart wondered if he had suffered a ruptured eardrum, he knew he would come out ahead in the form of heroic fame, making it all worth it.

Mr. Pike was on a roll. He hit on all of his football picks the previous weekend, netting him a tidy sum of cash. Rather than take his winnings, as he had done weeks before to buy his truck, Mr. Pike decided to leave it with his bookie and bet the entire sum. He wasn't going to foolishly bet it all on just one game and would continue to spread out the bets, lessening his risk. It meant taking more time watching and analyzing games, though it didn't matter to him as he loved everything about football. In his apartment were half a dozen large, high definition televisions and with all of them lined up on the wall, his living room looked like a sports bar. He also bought the best reclining chair on the market, allowing him to watch all of the games in extreme comfort.

He finished placing his bets for the week and hung up the phone as the boys for the next class entered the locker room. This was going to be a long week for him. A cold front had moved into Colorado and the temperatures had dropped considerably from the warm, fall days that had been going on for the last month. The weather forecast showed high temperatures would be just a little above freezing for the next week with a mix of rain and snow. Cold weather meant indoor activities and not playing football outdoors, where the boys could run off their boundless supply of energy. Basketball wasn't scheduled for a few more weeks, so he would have to go to plan B, which was good old-fashioned conditioning. Pushups, sit ups, shuttle runs, climbing a rope to name a few. Some of the boys would hate it, but so what? It was good for them.

The boys gathered around Mr. Pike, who was holding the end of a thick climbing rope attached to the ceiling. Stewart's eyes followed the rope from Mr. Pike's hand to the ceiling. How high was that? Twenty feet? Thirty feet? Whatever it was, it was too high. Stewart did not like heights at all and especially did not like the idea of hanging from a rope without any kind of safety harness or something to prevent him from falling to a certain death. He learned of this fear when his family drove one hundred miles from Denver to see the Royal Gorge, at one time the highest bridge in the world at 955 feet above the ground. As his family walked across, Stewart peered over the edge and looked at the tiny river and railroad tracks down below. He felt his legs turn to jelly and his stomach drop out of his body, forcing him to clutch his dad's arm the rest of the way. And now this madman wanted him to climb a rope?

"Okay everyone, listen up. This is how you climb a rope." Mr. Pike jumped and grabbed the rope above his head with both hands. "Grab tight and pull your body up towards your hands." Pulling his body upward, Mr. Pike clamped onto the rope with both of his feet. "Now grab the rope with your feet, one on top of the other with the rope in between. Hold tight with your feet, then straighten your body, reach up and grab again with your hands. Repeat this until you get to the top. When you get to the top, it's the reverse. Lower your feet, hold tight, lower your body, hold tight with your hands, lower your feet and keep repeating. Now watch."

Mr. Pike carefully showed the class how he moved his hands and feet for a few repetitions. "You guys see that?" The boys nodded their heads. "When you get really good you can do this," boasted Mr. Pike, as his feet let go of the rope and, using only his hands, quickly climbed to the top. The boys gasped in astonishment at this feat and whooped and hollered as he climbed down using only his hands. He descended to the floor and with the flair of a gymnast, let go of the last few feet of rope, landing perfectly on both feet. "Any questions?" he asked, extremely pleased with his feat of strength. "Now this is the goal. Everybody in this class must make it to the top. Everybody." He seemed to spend a few extra seconds gazing at Stewart and the other less athletic boys in the class. "The weather is going to be crap for the next week so you're all going to get a lot of practice. I'm going to test you all and if one person fails to make it to the top, all of you will run for the rest of the class."

The boys listened to this task in stunned silence. Raymond felt his face grow hot at the thought of this challenge. He knew he could climb the rope right away and he was certain the spastics in the class wouldn't be able to climb it, even if they had a full month to practice.

"Okay, we've got three ropes here, divide into groups and start climbing," ordered Mr. Pike. Raymond headed over to Stewart, who was already in a line, and cut in front of him.

"Listen, you fat blob. If you don't climb this rope, you're going to get it," threatened Raymond in a hoarse whisper. Stewart looked into Raymond's smoldering eyes and knew he meant every word of it.

Mr. Pike retreated to a chair across the gym and happily watched Raymond's exchange with Stewart. This was exactly what he wanted for a kid like Stewart. Peer pressure. Letting the other kids badger the weak ones into performing was a tactic he learned in football, and it worked surprisingly well.

04

THE TEST

BYRON THOUGHT THE MEETING with the new client went well. Charlie was superb, outlining what their firm could do for the client's various companies. Byron only had to say a few words, something he managed to do without feeling like he would pass out. He enjoyed meeting Angelo Moretti, a dapper sixty-year old who recently moved to the Denver area and re-located the headquarters for his businesses from the east coast. "It was time for a change," said Angelo, explaining the reason for the move. "Besides, Colorado's tax rates are more favorable than back east, so it made business sense."

Nodding his head, Byron agreed, as did Angelo's right-hand man, Bruno Russo. They were an odd mix, observed Byron. Angelo was like a kind grandfather and Bruno was the detail man who didn't seem to smile very much. Whatever the personalities, he had long observed, as long as it worked, it didn't matter how different they may be.

Angelo's main business was manufacturing gelato, a delicious Italian dessert he had learned to make from his grandmother back in Italy. His business was firmly established in the eastern states and now they were looking to expand to the western part of the country. Angelo also had other businesses, such as check cashing companies and auto body shops. Byron's job would be to coordinate tax strategies and minimize income taxes for these companies.

"We don't like paying taxes," stated Bruno, his eyes cold and flat. Who does? thought Byron while deciding to respond by simply nodding his head, along with Charlie.

Stewart's arms ached as he climbed into the car with his mother. He had been climbing that infernal rope all week in P.E. and couldn't get the hang of it. Near the end of the week he had improved to moving up a few feet from where he would start though he couldn't climb much higher beyond that point. In the middle of the week he had gone on the internet and found videos demonstrating how to climb a rope, but he wasn't able to get the hang of this combination of strength and technique. Raymond's shadowing presence and glaring stares didn't make it any easier. Stewart thought his only chance would be some kind of divine intervention, possibly in the form of an invisible hand from the heavens that would help hoist him to the top of the rope, to the cheering cries of his joyful classmates.

Nora drove them to Ethan and Nathan's large house just a few streets away from the Cambys. Their father, Dr. Jenkins, was a leading neurological doctor and very well-known for his treatment of epilepsy and other disorders of the brain. Stewart liked Dr. Jenkins, though he rarely saw him as he seemed to work almost as much as his dad. Why did it seem like most successful people had to work an awful lot?

Ethan and Nathan ran out of the house as Nora pulled into their driveway and climbed into the back seat.

"Good morning," said Nora cheerfully to the twins.

"Good morning, Mrs. Camby," they replied in perfect unison. She backed out of the driveway and proceeded to Dino's family's restaurant, a short drive from their home, for their usual Saturday morning breakfast.

The Spartan Restaurant was decorated to give customers the feel of a cozy taverna in Greece. Pictures of Greek villages overlooking the Mediterranean Sea covered the walls and the melodic sounds of a bouzouki played over the sound system. As usual, the restaurant was noisy and filled with diners hungry for the delicious meals cooked by Eleni, Dino's mother and head chef. Dino's father, Stavros, a burly man of medium height, was running around the restaurant, seating people and helping clear tables. His loud voice was easily heard above the noise of the restaurant, talking and laughing with various customers. He was extremely outgoing and all of the customers loved him almost as much as they loved Eleni's cooking. Stewart, Dino, and the twins sat at a table closest to the kitchen.

Dino's younger siblings George, Nick, and Maria emerged from the kitchen with plates stacked high with Eleni's special pancakes, eggs, and bacon, and brought them to the boys. Stewart poured a generous river of syrup over his pancakes that quickly flowed down the sides of the stack and mixed with the eggs and bacon. He grabbed his fork and began devouring the food.

"How can you eat those EGGS with all that SYRUP all over them?" asked Dino in a voice that sounded eerily similar to Stavros, especially his tendency to enunciate certain words in a sentence.

"Syrup goes with everything," replied Stewart incredulously.

"No, it DOESN'T," Dino argued. His younger brother George walked by and Dino snapped his fingers to get his attention. George did not like this at all and ignored Dino.

"Hey George," yelled Dino.

"What do you want?" George responded, clearly irked by his brother.

Dino pointed around at their table. "We need water."

"Why can't you get it?" demanded George.

"Because you're working and I'm not," said Dino as he glanced at Stavros who was walking their way. George knew Dino would complain to their dad, so he headed for the kitchen, fuming the entire way.

"How are my BOYS?" boomed Stavros in his thick accent.

"We're fine," responded Stewart and the twins. Stavros was pleased these boys were Dino's friends and did everything he could to accommodate them, knowing they were a good influence on his son. For many weeks, he let them eat for free. Soon enough, Nora and Mrs. Jenkins told him they expected to pay for their sons' meals. Stavros reluctantly obliged, though he always undercharged them and let the boys have as many helpings of whatever they wanted.

George walked out with glasses and a water pitcher and set them on the table.

"What took you so long?" questioned Stavros. George held up his hands in total exasperation and walked away as Dino smirked at his younger brother. Stavros was a demanding boss and didn't let up on anyone, especially his family. It was necessary for the entire family to work at the restaurant to keep down the costs, though Stavros made a few exceptions for Dino to be with his friends and Saturday breakfast was one of them.

Stavros noticed a group of four had entered the restaurant and turned to go to them.

"EAT everybody, EAT!" he directed the boys as he walked away. After he left, Eleni, a sturdy woman with jet black hair, marched out of the kitchen and looked sharply at Dino. She rattled off a sentence in Greek that sounded to Stewart like one long word spoken at the speed of light. Dino responded in a brief sentence that sounded apologetic. Eleni turned to the boys, her mood instantly bright and happy. Stewart appreciated how nice she was to them, as if she had instantly adopted them as family from the moment she met them.

"You boys liking the breakfast today?" she asked in her charming accent as thick as Stavros'.

"It's great!" declared Stewart.

"Bravo," said Eleni, clearly happy. She looked directly at the twins. "You two eat, eat, eat. Don't stop, I have more food for you." She then looked at Stewart. "You, not so much." She turned and headed back to the kitchen. Eleni's bluntness never failed to amuse the boys. Dino sheepishly shook his head.

"What did she say to you?" asked Stewart. Dino smiled. "She told me to stop being mean to George." They laughed and continued eating.

"Heard anything from aliens?" asked Ethan.

"Not yet," Stewart replied. "I finally got the major languages translated and have been transmitting them for a few days and haven't heard anything."

"Don't give up, it's going to work," said Nathan with a hopeful smile.

"Yeah, I'll keep trying," replied Stewart, with minimal conviction.

"We're still going to the mall after this, right?" mentioned Ethan, looking at the others.

Dino sighed. "I've got to get back to work. You guys have fun."

The large indoor mall was home to one hundred stores and restaurants spread over three levels. It was open, light and airy, with high ceilings and a water fountain in the center of the complex. Numerous benches surrounded the fountain, making it a good place to rest from shopping or hang out with friends. Mall security stood nearby, making sure everything remained peaceful for all visitors.

Stewart loved going to the electronics store and immersing himself with the latest gadgets. He never grew tired of surprising the employees with his knowledge. They were shocked when they first learned he was only thirteen and half-jokingly offered him a job.

Every trip to the electronic store was immediately followed by the mandatory trip to the food court. Stewart's favorite shop was a little bakery that made an assortment of Danish pastries. After reviewing the freshly baked pastries of the day, Stewart and the twins decided on a large kringle, a pastry with flaky layers of buttery dough and coated with a sugar glaze they would share at the fountain.

The boys made themselves comfortable on a bench near the fountain and sank their teeth into this wonderful kringle. Stewart finished his share of the pastry well before the twins and while wiping his mouth with a napkin, he noticed Sofie, Linh, and Debbie passing by on the other side of the fountain. The girls saw them and headed their way.

As Stewart looked at Sofie, he felt a small lump of kringle in his throat. Where did that come from? Why wasn't that in my stomach by now? He forced himself to swallow and chugged the rest of his drink. The girls approached and said hellos all around. Linh and Debbie met the twins last year and became friends during the many classes they had together. Ethan and Nathan effortlessly struck up a conversation with them. Stewart never understood how the twins were able speak so easily to girls. Why didn't their tongues feel like they were inflating in their mouths? He realized it was best to just enjoy the conversations around him and mumble a few one-word sentences when the opportunity presented itself.

Stewart felt his stomach churn as he spied the POP Sisters, dressed like they were on their way to a fashion show, head towards Stewart and the others. They stopped and Brittany posed with her usual look of contempt that was immediately imitated by Shelby and Courtney. The group stopped talking and looked at the POP Sisters.

"What are you guys doing here? The cheap clothing stores are on Lakewood Boulevard," scoffed Brittany who directed her words to Sofie. The POP Sisters laughed and walked away, pleased with themselves. Burning with anger, Stewart wished he had the super powers of Plasma Man so he could liquify their bodies with a lightning bolt. The faces of Sofie, Linh, and Debbie, happy and care-free just a moment earlier, now re-vealed a hurt that was impossible for them to mask. After an awkward silence, the girls said they had to leave and walked away.

Equally upset, the twins turned to Stewart. "Who do they think they are?" fumed Ethan. "They think they're better than everyone," griped Nathan.

"They're the worst," was all a disgusted Stewart managed to say.

That evening, Stewart carried bowls of pretzels and popcorn to the basement and set them on a table next to a large pitcher of lemonade. Plates of cookies and brownies were already on the table. Next to the table of food were two other tables and four chairs. On one of the tables were two large flat screen monitors attached to computers. One of the computers was for him, the other he had built out of spare parts for Dino. The twins would be bringing over their own equipment and Dino would arrive after the dinner rush at the restaurant had calmed down. The boys had local area network (LAN) parties once a month and alternated between Stewart's and the twins' homes. They stayed up late into the night playing computer games and munching on snacks. When they wanted to take a break, they flopped on the couches and watched movies on the huge television set. The basement was the perfect place for them to get together and make all kinds of noise without disturbing Byron, who insisted on getting eight hours of uninterrupted sleep each night.

The doorbell rang and Stewart ran upstairs. He opened the door and the twins entered carrying their computers, monitors and assorted cables. Stewart escorted them to the basement and they began hooking up their computers.

Spread across the couch, Stewart and the twins passed the bowl of popcorn while watching a superhero action movie. After a while, Dino hurriedly came down the stairs.

"Dude, what took you so long?" asked Ethan.

"Sorry guys, we were crazy busy tonight," replied Dino. "I'm lucky my dad let me out of there."

"Okay, let's get going!" shouted Stewart as he headed to his computer. The rest of the boys followed and they put on their headsets, ready for battle. Through the internet, they signed in to their favorite game, Age of Romans, which featured Roman-like warriors with special powers and weapons in a landscape similar to ancient Rome. Each boy had a unique character and as a team, they fought various battles against other teams either to protect their territory or to raid other territories. The boys worked exceptionally well together and had earned a very high ranking. They constantly beat teams featuring players much older than themselves, padding their egos and infuriating the teams they conquered. This was going to be the night they would accumulate enough points to reach the top tier of teams and would be able to go against the best players from all over the world.

The boys quickly guided their characters into position and began bludgeoning their opponents. Stewart's character, Volcanic-Gladiator, dominated every opponent that came its way. "This is going to be a good night!" crowed Stewart, as Volcanic-Gladiator continued to wipe out the enemy, turning them into wisps of vapor. Suddenly, the power went out, leaving the boys in total darkness and groaning loudly.

"Are you KIDDING me! This is RIDICULOUS!" fumed Dino.

"What the heck? We were destroying them!" said Nathan.

"We just lost." complained Ethan, sinking in his chair.

If a game was terminated before completion, the team leaving the game lost considerable points. Stewart turned on his cellphone flashlight and illuminated the boys' faces. "Power outage," he surmised. "I'll check the circuit breakers." He got up from his chair and as he reached the stairs, the lights came back on. The boys cheered and Stewart returned to his seat. "I'm going to talk to my dad about getting a backup generator. We can't have this happen again." The boys grabbed snacks from the plates and powered up their computers, ready for more warfare.

"We've got a lot of ground to make up," said a determined Stewart.

Ethan took off his headset. "You know what I've been thinking about today? We should figure out a way to get back at Brittany." Puzzled, Dino looked at him. "What did she do?" he asked.

"They were horrible to Sofie and her friends at the mall," explained Stewart. "Their own special brand of horribleness."

"Ethan's right!" Nathan passionately declared. "They need to be taught a lesson."

"Someday, somebody will. And when it happens, I hope we're all there to see it," said Stewart.

Nora sensed something wasn't quite right that Monday morning when Stewart barely ate his breakfast. Lost in thought, he would take a bite and push his food around the plate while staring out the window.

"Honey, is everything okay?" Nora asked, trying not to sound too concerned. Stewart continued to stare out the window with a blank expression.

"Yeah, everything is fine," Stewart replied.

"Are you sure?" pressed Nora.

Stewart looked back at his plate and set down his fork. "I'm not hungry." He stood up and pushed in his chair. "Can we go to school a little earlier today? I have a lot to do."

"Yes, of course. I'll put the dishes away while you brush your teeth," said Nora, trying to be cheerful. It was hard to be a mother in moments like these, she thought to herself. It pained her not to see her son in good spirits, yet she realized there wasn't much she could do about it. Too much prying would only make Stewart more reluctant to speak, so she thought it best to wait until he was ready to talk about whatever was on his mind. And for Stewart to say he wasn't hungry, something must be bothering him.

Mr. Pike finished taking roll in P.E. Tension filled the air as this was the day that every boy faced climbing the rope. Every one of them wanted to climb to the top and all of them, including Stewart, did not want to be the boy who failed and caused the class to run the rest of the period.

The first boy to climb the rope was Raymond, who scampered up the rope like a sailor. He reached the top and for good measure, slapped the ceiling with the palm of his hand before descending to the bottom. Many of the boys clapped as Raymond accomplished the climb, excited to be off to such a good start. Mr. Pike called off the next names, and all of those boys successfully reached the top. His strategy for the order of the boys was based on having watched them practice the prior week. He called the best rope climbers first and saved the weaker ones for later, with Stewart being last. Allen, a small boy with a slight frame was going to be next to last and if Allen didn't make it, the boys could blame him for running. In theory, this gave Stewart less than a 100% chance of being the goat of the class, while in reality, Mr. Pike knew Allen had a shot of making it up the rope, so Stewart's odds of making the class run were excellent. Mr. Pike secretly hoped Stewart would fail and the wrath of the boys would light a fire under that large behind of his and make him think of doing something about his physical condition.

It was Allen's turn to climb and all of the boys ahead of him had made it the entire way, though the last few had struggled and barely touched the metal collar at the top of the rope. Allen looked upwards, spit on his hands and started to climb. Slowly but surely, he inched his way up the rope. The boys clapped and shouted encouragement as he climbed closer and closer to the top. He finally reached the top, and like Raymond, slapped the ceiling to the cheers of his classmates. Allen's face broke into a gigantic grin and he practically flew down the rope, smothered by pats on the back when he hopped to the floor.

Stewart stepped to the rope knowing the success of the rope climb rested squarely on his shoulders. Taking a deep breath, he imitated Allen by looking upwards and spitting on his hands. Bending his knees, he jumped and grabbed the rope. With both legs swinging under him, he struggled to get his feet to clamp onto the rope. Not a good beginning, he thought. Surprisingly, his classmates started encouraging him. Fumbling, his feet finally found the rope and he clamped them tightly together. Classmates cheered as he slowly pulled his body up the rope.

Feeling more confident, Stewart managed to repeat this sequence a couple of more times with his eyes focused on the ceiling. How high was he? Ten feet? Fifteen feet? He looked down and saw he was only four feet off of the ground. His arms trembled and he could feel his strength fading. The boys clapped louder and louder. Moved by their support, Stewart strained to keep climbing. He inched another couple of feet higher as the boys kept clapping. Tiring, he stopped for a moment to rest. The class gasped as he slid a few inches down the rope. He recovered, and clenching his teeth, climbed a couple more feet to the cheers of his classmates. Then, his arms began to shake. The boys groaned as he stopped. Stewart's arms began shaking more and more. He tried to fight on and found he couldn't move. It was as if his arms had lost all feeling and strength. Helpless, he hung on the rope. The clapping died down as the boys realized the end was near. Raymond stepped forward, his face red with anger.

"Climb that rope you maggot-faced weasel!" he shouted at the top of his lungs. Stewart froze as the words slammed his ears with the weight of a sledgehammer. He felt dizzy as the blood seemed to drain from his head. Slowly, he slid down the rope and dropped to the floor with a thud. The room was deathly silent.

After a long moment, Mr. Pike stood up and slowly pointed to the basketball court. "Line up under the basket."

With emotions ranging from anger to sadness, the boys spread out on the line. Stewart lined up at the far end with a noticeable gap between him and the others, as if he had suddenly contracted leprosy. Mr. Pike stood before them. "Run to the other end, touch the wall, then run back and touch this wall. And I want all of you to understand something." Mr. Pike paused as he cast his gaze across all of the boys. "You are gonna run hard. You are gonna run until you feel like puking. If I see anyone dogging it in the twenty minutes we have left, the whole class is gonna do nothing but run the rest of the week. We'll run and run and run some more. Got it?

Everyone looked at him in near panic, then over at Stewart, who stared at the floor while feeling the heat from the glare of every classmate. Mr. Pike looked at his watch. "Ready. Go."

The boys sprinted to the other end of the court, touched the wall and sprinted back, repeating this sequence over and over and over. Stewart kept his head down the entire time, ashamed to make eye contact with any of his classmates, all of them running as if their lives were at stake.

Every muscle in Stewart's legs ached as he walked to the bus after school. He had never run so much in his life and he discovered running in the gym was worse than running laps around the track. Instead of a steady pace, running indoors meant constant stopping, turning, and starting, every time he touched a wall. The twenty minutes of running on the basketball court felt like an eternity that would never end.

Hobbling to the bus, he wished his mother wasn't at the hairdresser so he could call her for a ride home. He wasn't looking forward to walking the few blocks to his house from the bus stop and certainly didn't need the exercise for the day. Stewart climbed the stairs into the bus and slumped into the first seat behind the driver, grateful the other students always wanted to sit at the back, leaving this seat open for him.

The bus reached Stewart's stop and came to a halt. Stewart took one step down the stairs and his legs nearly buckled. He grabbed the bar and turning sideways, continued slowly down the last few steps. Wincing in pain, he hopped to the ground and began walking in an odd shuffle down the street.

The doors started to close, and then re-opened. A boy stepped down the stairs and jumped to the ground. It was Raymond. He had been in the back seat and ducked out of sight when Stewart climbed aboard. Walking quickly, Raymond caught up with Stewart as he turned down the street. Grabbing Stewart by the back of his collar, Raymond forcefully dragged him to the closest yard near a large row of bushes.

Stewart was completely taken by surprise and wasn't able to react as Raymond threw him to the ground and jumped on him. Raymond's eyes smoldered as he drew back his arm, his hand balled up in a fist and his other hand clutching Stewart's throat.

"You're gonna get it for all of that running!" hissed Raymond. Just as he was about to punch Stewart in the face with every ounce of strength in his body, he stopped and looked at the grass. A few feet away from Stewart was a fresh pile of dog poop. An evil grin spread across Raymond's face as he unclenched his fist. He leaned over, scooped the poop in his hand and smeared it all over Stewart's face and through his hair. Stewart struggled to free himself, which was impossible with the weight of Raymond on his chest. Raymond tried forcing the poop into Stewart's mouth while he thrashed about underneath him. Stewart clenched his lips together until his jaw ached.

Raymond rolled off of Stewart and vigorously wiped his hand on the grass. He jumped to his feet and towered over Stewart who was crying and gagging.

"Go home to your mommy, you worthless piece of garbage," gloated Raymond as he took a few steps backwards, turned, and sprinted out of the neighborhood.

Stewart rolled over and vomited. The stench was so overpowering he continued vomiting as he cried. Heaving, he climbed to his feet and ran as fast as his body would allow him to run.

Stewart flung open the door to his house, dropping his backpack as he stepped inside, slammed the door shut, and ran up the stairs to his bathroom, gagging and coughing the entire way. He ripped off his clothing, turned on the shower, and stepped under the water. Grabbing a bar of soap, he scrubbed his face until his skin was raw. After countless scrubbings, he stopped and leaned against the wall as the water continued to pour over him. His head started to clear and he could think of only one thought. Raymond was going to pay for this, he vowed. Nothing else mattered. Raymond would pay.

05

RECOVERY

LYING ON HIS BED, Stewart stared at the ceiling and replayed the sequence of events that led up to this horrible afternoon. He wasn't strong. He couldn't climb a rope. While he tried his best, the boys still had to run for half of the class. Did he deserve Raymond's wrath for this? His eyebrows scrunched in a deep frown. No, he did not deserve Raymond's wrath. He couldn't bear to think of Raymond's exact actions on that yard for the mere thought of it made him instantly nauseated.

Nora returned from her errands and noticed Stewart's backpack lying on the floor by the front door. She found this very odd, as he always brought it with him to his bedroom. Taking hold of a strap, she brought it upstairs and found him on his bed.

"Are you okay?" asked Nora as she set his backpack on the desk.

"I'm fine," replied Stewart blankly.

"You don't seem fine," said Nora as she went over to him and felt his forehead. "Hmm, well, you don't have a fever."

Stewart turned his head towards her. "I'm okay, mom. Really, I'm okay." Nora withdrew her hand from Stewart's forehead and after a moment, turned to leave the room.

"Let me know if you need anything," volunteered Nora.

"Okay," Stewart's replied half-heartedly. Nora paused, desperately wanting to say something, thought better of it, then left the room.

Nora brought a plate of pork chops to the dining table and set it down next to a plate of vegetables and a basket of bread. Byron was working late, so the table was set for two. She left the room and stopped at the stairs.

"Time for dinner!" shouted Nora. No reply. "Stewart, it's time for dinner!" No reply. She headed up the stairs and reached his darkened room. Flipping on the switch, she found Stewart lying in the same position. "Honey, please come downstairs, dinner is ready."

"Go ahead without me. I'm not hungry," Stewart said while staring at the wall. Nora was now convinced something was definitely wrong. She again placed her hand on his forehead. He didn't feel unusually warm, so she placed her hand on neck and felt his glands under his jawline to see if they were swollen. Nothing unusual there, either.

"I'm going to call Dr. Thompson tomorrow morning and see if we can get an early appointment."

"Don't call the doctor," protested Stewart. "I'm fine. It was just a tough day at school."

Nora wasn't convinced. "Well, we'll see how you feel by tomorrow. If you get hungry, I'll have a plate ready for you." She left the room and headed downstairs, frustrated and concerned at the same time.

Later that evening, Byron pulled into the garage and stepped out of his car carrying his briefcase. He pushed the button to close the garage door and climbed the two steps into his house, tired from another long day at the office.

Entering the kitchen, he found Nora washing dishes. He set down his coat and briefcase on the table, walked over to her and gave her a kiss on the cheek.

"How is he?" asked Byron.

"Asleep," replied Nora.

"Good. Hopefully, he'll feel better in the morning," said Byron thoughtfully. Nora placed the dish towel on the counter and opened the oven. She took out a plate covered with foil and set it on the table. Byron loosened his tie as he sat down. He removed the foil and smiled at Nora. "This looks delicious."

"I hope it's still warm," said Nora as she sat down to keep him company while he ate his dinner. She pushed the butter dish over to him. "You look tired." Byron nodded and put down his fork.

"I've been pushing it pretty hard these last few months. I can't believe how busy we are and we seem to just keep getting busier. It's good for business." Byron closed his eyes as he rubbed the back of his stiff neck.

Nora looked at him with the same concern she felt earlier for Stewart. "It may be good for business, but is it good for you?" Byron pondered this question for a few moments. "I don't know," he finally replied.

The sun barely peeked over the horizon the next morning as Nora knocked on Stewart's bedroom door. "Come in," was Stewart's faint reply. Nora pushed open the door and found Stewart under the covers. "Honey, you're going to be late." Stewart pulled the covers up to his ears. "I don't want to go to school today."

Stewart tried not to roll his eyes as Nora placed her hand on his forehead. Again, she was puzzled that he wasn't feverish. "I'm going to call Dr. Thompson," said Nora.

"Mom, I'm not sick. Really, I'm not sick. I just don't want to go to school." Stewart had never uttered those words before. Nora sat beside him on the bed. "Why don't you want to go to school?" she asked gently. While Stewart thought of an answer, his face tightened and his chin trembled. He couldn't hold back any longer and burst into tears. Nora held his head in her arms. Stewart wiped his eyes and looked up at her. "I...I couldn't climb the rope," said Stewart, completely defeated.

"Which rope?" asked Nora.

Stewart shook his head back and forth. "The rope in P.E. We had a test and I couldn't climb it."

Nora felt badly for him and was greatly relieved to finally hear what was bothering him. "Did you try your best?"

Stewart nodded vigorously. "I did. Everyone was counting on me and I let them down." More tears welled up in his eyes. Nora hugged him tightly and found tears forming in her eyes. "As long as you tried your best, that's all that matters."

Stewart pulled back from her and wiped his eyes. "Can I stay home today? Just today, I promise."

Nora thought about it for a long moment. He never misses a day and his grades are terrific, except for that blasted P.E. class. Maybe a day off would be good for him. "Okay," she said, "One day should be fine." Stewart lurched forward and squeezed Nora in a tight hug. He was relieved to tell her part of what happened that day, though he wasn't going to tell her everything. He also wasn't going to tell his friends. It was too humiliating.

Stewart remained under the covers for the rest of the morning, at times dozing, the rest of the time lying motionless with his eyes closed. Nothing seemed fun to him. No matter what he tried to think about, he couldn't concentrate and quickly lost interest in the subject. He tried thinking about the messages he sent to space and wondered if he would ever receive a response. Maybe he should have tried sending a message in Pig Latin, since the other languages weren't working. The more he thought about it, the more depressed he became, so he decided to think of something else. He imagined Sofie flying into his room with wings of an angel and playing her flute. That would definitely lift his spirits. Stewart glanced at the window, hoping his wish would come true.

"Honey, I have an idea," said Nora peeking into the room and causing Stewart to jump at the sound of her voice. "Let's have lunch with your father." Stewart's eyes brightened. "But only if you think you can eat lunch." Stewart climbed out of bed.

"I am getting kind of hungry," he acknowledged. "When can we go?"

"We can leave as soon as you get dressed," said Nora, closing the door behind her as she left the room.

Seated at a table in a cozy downtown Italian restaurant, Byron and Nora watched Stewart eat the last few bites of his lasagna. Stewart set down his fork and patted his stomach. The waitress approached their table. "How was it?" she asked Stewart.

"That was the best lasagna!" exclaimed Stewart. The waitress smiled as she handed Byron the bill. "Glad you enjoyed it," she said as she took his plate. Byron took out a credit card and handed it to the waitress.

"How about going for gelato?" said Byron, looking directly at Stewart.

"What's gelato?" Stewart asked quizzically. Byron looked at Nora. "He hasn't had gelato?" Nora shrugged her shoulders. Byron looked back at Stewart. "It's an Italian version of ice cream. My new client has a chain of stores and one of them is down the street. Let's go give it a try."

Stewart scooped a huge spoonful of chocolate gelato out of a bowl and stuffed it into his mouth. His eyes glazed over with pure joy. "This is amazing! It tastes so good! This is the best day ever!" declared Stewart. Byron and Nora smiled, with Stewart showing he was well on his way to getting over his doldrums.

- - - -

Staring straight ahead, Stewart stood in line and ignored the glances of his classmates in P.E. He heard his name whispered by a few of the boys and continued to stare ahead, believing if he didn't make eye contact with any of them, he would be safe inside his imaginary protective shield. Raymond tried provoking him seconds earlier by bumping Stewart as he went to his place in line. Although the bump knocked him back a step, Stewart ignored him. Seeing no reaction from Stewart, Raymond turned to him and loudly sniffed the air.

"What's that bad smell?" taunted Raymond. The other boys took notice and watched as he sniffed around Stewart. "Stewie, have you been rolling around in dog crap?" While Raymond laughed uproariously at his question, Stewart thought this was a perfect time to see if he could send a lethal ray of signals from his brain that would cause Raymond's head to explode. Stewart closed his eyes and concentrated so hard on Raymond, his own head started aching.

The boys scrambled to their places in line as Mr. Pike strolled out with his clipboard and began calling names. "Arnett."

"Here," said Ronald. Ronald's last name was actually Arnett-Sanderson-Curry-Langley. Both of his parents had hyphenated last names and hadn't been able to agree on which names to use, so their children were stuck with their entire combined last names. After hearing this explanation on the first day of school last year, Mr. Pike snorted in disgust and said he was just going to call him Arnett, which didn't seem to bother Ronald. Mr. Pike had difficulty with any kind of last name that wasn't ordinary. When he first read Dino's last name on the roll sheet, he stumbled so badly after the first syllable, he told Dino he would just call him Petro. The boys naturally changed it to Petroleum and whenever class clown Larry Weber would see Dino, he always asked him if he had gas.

"Burns," barked Mr. Pike, looking at his clipboard. "Here," said Raymond. "Cam-bee." Stewart looked firmly ahead. "Here." Mr. Pike glanced at him and continued with the others. I am not going to look at him today, thought Stewart, and maybe not for the rest of the year.

Mrs. O'Brien instructed the class to go to the last chapter of "Huckleberry Finn." Stewart fought the urge to rip the pages out of the book and hurl them to the floor, knowing they were finally near the end and would hopefully move on to something more interesting, like science fiction. He thumbed through the pages and found the last chapter. Looking up, his eyes rested on the back of Sofie's head and her golden locks. His mind started wandering. Drifting, drifting....

The red light on the instrument panel flashed as the siren blared, warning that the starcraft was out of fuel. Captain Stewart Camby of the First Inter-Galactic Space Division prepared to crash land his starcraft on the dark, scorched terrain of Herculon. The lush gardens and forests of this planet had disappeared under the occupation of Raymond the Terrible and his forces of evil. Captain Camby pledged he would expel him from this planet, but for now, his mission was to rescue Queen Sofie.

The starcraft nosedived towards the planet and right before impact, Captain Camby expertly lifted the nose, allowing it to land on its belly and slide to a halt. He crawled out of the burning vessel moments before it exploded and ran to the castle. Armed guards rushed to greet him with weapons drawn. Captain Camby pulled out his electrolaser and with lightning bolt power, zapped them into dust. Running down the hallway, he came to the stairs leading to the dun-

geon, zapping everyone who got in his way. Descending the stairs, he reached the dungeon and began looking for the Queen. He found her chained to the wall and fired his electrolaser at the bars to her cell. Sparks flew everywhere as the bars disintegrated. He walked to her and was about to zap the chains on her wrists and realized the chains would conduct the current of the electrolaser into her body, resulting in instant death. Somehow, he would have to cut the chains. His mind raced as he tried to think of a way to free the Queen who was in desperate need of food and water.

Hideous laughter filled the dungeon. Captain Camby whirled around to see Raymond the Terrible pointing a ray gun directly at him.

"Drop your weapon," ordered Raymond the Terrible. Captain Camby stood tall and looked at him straight in the eye. "Surrender and you live," said a defiant Captain Camby. He pushed a button on his belt and a protective shield surrounded him. Raymond the Terrible smiled his sinister smile and pulled the trigger. The rays from his weapon bounced off the protective shield in a shower of fireworks. Raymond the Terrible's eyes widened with terror as Captain Camby coolly pointed his electrolaser at him and....

"Stewart?" said Mrs. O'Brien. "Did you hear the question?" Not again, thought Stewart. This woman has horrible timing. Why couldn't she let him finish off Raymond and save mankind?

"I'm sorry," replied Stewart sheepishly, ignoring the smirking faces of his classmates. "Please repeat the question."

- - - - -

Stewart couldn't wait for French class to end so he could go home. It was almost unbearable seeing Raymond throughout the day, though he knew he would have to get used to it, as neither one of them would be going anywhere. At least he wasn't. Raymond, he hoped, would do something really stupid and end up locked away in a deep hole in the ground.

Last year, Stewart and the twins signed up for French because a foreign language was required throughout middle school. They had all read "The Three Musketeers" before they entered middle school and envisioned themselves riding horses, swinging swords, and rescuing fair maidens in distress. Ms. Robitaille, their petite teacher, allowed them to choose names for themselves to be identified in class, so Stewart chose Porthos, Ethan chose Athos, and Nathan chose Aramis. Little did they know they would soon be trying to pronounce words that defied pronunciation and be exposed to the confounding world of nouns with genders, elision and nonsensical irregular verb conjugation. Did the Musketeers have to do this? Probably not, groused Stewart. If he had to do it over again, he would have signed up for another language. Why couldn't the school offer a language more interesting to boys his age such as Elvish or Klingon?

In an effort to inspire him in his French studies, Nora took Stewart to Paris for ten days at the beginning of last summer. Byron was too busy, so it was just the two of them on this trip. Nora encouraged Stewart to speak French as much as possible and to his dismay, found he was barely able to say anything beyond the basic greetings. He needed work on his pronunciation and when he did manage to make himself understood, the response was far too fast for him to comprehend. He wished Dino had come with them and served as their interpreter. Dino was also in the class and was called D'Artagnan, the fourth Musketeer. Dino easily learned French and quickly became Ms. Robitaille's favorite student. Despite his difficulty with the language, Stewart and his mother had an enjoyable time seeing the sights of the city and feasting on wonderful pastries and French cuisine.

What impressed Stewart the most was how it seemed most of the men in the city spent the afternoons, seated at sidewalk cafes while watching pretty women walk past them. Why didn't they have to work all day like his dad? When he returned from the trip, he asked Byron if he knew anyone in Paris, so he could call them and ask how they were able to spend the afternoons at sidewalk cafes, but his dad didn't seem all that interested in finding out their secrets.

Stewart and the twins walked through the school doors to the drop-off zone, where Nora patiently waited for them. Stewart did not want to ride the bus home for the time being and was happy that his mom didn't mind picking him up for now. The boys climbed in the car and Nora accelerated down the street.

Nora enjoyed listening to the boys talk about their day as she drove, especially when the twins finished each other's sentences so seamlessly, it almost sounded as if just one of them were speaking.

Turning down their street, they saw a moving van parked in front of the house that had been for sale. A team of movers unloaded furniture and boxes from the truck and scurried into the house. Nora slowed down and craned her neck to get a good look while they passed.

"I wonder who we have for new neighbors?" mused Nora. Mildly interested, the boys watched the movers for a moment and resumed talking to each other as Nora pulled into their driveway and parked. The boys jumped out of the car and ran inside, eager to gorge themselves on the fresh doughnuts Nora was going to make for them.

Nora took a pair of tongs and removed the doughnuts from the bubbling oil in the fryer. She placed them in a paper grocery sack containing sugar and Stewart vigorously shook the sack. He stopped shaking the sack after a few seconds and placed the doughnuts, now coated in sugar, on three plates. Grabbing the plates, the boys ran up the stairs to Stewart's room.

With rings of sugar around their mouths, the boys chomped on their doughnuts while hovering over Stewart's computer monitor.

Impressed, Ethan shook his head as he looked at the screen. "Look at this log of messages. There must be thousands," he said. "Do you know how many messages have been sent?" asked Nathan.

"Close to a hundred and fifty thousand," replied Stewart. "And I haven't heard a thing. Not a thing." The twins sat on the bed as Stewart put his elbows on the desk and rested his head on his hands while staring at the screen.

"I feel like I have tried everything and nothing works. I don't know what else to do. Maybe this is just a waste of time. Nobody else has made contact with aliens so I guess I shouldn't be surprised I haven't heard anything," lamented Stewart.

"That's because it's never," started Ethan, "been done the right way," finished Nathan.

"What is the right way?" Stewart asked, not expecting an answer.

Ethan shrugged his shoulders. "I don't know."

"Snow," quipped Nathan.

"Bro," Ethan said with a satisfying grin. They gave each other a high five while Stewart slapped his forehead in annoyance.

They ate their doughnuts while contemplating this dilemma. Stewart took a huge bite when suddenly, his eyes widened and he jumped to his feet. "I've got it!" he exclaimed, chunks of doughnut flying out of his mouth as he spoke. "The aliens don't speak at all!"

"What do you mean?" said Nathan.

Stewart began pacing the room. "Maybe some do, but maybe the ones within reach of our ability to send messages don't communicate as we do. Maybe they have advanced beyond talking."

"So how do they communicate?" wondered Ethan.

"They communicate with their minds!" shouted Stewart. "Ahhh!" said Ethan and Nathan at the exact same moment and for the exact same length of time.

"Just like you two," continued Stewart. Ethan and Nathan frowned, puzzled by this comment.

"We can't communicate with our minds," said Ethan.

"We've tried and it hasn't worked," added Nathan.

"I think you do communicate with your minds and you don't notice it. Maybe not like when you talk to each other, but you seem to know what each other is thinking. Maybe it's because you're twins and your brain waves are pretty much the same." Ethan and Nathan looked at each as they considered Stewart's comments.

Stewart stood before them and did his best impersonation of an attorney making his case, dramatically pointing a finger at Ethan. "What about the time you were visiting your grandmother and you fell out of a tree and broke your arm?" He turned to Nathan, pointing his finger at him. "You grabbed your arm at the same moment as Ethan broke his arm, saying it hurt like crazy. And you weren't with Ethan, you were with me!" stated counselor Stewart, impersonating his favorite television attorney. "There are lots of other times you guys have done stuff like this. It blows my mind every time this happens."

"It's an interesting theory," pondered Ethan.

"So how are you going to communicate with just your mind?" asked Nathan.

Deep in thought, Stewart paced the room. "I don't know. But I'm going to figure it out."

- - - -

Stewart lay in bed that night and stared into the darkness. His parents had gone to bed and the house was completely quiet. He enjoyed these moments of stillness, lying quietly without a sound in the house, his mind racing with thoughts. The feeling of his brain going into overdrive with thoughts was always exciting, so much so, that on a couple of occasions, he couldn't sleep the entire night. The few times this happened, he got out of bed as soon as he heard his dad go downstairs and followed after him. They would chat for a few minutes before his dad left for his office.

The downside to staying up all night was the next day in school was always a disaster, as his brain would shut down in the early morning and all he could think about was going to sleep. Stewart decided he didn't want to go through with that, so he tried to make himself relax and clear his mind of any thoughts. Clearing his mind was not easy, especially when he was trying to figure out something as exciting as communicating with just his mind. Rolling over in bed, he realized it was going to be a long night.

06

NEIGHBORS

STEWART HAD NOT BEEN able to fall asleep until sometime after midnight and was in a very deep sleep the next morning. Nora heard his alarm ringing and after a few minutes, realized Stewart was still asleep. She went to his room, turned on the light and opened the curtains. Stewart remained sleeping, so she went to him and gently shook him by the shoulder. "Stewart Honey, wake up." Stewart groaned and rolled over with his back to Nora. She shook him again, a little harder this time. "Stewart, wake up."

Opening his eyes, he blinked a few times and saw his mother's face come into sharper focus.

"Are you awake now?" she asked.

"Yeah, I'm awake," mumbled Stewart.

"Okay, I'll see you downstairs," said Nora as she walked away from bed. Stewart sat up as she left and rubbed his eyes. He leaned back on his pillow and replayed the dream he was having just before his mother came to the room. In the dream, he was flying with a machine he intended to invent someday. It would be strapped to his back, but instead of a bulky jet pack that only allowed a person to fly upright, his invention would be small and light, and allow a person to fly while lying horizontally. The challenge would be to figure out how it could be designed so it could transmit enough energy through a lightweight device to lift and propel a human body that wasn't designed for flight.

The flying machine would have to be his second invention, because his first invention was going to be the machine to transmit thoughts to space. Despite how much he loved the sensation of flying in his dreams, the idea of making contact with aliens was more important to him. He believed the aliens would be a far more advanced species than earthlings and it was quite possible they had already invented a flying machine. If that were to be the case, it didn't make sense to him to spend time inventing such a machine before meeting them.

Stewart finished eating a bowl of cereal just as Nora entered the room holding her purse.

"We need to leave soon, please go upstairs and brush your teeth," requested Nora. She stopped and looked at Stewart, noticing the hair on the back of his head sticking straight up in the air. Distressed, she walked to the sink as Stewart rose from the table.

"Come here," she ordered. As Stewart walked to her, she turned on the water and felt to see if it was warm. She guided his head down into the sink and shoveled water on the back of his hair. Turning off the water, she took a towel to his head and ran it vigorously through his hair. "Okay, upstairs, please hurry. I'll be waiting in the car." Stewart scampered upstairs as Nora headed for the garage.

Carrying his backpack, Stewart ran out of the house and jumped in the car. Nora looked at the matted mess on the back of his head with a big clump of hair standing upright like a tree refusing to bend in hurricane winds. "You didn't comb your hair," she commented with a hint of irritation.

"You said to brush my teeth," said Stewart, who thought he had done a good job of following directions.

"Yes, but I assumed you would realize you needed to comb your hair after I ran water over it." She tried to push his hair down with her fingers. Stewart resisted and leaned away from her. "Mom, it looks fine. Nobody will notice. Nobody will care." "Well, I care," said Nora. Stewart sighed as he knew she would say those very words. He was in a hurry and had simply forgotten to comb his hair. Why was it a big deal?

Nora put the car in reverse and backed out of the driveway. Reaching the street, she slowly drove past the house where the moving van had been parked the day before. The couple who had looked at the house with the realtor lady, walked with a boy and a girl to their car in the driveway.

"Our new neighbors look like a nice family," observed Nora. "The boy and girl seem to be around your age, don't you think?" Stewart glanced at them as they drove by and shrugged his shoulders. "I guess so," he replied. His thoughts turned away from the new neighbors as they drove past to the more important task of trying to figure out how to create his mind machine.

No matter how hard he tried, Stewart was having trouble concentrating in math class. It wasn't Sofie's golden locks distracting him for once, it was the mind machine. Ideas for the machine kept popping into his head. He was hoping that the right idea would come to him soon because until then, he feared he wouldn't be able to concentrate in any of his classes. Mr. Leiker stood at the chalkboard, filling it with equations that led to solving the problem of the day. Stewart was grateful the problems became more complicated, because it forced him to pay more attention to what Mr. Leiker was saying and would help him get his mind off the machine. He looked up at the chalkboard and began copying the illustrations.

Halfway through the class, the door opened and a woman from the front office escorted the boy and girl from Stewart's neighborhood into the class. Mr. Leiker put down his chalk and met them by the door. The woman said a few words to him and left the room. Mr. Leiker led the boy and girl to the front of the class.

"Okay, class, this is Alex and Annie McKnight," he announced to the students. "They just moved here from Houston, Texas." He motioned towards the empty desks in the class. "Please, take a seat." Mr. Leiker went back to the chalkboard and continued with the lesson.

Naturally, the entire class was distracted by the new students. Alex caught everyone's attention, especially every girl, as he made his way to the back of the room. He was almost as tall as the twins and had a wiry, muscular build. He had jet black hair and blue eyes and walked with the easy motion of a panther.

No one seemed to pay much attention to his sister, Annie, as she took her seat in the row next to Stewart, directly across from Sofie. While Alex wore a colorful t-shirt with a silhouette image of a skier on the back, Annie wore a sweater that reminded Stewart of Mrs. Darby, their ancient librarian who wore sweaters even in good weather. Annie also had jet black hair and blue eyes just like her brother. Unlike Alex, who exuded a quiet confidence from the moment he entered the room, Annie seemed somewhat withdrawn. She wore large glasses and a navy-blue beret. Stewart had seen that style of beret last summer when he was with his mother in Paris. Maybe she had been to Paris. If so, he wondered if she had also been dragged into every clothing store on the Champs Élysées as his mom had done with him. She explained that she only wanted to go into the shops to look at the stylish Parisian clothing. This didn't make sense to him. How could anyone have fun just by looking at clothing? Nora ended up purchasing a few items and he was glad to see it made her happy. She rewarded Stewart for being a good sport by buying a treat from every bakery they passed, making the clothes shopping experience bearable for a boy his age.

Students poured out of the classrooms and into the hall as the bell rang. Stewart, the twins, and Dino walked together towards their next class. Alex and Annie stepped into the hall and stopped to consult a class schedule. After a brief discussion, they headed down the hallway in the same direction as Stewart and the others.

Stewart and his friends stopped outside of their science class to hang out since they still had a few minutes before the bell rang. Alex and Annie walked towards them, pausing to glance at the classroom numbers. They found the correct classroom, which happened to be Stewart's next class, and walked towards the door.

"Hey," said Ethan to Alex and Annie as they approached.

"Are you guys twins?" asked Nathan.

"No," replied Alex in a soft Texas drawl. "I'm a year older."

"I skipped a grade," said Annie proudly, her drawl barely detectable as if she was trying to hide it. Everyone seemed impressed by her comment. Everyone except Stewart. People showing off their intelligence bothered him. His dad was the smartest person he has ever known and he didn't flaunt his intelligence. In fact, he was very humble, a quality Stewart admired and tried to emulate knowing he, too, was pretty darn smart.

Science class ended and as they left the room, Ethan told Alex about the prank Stewart and Nathan had pulled on Brittany and Shelby, careful not to let the POP Sisters hear the story. Alex laughed as he heard about the mayhem they had caused and at the animated way Ethan recounted the incident. They reached an intersection in the hallway and the twins, Dino, and Annie headed towards study hall, while Stewart and Alex turned in the direction of their P.E. class. Stewart found Alex easy to talk to as they walked towards the locker room and thought it may be good having a friend in this class. At least it couldn't hurt.

Stewart and Alex walked out of the locker room, dressed for the class. It was obvious Alex was the new student as his shirt was brighter than the others and had creases from being just pulled out of a box. Alex followed Stewart to the basketball court sideline where Stewart pointed for him to stand between Larson and Morgan. Stewart went to his place next to Raymond and as he stepped backwards behind the line, Raymond stuck out his leg. Stewart tripped and fell hard on his back. The rest of the boys chuckled as Stewart lay there for a moment, grimacing in pain. Raymond innocently looked away as if he didn't notice what had just happened.

The boys at Alex's end of the line had no idea what was happening and all they could see was Stewart lying on the floor. They watched as Stewart rolled over and climbed to his feet. Alex wondered why no one helped him up and thought the big kid next to Stewart was acting strange. Strange enough to have caused Stewart to fall?

Mr. Pike emerged from the locker room with his clipboard and bag of footballs. He strutted to the boys, held up his clipboard, and began reading names. "Larson," said Mr. Pike, now at the middle of the line and staring at the list. "Here," responded Larson. "Morgan," continued Mr. Pike. "Here," replied Morgan, the boy on the other side of Alex. Confused, Mr. Pike glanced up from his clipboard and looked at Alex.

"Who are you?" asked Mr. Pike in his normal gruff tone.

"Alex McKnight, sir," replied Alex. Mr. Pike squinted at his clipboard. "Okay, I see your name. It's at the bottom. You're the new kid." Mr. Pike quickly assessed him. Good size and an athletic build on this kid, he thought. We'll see what he can do.

Mr. Pike resumed calling out the rest of the names and ordered them outside to run laps and meet on the football field. The boys headed for the exit doors and Alex jogged over to Stewart, who was at the rear of the pack.

"How'd you end up on the floor?" asked Alex. Stewart glanced at Raymond who was at the front of the pack and close to the door.

"I tripped," said Stewart quietly.

"Who tripped you? The big fella?" pressed Alex. Stewart nodded his head. "Boy, that was not cool," said Alex. "Not cool at all."

Alex and Stewart reached the track behind the others. "Mind if I go ahead?" Alex asked as he picked up the pace. Surprised at the question, Stewart waved him ahead and watched as Alex effortlessly increased his stride and soon joined the boys further down the track. After one lap, Alex was thirty yards ahead of the rest of the boys. He finished the second lap more than sixty yards ahead of the next boy to finish and began stretching.

Wow, that kid can run, observed Mr. Pike. He made it look easy and he wasn't even breathing hard. He wasn't as lean as the top runners Mr. Pike had seen on the track team, though the new kid was definitely strong, cowboy strong. Mr. Pike had played with guys like that in college, guys that didn't look intimidating, but could run all day and then deliver bone-crunching tackles that would cause helmets to fly all over the field. He was going to have to see more of this kid in action.

Mr. Pike ordered the boys to their areas on the football field to spend the rest of the class playing flag football. He assigned Alex to Stewart's team since they were the worst in the class, and today they would be matched against the best, with Raymond leading the way.

Stewart's team had the ball first. Rushing the quarterback, Raymond knocked over a couple of kids and threw his hands in the air as the quarterback tried to pass. He deflected the ball in the air and caught it as it came down. He bolted for the goal line, thinking he had an easy touchdown. Just before he got there, Alex sped over to him and pulled his flag. Angry, Raymond slammed the ball to the ground.

On the next play, Raymond, playing quarterback, backpedaled while looking for one of his friends. Alex, playing back on defense, followed Raymond's eyes and ran to the boy where Raymond was looking as soon he threw the ball. Stepping in front of the boy, Alex intercepted the pass and ran towards the goal line. Raymond ran to him as fast as he could, wanting to slam this new kid to the ground as if playing tackle football. Alex stopped, faked Raymond one way and quickly cut the other way, leaving Raymond grasping at nothing but air while he galloped for a touchdown.

Stewart and his teammates ran over to Alex, cheering like they had just won a championship. Raymond kicked the dirt and headed to the other side of the field. Mr. Pike watched from the other half of the field while hiding a smile. This kid definitely has "it," he observed. He was going to get on the phone with the high school coaches later that day and let them know he had found their next star.

The cafeteria was noisy with chatting students. Stewart and his friends were already sitting at their customary table when Alex and Annie emerged with their trays of food. Nathan waved them over to their table. Stewart was fine with Alex sitting with them, but Annie too? Maybe she will get tired of listening to them talk about boy stuff and end up sitting with the girls. Sofie's group at the next table would work out good for her, definitely not Brittany's table. They would eat her alive.

Alex sat down next to Stewart, oblivious to virtually every girl in the cafeteria sneaking glances at him. Annie noticed their glances, rolled her eyes and let out a barely audible scoff as she sat next to Alex.

Sitting across the table from Alex, Dino looked up at him while he ate. "Do you play computer games?" he asked. Alex nodded. "What's your favorite?" Dino inquired.

"Age of Romans, probably," Alex replied. "I play that game," said Annie. Surprised, the boys looked at her. "Volcanic-Gladiator is the best character," she said in a barely detectable drawl. Hmmm, maybe this girl won't be so annoying after all, thought Stewart.

"What about a Romatron?" asked Ethan, testing her knowledge of the game.

"A Romatron stinks," Annie replied dismissively.

"You're RIGHT!" said Dino slapping the table and looking at the twins, who smiled, enjoying the fact that a prior conversation about Romatrons still bothered Dino.

While the boys and Annie continued eating, the POP Sisters, seated a few tables away, whispered to each other, while turning around to look at Alex.

"The new boy is hot!" whispered Brittany to Shelby and Courtney.

"Who is he?" asked Courtney.

"Alex McKnight," replied Brittany.

Courtney turned back to the girls after looking at Annie. "The girl sitting next to him is his sister, right? What's her name?"

Brittany scoffed. "Who knows? Who cares?" she chortled, her voice rising slightly above a whisper. "The way she's dressed, she might be his grandmother!" The girls covered their mouths as they burst out laughing.

Alex looked around the room as they all finished eating. "What do y'all do for the rest of lunch hour?"

"It depends," Stewart responded. "If it's nice weather, we go to the courtyard or outside to the benches on the south side. If it's cold, we just stay here."

"Most of the time we stay here because Raymond and his friends usually ditch study hall and hang outside," said Ethan. "We try to avoid them, especially Raymond," added Nathan.

"Who's Raymond?" asked Alex.

"He's the biggest jerk in the world and happens to go to our school," said Stewart, practically spitting out the words. "He's the big kid in P.E."

Alex sat back and reflected on their comments. "Yeah, he does seem like the kind of guy you want to stay away from."

The boys spent the rest of the lunch hour talking and getting to know each other. Now and then Annie contributed to their conversation, though most of the time she was content to listen to them.

The bell rang and the students rose from their tables and dropped off their trays and trash as they left the cafeteria. Alex noticed the boys walked hesitantly as they passed through the cafeteria and into the hallway, their eyes worriedly searching the students heading towards them. After a few moments, they all seemed to relax and resumed chatting with each other. Alex leaned over to Stewart as they walked down the hall.

"What's going on?" asked Alex quietly.

"Looking to see if Raymond is coming," said Stewart cautiously. "He must be terrorizing someone else right now." Alex shook his head upon hearing this and continued down the hall with the others.

The students filed into band class and went to their seats to set up their instruments. Alex and Annie followed them into the room. Not knowing where to go, they approached Mr. Stimple. He picked up a chair and led Annie between the clarinet and flute sections. "Make room," he asked the students, who moved aside so he could set down the chair. Annie sat in the chair and began assembling her instrument. Mr. Stimple was clearly pleased at her presence.

"We finally have an oboe player," he said aloud to the students near him. Ted Kendricks was their only oboe player last year and his family had moved over the summer. Mr. Stimple did not like conducting a band with a missing instrument and he couldn't persuade any of the students, especially the clarinetists, to switch to the oboe. Though Stewart thought the sound coming from an oboe was interesting, it was smaller than a clarinet, so he definitely was not going to change instruments.

Mr. Stimple led Alex to the trumpet section and placed a chair for him at the end of the row. "I'm sorry," Mr. Stimple apologized. "I have to put you in last chair for now until I hear you play." "Yes sir, I understand," said Alex pleasantly.

Mr. Stimple's policy was to place the best student for each instrument in first chair, then the rest in order of ability down to last chair. Stewart didn't mind being second chair in his section. First chair was Lucy Porter. She was very good and loved the clarinet so much, she was known to practice for hours. Stewart watched Alex as he opened the case and removed his trumpet. This kid runs like a deer and plays the trumpet, marveled Stewart. Is there no end to his talent?

Stewart talked with his friends, waiting for French class to begin. Annie entered the room without Alex, who was taking Spanish. This was the only class Stewart did not share with Alex and P.E. was the only class he did not share with Annie. He was going to be seeing a lot of these McKnights.

Ms. Robitaille greeted Annie in French, and Annie responded flawlessly. With a smile of approval, Ms. Robitaille pointed for Annie to sit in an open desk next to Stewart. This girl is going to give Dino a run for his money, thought Stewart, as Annie took her seat near the Four Musketeers. Annie smiled at the Musketeers as she opened her notebook, clicked her pen and looked at Ms. Robitaille, ready to take notes. Self-conscious, the Musketeers opened their notebooks and grabbed their pens, wanting to show Annie they were also serious students.

For the second year of French, Ms. Robitaille spoke almost entirely in French and began class with questions relating to the homework assignment. Annie raised her hand after every question, surprising Stewart, as this was only her first day with them. How could she possibly know the assignment? They found out later her old school used the same textbook and she had already read the entire book before they moved.

Ms. Robitaille was overjoyed that more and more students were raising their hands. She normally had to beg students to answer questions and would then have to guide them to an answer, making her feel like she was constantly forcing a confession out of a prisoner. Stewart looked around and saw his friends waving their hands to be called upon. This is turning into a competition, he thought. What is going on here? Had his friends forgotten their vow of "All for one and one for all?"

And before he realized it, when the next question was asked, Stewart raised his hand.

Mr. Pike hung up the phone, jumped to his feet, and threw a fist in the air. He hit on all of his picks last weekend and his winnings had grown close to twenty thousand dollars. Rather than take the money the last few weekends, he rolled them over into the new bets, substantially increasing his pile of cash. Just seconds ago, his bookie had called to tell him they would give him credit, meaning he could bet the cash he already had with them and an amount they would "lend" to him, allowing him to increase his bets even more.

He paced back and forth in his little office so he could absorb this information. It meant taking a big risk for the amount "loaned" to him, as he had heard of people who lost their bets and couldn't repay the loan. However, with his ability to make picks, he didn't believe he would lose and began thinking of all of the ways he would eventually spend his money. He would retire from teaching and buy a big house with enough garage space for a boat, motorcycle, ATV, and a classic muscle car. This was a dream of his for many years and it was coming closer to being a reality. He just had to keep making the right picks, something he was certain would not be a problem.

Stewart emerged from the front doors of the school and looked for his mom, who usually parked close to the entrance. The drop off/pick up zone was unusually crowded that afternoon and Nora was not in her customary spot. Stewart scanned the area, looking for her car. If the drop off/pick up zone was too crowded, parents had to wait in the parking lot on the south side of the school. Not seeing Nora, Stewart headed to the other lot, a short walk away.

He couldn't see his mom's car as he made his way to the crowded parking lot and assumed it was behind one of the large SUV's that were everywhere. Stewart stopped cold. Raymond was approaching from his left. Stewart calculated they would cross paths right before reaching the cars. Raymond had not yet seen him, so Stewart had seconds to figure out what to do. If he made a run for it, Raymond was sure to notice him and would probably chase after him. Without knowing where his mom was, Raymond would quickly catch him.

Realizing Stewart wouldn't be able to find her as she was parked behind a large van, Nora stepped out of the car and walked until she could see him standing on the sidewalk.

"Stewart! Over here," she yelled, waving her hand.

Raymond spotted Stewart at that moment and started running to him. Stewart ran towards his car with Raymond in hot pursuit.

Returning to her car, Nora opened the door and lowered herself onto the seat. Stewart rushed to the other side, frantically reaching for the door. Suddenly his face was pressed against the window, his features completely distorted. Raymond had caught him and shoved him hard against the door. Nora jumped out and faced Raymond.

"Let go of him!" she yelled as she began to walk around the car. Raymond paused before letting go of Stewart. Nora walked up to Raymond and folded her arms. "What do you think you're doing?" she demanded, shocked as well as angry. Raymond gave her a cocky grin and walked away leaving Nora completely flabbergasted. Stewart jumped into the car as she walked back to the other side and opened her door.

"Who was that?" she asked, still ready for battle.

"Raymond. The biggest jerk ever," replied Stewart, biting each word.

"Well, we're going to talk to the principal about him."

"No," said Stewart. "Let's just go home."

"Stewart, we have to go inside and tell someone. Otherwise, he'll keep behaving like this."

Stewart shook his head and stared out the window. "I want to go home." Nora sat there for a moment, trying to figure out what to do. "I'm going to talk to someone in the office," she said, opening her door. Stewart reached over and grabbed her arm.

"Mom, it will only make it worse. He bothers everyone. Let's just go home. Please." Stewart looked at Nora, his eyes pleading for her to stay. "Please." he repeated. Nora relented and closed her door. Nora looked at him, wondering how often this happened to Stewart. Was it just this boy that tormented him or other boys? Did this happen to his friends? And why was he so afraid to report this kind of behavior? She thought of numerous other questions and decided she would talk about this with him another time.

They drove in silence until they reached their street. As they passed the McKnight house, Nora, much calmer, turned to Stewart. "Did you meet the new neighbors?" she asked.

"Yeah, I have both of them in most of my classes."

"Are they nice?"

"I guess so."

"We should have them over so we can get to know them better. What do you think?"

"Sure."

Stewart's brief answers always bothered Nora though she understood he was still upset from the incident with Raymond in the parking lot.

"I can make cinnamon rolls whenever you want to invite them over."

Stewart's features started softening and his jaw finally relaxed, as he had been clenching it the entire drive home. "That sounds really good," said Stewart.

Nora smiled as she pulled into their driveway, relieved that a fresh batch of cinnamon rolls could still be counted on to make him feel better.

07

TO THE RESCUE

STEWART WATCHED THE LOG of messages scrolling across the monitor, updating every transmission. Another hundred thousand or so messages in various frequencies and in hundreds of languages had been transmitted since the twins were last over to his house. Though they had discussed the possibility of aliens communicating in a non-spoken language, Stewart continued to let his computer automatically transmit messages, hoping for a reply until he could think of a better way to communicate.

He found the internet had good information on an amazing number of topics, so he clicked on his web browser and queried "transmitting signals from a person's brain." Since this was an unusual request, he thought there wouldn't be much information about this subject.

The browser returned a handful of interesting topics with a few of them mentioning something about telepathy. He queried that subject and found numerous responses. After reading the first dozen, he leaned back in his chair, pondering this information. Surely the twins used telepathy in some form, he thought. How did they do it? Possessing remarkably similar DNA would obviously contribute to their ability to silently communicate. If their brains were like shortwave radios, they would be able to transmit and receive signals, although they would be communicating with thoughts instead of radio waves. So how does one go about transmitting and receiving if one isn't a twin? Stewart closed his eyes as he leaned further back in his chair. There has to be an answer, somewhere, somehow…

Stewart's eyes opened wide as he lurched forward in his chair. "I've got it!" he shouted.

Panting from running down the street, Stewart approached the twins' house and repeatedly rang the doorbell. Impatient that no one immediately came to the door, he rang a couple of more times for good measure. Ethan, clearly agitated, threw open the door.

"Dude! Stop ringing! You're going to tick off my dad!"

Stewart stepped inside as Nathan walked into the entryway. "Sorry," he said quickly. "Can we go to your room?"

"Sure," said Ethan, leading them down the hall.

Stewart closed the door after the boys entered Ethan's room. Ethan sat on his bed while Nathan sat in a chair at his desk. Stewart remained standing, too excited to sit.

"I was reading about EEG tests and how they record the brain's electrical activity from electrodes attached to a person's head. Thoughts are activities of the brain. Why can't thoughts be captured and transmitted from a machine that takes the apparatus used for an EEG to another level?"

"How are you going to take it to another level?" asked Ethan.

"We watched our dad do EEG tests for his epilepsy research last summer and his equipment can't do anything like what you're talking about," said Nathan.

"I know," said Stewart. "My idea is for electrodes to be placed on the head and hooked to an amplifier to boost the power of the brain's thoughts and transmit it from there."

"The electrodes for an EEG test are hooked up to an amplifier which allows the signal to be interpreted. You're thinking of doing something that already exists," argued Ethan.

"Yes," said Stewart, "but these electrodes are based on waves within the electromagnetic spectrum!" said Stewart, his voice rising with excitement. "That is the problem! Our thoughts are not within the electromagnetic spectrum! They are on a spectrum unknown to man. That is why no one has come up with a way of communicating by thoughts. We only know about the electromagnetic spectrum."

"So how do you invent a machine that can work on a different spectrum?" asked Nathan.

Stewart stopped pacing and for a moment appeared unsure of his next step. "Well, I need to create an amplifier that magnifies my thoughts so they can be transmitted to outer space and hope there is something out there that can receive those thoughts. I was thinking of a device that goes on my head like a football helmet so it is close to my brain and can capture the thoughts with a power source to amplify and transmit." Stewart and the twins sat in silence as they each pondered Stewart's idea.

"I don't like the idea of the football helmet device," stated Ethan.

"Why not?" asked Stewart, somewhat surprised.

"If you're not careful, it could fry your brain," answered Nathan.

"Oh. Good thought," acknowledged Stewart. The boys resumed thinking of a solution to Stewart's problem for a while longer. Suddenly excited, Ethan jumped to his feet.

"I know! You use an intermediary," suggested Ethan.

Stewart frowned. "What do you mean?"

Nathan tapped his head. "Another brain."

"I'm not following," said a puzzled Stewart.

"The other brain receives your thoughts and you amplify that brain so if something goes wrong, it's not your brain that gets fried," suggested Ethan.

"That makes sense. So where do I get a brain?" asked Stewart.

"Our dad's lab," replied Ethan. "He has lots of them in jars from all of his tests. We go to the lab and take a brain that he's finished analyzing."

"This sounds really weird," sighed Stewart. "Like something out of a horror movie."

Ethan jumped to his feet. "There was a brain in the lab that was really interesting. It was from a genius who dealt with epilepsy his whole life. What was unusual about this guy was that he was a criminal genius."

"He pulled off some major crimes and it took the FBI forever to catch him. My dad was asked to study his brain to see if they could understand his criminal tendencies.

"Should we use a brain from someone like that?" wondered Stewart.

"There are a few others to choose from, but I think it would work best to use a brain with a mind as smart as his was," said Ethan.

Stewart thought about it for a moment. "Let's get it."

- - - -

Lying under the covers, Stewart stared at the ceiling in the darkness of his room. He glanced at his clock and saw that it was just before midnight. It was going to be difficult to get up in the morning, but he didn't care. His visit with the twins was a great breakthrough in his quest to communicate with aliens and the possibilities that lay ahead were too exciting. The moment he returned home from the twins' house, he ran to his room and began working out as many details as he could think of for his incredible machine.

The twins thought Saturday would be the best day to get the brain. It was important for the lab to be empty so no one could put a stop to their plan. The twins knew their dad wouldn't allow them to use the brain even though he was done with his research, so they would have to do it without his knowledge. They didn't think they would be violating any laws and they assumed the worst thing that would happen to them if they were caught would be a stern lecture from Dr. Jenkins. Listening to a stern lecture was definitely worth the risk. Just one more day of school this week and it would be Saturday. Stewart couldn't wait.

- - - -

Stewart dreamed he was in a lab, ready to insert a brain into a Frankenstein-like monster and bring it to life from the energy of the lightning storm that crashed around him. Townspeople were marching with torches and pitchforks to his castle on the hill to stop the experiment. A siren from the police car leading the mob was blaring. Foggy-headed, he sat up in bed and realized he had been dreaming and the blaring noise was his alarm. His thoughts turned to the brain and his machine, and he instantly felt energized. Eager for the day to get going, he hopped out of bed, knowing each hour that went by would be an hour closer to Saturday.

Nora backed out of the driveway and drove to the McKnight's house. She had brought a tray of cinnamon rolls to them the day before and spent an hour visiting with Alison, Alex and Annie's mother. Alison was touched by Nora's welcome and invited her in for a cup of tea so they could get to know each other. Nora offered to help her when she saw all of the boxes that had not yet been unpacked. Alison mentioned she was used to it as this was their third move in the last five years. Her husband Andrew worked in the oil business and had been transferred from the company headquarters in Houston to manage the Denver office. Each year they would spend the week of spring break skiing in the glorious mountains of Colorado, so they were happy when they learned where Andrew was going to be transferred. The family hoped they would be able to stay for many years to come.

Alison agreed that driving the kids in the morning made sense since the bus seemed to come so early and alternating driving days would be a good schedule.

Stewart did not like to wait, which is why he did not carpool with the twins. They were never ready when Nora would go to their house and were always late picking him up, and after hearing his daily complaints, they all decided it would be best if they went to school separately. Much to Stewart's relief, as soon as Nora pulled up to the curb, Alex and Annie stepped out of the house. Alex was wearing another colorful shirt and Annie wore another sweater. This one is even more frumpy than the one she wore yesterday, thought Stewart. Was it possible he had seen that sweater on Mrs. Darby? Were Annie and Mrs. Darby participating in a sweater exchange program? He would have to pay more attention to Mrs. Darby's sweaters from now on.

"Good morning," sang Nora cheerfully as they climbed into the car.

"Good morning ma'am," answered Alex politely. "Good morning," said Annie.

"How did you like your first day of school?" asked Nora. Stewart found himself covering his eyes at Nora's questions. Didn't she know kids don't like to be questioned?

"It was okay," Alex again answered politely.

"What are your favorite classes?" asked Nora, furthering the interrogation to Stewart's dismay.

"P.E.," said Alex, causing Stewart to laugh.

"French," said Annie brightly. Oh, no, thought Stewart. Here we go.

"Oh, you like French?" asked Nora.

"Oui, madame," replied Annie.

"Very good," said Nora, clearly impressed. "Have you been to France?"

"Not yet. Someday," replied Annie wistfully.

"We went last summer. Has Stewart told you about it?" volunteered Nora.

Annie's face brightened immensely as she looked at Stewart. "No, he hasn't told me." Annie looked back at Nora. "I can't believe you've been there. How was it?"

"It was wonderful. We are definitely planning to go again. There was so much we didn't have time to see."

"Take me with you!" begged Annie.

"Yes, take her next time," chimed in Stewart. Nora laughed, thinking he was kidding. Stewart, however, wasn't kidding.

Annie sat back in her seat, her thoughts filled with sights of Paris. And Stewart. She peeked at him. He was cute, with a nice smile and perfect white teeth. For the rest of the drive to school she envisioned Stewart speaking French to her from the steps of the Eiffel Tower.

Friday was Stewart's favorite day in math class. Mr. Leiker either gave them a short quiz or a test and on this day, the class would be given a test. Tests were supposed to take the students the entire class to complete though Stewart was usually finished in fifteen minutes. Mr. Leiker would give him a hall pass to the library, and Stewart would go read about outer space. Today, he was anxious to go to the library and work on his ideas for the brain machine.

Mr. Leiker rambled through his customary instructions. Everyone must keep their eyes on their own paper and keep it face down until he said to begin. After everyone received their test, Mr. Leiker gave them the go ahead to begin. Stewart flipped his over and quickly answered the questions.

Finishing the test in fourteen minutes, Stewart rose from his seat, grabbed his backpack and walked to Mr. Leiker's desk. Mr. Leiker had the hall pass ready and handed it to Stewart as he turned in his test.

Annie looked up, astonished to see Stewart leave the room. She was only halfway through and he was already finished?

How could this be? She had always been the smartest kid in all of her classes. Quickly glancing around the room, she saw that everyone else was still working on the problems. Well, maybe this time she was the second smartest kid in the class. What an odd feeling, she thought and found herself smiling. Stewart was cute and very smart, a combination she found appealing.

Mrs. Darby peered at Stewart's hall pass as he stood at her desk in the library. He thought it was humorous that she scrutinized his hall pass every time, checking to see if it was a forgery. While she examined the pass, he looked at her sweater, and took a mental note of the details. He liked to name her sweaters and called this one "The Great Outdoors," as the design was of mountains, with a lake, and a couple of moose standing among the trees.

She handed the pass back to Stewart. Despite her age, Mrs. Darby projected a no-nonsense air about her that was well suited to being a librarian. She insisted on complete quiet and everyone returning books to their proper place on the shelves. As he took the pass from her, Stewart found himself thinking of her on the deck of a pirate ship wearing a large hat with a feather in it, patch over one eye, and a parrot on her shoulder, making sure the pirates ran a tidy ship. He went to a table in the corner of the library, away from the other students quietly studying, and pulled out the notes on his machine. He had a little more than half an hour before the bell and wanted to use this time to figure out a couple of problems he saw with developing his invention. While the twins had come up with a great idea, there were many issues he needed to solve. He wasn't discouraged because he expected it to be a tremendous challenge. If it were easy, his idea would have already been invented by now.

The boys went to their teams on the football field while Stewart finished his last lap. Mr. Pike usually had the four teams play each other on a rotating schedule, but today, he had the same teams play each other so he could watch Raymond play more against the new kid. After attendance was taken, Mr. Pike took Raymond aside and told him to match up with Alex when he was on defense.

Raymond's intensity made it clear he was determined to stop Alex. This was something Alex constantly dealt with as he always ended up drawing the other team's best defender. It didn't bother him to always be matched up with the best players as he found the tougher the competition, the more fun he had. He couldn't wait for the game to begin.

The center snapped the ball to the quarterback and Raymond ran hard at Alex, planning on immediately taking him out of the play with a shoulder to the chest. Alex danced around Raymond with such astonishing quickness, it appeared Raymond was nailed to the ground. With this maneuver, Alex was wide open. The quarterback threw the ball to him and Alex raced for a touchdown with speed no one in the entire school had ever seen.

Raymond's team couldn't move the ball for a first down and punted to Alex's team. On the first play of this new series, Raymond crowded the line and just before the snap, flew across the line and threw his shoulders into Alex's chest, sending him flying backwards onto the ground. Alex jumped to his feet and walked over to Raymond.

"What's your problem? The ball wasn't hiked," said Alex evenly, looking Raymond straight in the eye. Raymond grinned.

"What's the matter, can't take a hit?" sneered Raymond.

"I can take a hit. But this is flag football. Pull a flag. If you can," Alex replied still looking Raymond in the eye. Raymond gave him a hard shove to the chest and Alex stumbled back a few feet. His eyes narrowing, Alex purposefully walked towards him, stopping as Mr. Pike, watching on the sideline, began blowing his whistle. Watching the confrontation unfold, Stewart's stomach turned, knowing Raymond wouldn't hesitate fighting with Alex. He was greatly relieved to hear Mr. Pike's whistle.

"Okay, that's enough," ordered Mr. Pike, not wanting to deal with the paperwork in the office if a fight broke out. "Raymond, take your team and switch fields with Johnson's team."

Raymond and his team trudged to the other field. Mr. Pike smiled, pleased to see Alex stand up for himself. If this kid will stand up to the biggest kid in the school, he will stand up to anybody, he thought. Good stuff for a football player.

The boys finished lunch and chatted in the cafeteria when the bell rang. Stewart picked up his tray, happy lunch period was over. He wanted to talk about his ideas for the machine so badly with the twins and Dino but couldn't do so with Alex and Annie sitting with them. He thought about telling Alex and decided against it. Other than the twins and Dino, he didn't want anyone to know about his ideas and told his friends to keep it a secret. It was too early for anyone else to know what he was up to.

Alex spotted Mr. Leiker coming out of the teacher's lounge, next to the cafeteria, and went over to ask him when they could meet for extra help. He struggled on the test that morning and knew he better get a little help before he fell too far behind. Although it was the same material they had studied in Houston, he didn't have as strong a grasp on the equations as the others. Annie, of course, did not have any problem with the material.

Shortly after Alex left, Stewart and his friends deposited their lunch trays and left the cafeteria. He finally had a chance to tell them his ideas for the machine and was so caught up in the conversation that he forgot to look for Raymond. Unfortunately, they found themselves looking up at Raymond, Damon, and Willie, who quickly steered them to the lockers.

Raymond stuck out his hand. "Hand it over," he said curtly. The boys dug into their pockets.

"What are you guys doing?" asked Alex. After his discussion with Mr. Leiker, he saw Stewart and the others being led to the lockers. Knowing there was no reason his new friends would go with Raymond, he jogged over to them.

Raymond's face grew tight as he looked at Alex. Damon and Willie stood next to Raymond and the three of them did their best to glare at Alex. Alex looked at them calmly. Stewart and his friends watched in disbelief as Alex refused to be intimidated.

Raymond, Damon, and Willie walked to the other end of the locker bay and stopped inches from Alex's face.

"Mind your own business," snarled Raymond.

Alex did not flinch. "Leave them alone."

Raymond clenched his fists.

Mr. Leiker, seeing Alex run to the lockers, sensed something was wrong and followed him.

"What are you boys doing?" demanded Mr. Leiker.

Raymond unclenched his fists and looked at Mr. Leiker. "Nothing," said Raymond, shooting a look at Stewart, who scoffed at his lie.

"It better be nothing," said Mr. Leiker firmly. "Everyone, be on your way."

Stewart and his friends quickly hustled back to the hallway and walked towards their class. Raymond, Damon, and Willie lingered and glared at Mr. Leiker for a moment, then headed for the cafeteria. Mr. Leiker took a deep breath. Even though he was the adult, he realized that Raymond and his friends were much larger than he and if the three of them ganged up on him, there would be nothing he could do about it. This encounter brought up unpleasant memories of being bullied by the same kind of guys when he was in middle school. Bad memories that never go away, just retreat to the back of the mind. He would be very happy when Raymond and his friends would be moving on to high school.

Byron, his head buried in his work, did not immediately notice Charlie enter his office. It was early evening and the sun had set for the day. Byron glanced up from his computer screen as Charlie sat in a chair on the other side of his desk.

"How are you doing?" asked Charlie.

"Okay, I guess. Why do you ask?" replied Byron.

"Are you starting to feel the grind? I am and it isn't even tax season yet. Our business is doing great but I'm worried about the load. We're going to need to add staff."

Byron looked away. The idea of hiring people other than Bernie made him feel extremely uncomfortable.

"Look, I know how you feel about adding staff. We're a victim of our own success. If we keep adding clients at this rate, we're going to be underwater very quickly. I feel like we're getting close to that point, don't you?"

Byron leaned back in his chair and thought about Charlie's comments for a moment. "We may be."

"Well, please think about it over the weekend and we can discuss it next week. Sound good?"

"Sounds good," replied Byron.

"I'm calling it a day, it's been a long week. What do you say?" suggested Charlie as he stood from the chair.

"It wouldn't hurt to call it a night. I just need another hour," said Byron.

"One hour. That's all you get," joked Charlie. "See you Monday."

Charlie returned to his office and shut down his computer. He hoped Byron would give his comments serious consideration over the weekend. Byron was the hardest working person he had ever been around. He believed his motivation came from trying to prove something to those who had given him a hard time throughout his life. Though Byron's drive was admirable, he knew it would come at a price, a physical or mental toll that he didn't want either one of them to face.

08

HALLOWEEN

THE BOYS TALKED EXCITEDLY while they ate breakfast at their usual table near the kitchen at the Spartan Restaurant. Alex sat with them, having been included as the newest member of their group. He appreciated how quickly they befriended him after moving to the neighborhood. Having every class with at least one member of the group also made it easier for him to get to know them. He quickly became aware they were all smart, hardworking kids, similar to his friends back at his former school in Houston. The only difference was that none of these kids played sports. In Texas, his friends played all sports, especially football.

Overall, it didn't matter to him if they didn't like sports as he enjoyed their company and found hanging around them made it easier to get over moving away from his friends.

Alex's family was supposed to move during the summer, but there were delays and the move kept getting pushed back. Though the late move worked out well from a football standpoint because it allowed Alex to play a complete season with his team, it was difficult as far as his studies were concerned.

The boys planned their strategy for trick-or-treating while they ate breakfast. For days, Stewart had been so consumed with his machine, he hadn't been thinking about Halloween. They decided to wear the same costumes as last year. Nathan had found a company on the internet that sold a wide variety of outfits, and he came across a Spartan soldier ensemble. He called his friends to see if they would be interested in forming a Spartan army.

The costumes came with a plumed helmet, tunic, chest plate, shin armor, sandals, sword, and shield. The boys were initially disappointed to find the armor, shield, and sword were made of plastic, but after wearing them for hours, they were grateful they weren't made of heavy metal. The boys would be able to wear them for one last year, as next year they would be in high school and they all assumed high school kids didn't go trick-or-treating.

After describing their outfits to Alex and recounting their slightly exaggerated tales of last years' Halloween outing, Dino, the elected and rightful leader of their Spartan army, stopped eating and looked at Alex. "Sorry there isn't time to order a soldier costume for you. You would make a GREAT Spartan."

Alex shrugged his shoulders. "Not a problem. I'll come up with something."

Eleni walked out of the kitchen and went over to their table.

"Food is good today?" she asked. All of the boys responded enthusiastically. "And who is this one?" she said, looking at Alex.

"Alex. He just moved here," replied Dino. Eleni's eyes grew wide.

"Alex? Nice looking boy! You Greek?"

Alex shook his head. "No ma'am."

"Too bad," she said patting him on the shoulder as she started to walk back to the kitchen. "You have name like Greek." As Eleni returned to the kitchen, Dino leaned towards Alex.

"It's good you're not Greek," confided Dino.

"Why is that?" asked Alex.

"Because she would start fixing you up with my cousin."

"I'm only thirteen!" laughed Alex incredulously.

"It doesn't matter," said Dino. "She said it's never too early to start matchmaking. You wouldn't like my cousin. She NEVER stops talking."

While the others talked, Stewart tried to calmly eat the rest of his breakfast, even though his stomach was doing backflips. He hardly slept that night thinking of the mission he and the twins would be undertaking that day. The plan was to go through their normal Saturday morning routine so their parents wouldn't think they were up to anything. After breakfast they would go to the mall and take a bus to the lab. If they could get in and out as quickly as planned, they would be able to catch a bus back to the mall and be waiting for Nora. A brilliant plan, reflected Stewart, as he took another bite.

Stewart looked at his watch as Nora drove the boys away from the restaurant. They were going to drop Alex off at his house and continue to the mall. In front of everyone, Stewart had invited Alex to go the mall with them, knowing Alex had already mentioned he was going to spend the morning with his dad. By inviting him, he knew his mom wouldn't think he was rude and insist that Alex go with them.

Alex's cell phone rang. "Hello." Alex nodded his head. "Okay. Goodbye." Alex put his phone back in his pocket and looked at Stewart and the twins.

"My dad has to work this morning, so I can go to the mall with you guys."

Nora glanced at Alex in the rearview mirror. "Well, that had a nice way of working out."

Stewart's eyebrows raised to the top of his forehead as Alex announced he was now free for the morning. He looked at the twins, who had similar expressions.

Alex noticed Stewart's expression and looked at him quizzically. Stewart placed his hand on his chest. "Heartburn," he said to Alex. "Ah," responded Alex.

Stewart glanced at the twins as he turned back in his seat. Their eyes seemed to be saying "What do we do now?" He tried to make his eyes say "I don't know!" before turning forward in his seat.

Nora pulled over to the sidewalk near the main entrance to the mall.

"What time should I pick you up?" she asked Stewart. He looked at the others as if they were figuring it out at that moment.

"I don't know. How about after lunch? One o'clock?" suggested Stewart. Nora looked at the other boys. "Will that be okay with your parents?" she asked. The twins and Alex assured her it would be fine with their parents.

"Okay, I'll meet you right here at one o'clock," she confirmed as the boys climbed out of the car.

The twins immediately looked at Stewart, gesturing with their heads towards Alex. Geez, thought Stewart, a herd of buffalo storming through the mall would be subtler than their gyrations. Trying to figure out what to do in a split second was not going to work, he realized, so he decided to come clean with Alex.

"Alex," started Stewart.

"Yeah?" said a puzzled Alex, wondering where this conversation was going.

"We have something to tell you." The twins' mouths simultaneously dropped open as they realized what Stewart was about to say.

"We're not at the mall to go to the mall," said Stewart, realizing he wasn't making sense. "I mean, we're going somewhere else."

Alex folded his arms. He wasn't sure he liked the sound of this. Not that he was a goody two-shoes, but he wasn't the type of kid to get into mischief, either. "Where are we going?" he asked.

"We're going to a lab where their dad does research," said Stewart, pointing at the twins.

"Why are we going there?" Alex inquired. Stewart looked at the twins, knowing how this was going to sound.

"Uh, we're going to borrow a brain," explained Stewart. Alex looked at them completely bewildered.

"Sounds weird, huh?" offered Stewart.

"It sure does!" blurted Alex.

"I have an idea for inventing a machine and we need a brain to make it work."

Alex laughed. "I'm sorry, this sounds ridiculous. Doesn't this sound ridiculous?" he asked, looking at Ethan and Nathan.

"It does," said Stewart, checking his watch. "We have ten minutes to get to the bus stop and catch the bus. I'll explain it to you as we go. After I tell you about it, you won't think it's ridiculous, I promise."

Alex looked at Stewart, then the twins, and could tell from their expressions they were serious. In the few days he had been around them, he knew they weren't the kind of kids to do something that would get themselves in big trouble, so as strange as this all sounded, he found himself willing to trust them. "Okay," he said after a long moment. "Let's go to the bus stop."

A white bus with an advertisement of a popular hamburger chain emblazoned across its side slowly came to a stop. The boys hopped off the bus and headed down the sidewalk leading to the entrance of a building. Stewart looked at his watch and noted that the trip had taken almost thirty minutes.

The lab was located in a three-story structure with a rock and wood exterior similar to the design of a ski lodge. The building was built only a few years ago for the purpose of being a medical center and all of the offices were filled with doctors of various specialties.

Stewart observed there were only a couple of cars in the parking lot, a good sign. The twins confirmed that none of the researchers would be there that day, because the lab was closed on weekends. Stewart wondered if they had flat-out asked their dad for the lab schedule, a clumsy act certain to arouse suspicion. Fearing the worst, he expected to see helicopters appear in the sky with swat teams hanging from ropes, ready to land on the roof.

The boys walked to the entrance and Ethan pulled on the door. It was locked.

"What?" exclaimed a surprised Ethan. "Wait, I've got the spare key." He fished a key out of his pocket and inserted it in the lock. It didn't unlock the door. "I don't understand," said Ethan, looking at the key.

"Let me see that," grumbled Nathan as he took the key. "It's for the lab. It won't work for this door. I thought you were getting both keys!" Ethan put his hands on his head.

"Dude, I forgot the other key," lamented a pained Ethan.

"So how do we get in?" Stewart wondered aloud to no one in particular. While the boys stood by the door, Stewart noticed the elevator doors opening.

"Hide!" he yelled. The boys ran to the side of the entrance and dove behind the juniper bushes planted on each side of the doors. They landed in one large pile with Ethan on the bottom. "Get off me!" he managed to say, gulping for air. The boys slid off of Ethan, crawled to their feet, and peeked over the bushes. A man carrying a briefcase opened the door and emerged from the building. He headed down the sidewalk, with the door closing ever so slowly.

When the man walked just far enough past them, Alex leaped over the bushes and ran to the entrance, sticking his hand in the door right before it closed shut. He performed this maneuver so quickly and so quietly that the boys needed a moment to comprehend what they had just seen. Alex waved for them to come to the door.

Stewart and the twins scrambled around the bushes and ran inside the building. Ethan pushed the "up" button for the elevator and the doors opened. Once inside the elevator, Nathan pushed the third-floor button and the doors closed.

Upon reaching the third floor, the elevator doors opened and the boys stepped into the hall, with Ethan and Nathan leading the way. They came to a stop at the door leading to the lab and Ethan inserted the key in the lock. He turned the handle to the door and opened it, a big smile on his face. They entered the suite with Ethan closing the door behind them.

"Follow me," said Nathan heading down the hall and into another room filled with tables, microscopes and various types of scientific equipment. He opened another door and they crammed into a small room with shelves placed along the walls. The boys stared at the numerous jars with labels lining the shelves.

"Here they are," announced Nathan, with a sweep of his hand.

"Where is the brain you were talking about?" asked Stewart.

"It should be over here," Ethan replied as he went to a corner where there was an empty space between two other jars. "It's not here!" he exclaimed.

"What would they do with it?" asked Stewart, starting to panic at the thought of not leaving with a brain.

"I don't know," said Ethan, trying to remain calm. "Okay, let's take another one." He scanned the rows of jars and came to a stop at the other end of the room. "Hey!" shouted Ethan. "This one will work great!"

Stewart looked at the label. "Do you know anything about this one?"

Ethan leaned over Stewart's shoulder and peered at the label. "Oh yeah. This one was different from the other ones. My dad studied this lady's brain right after she died to see if there was anything that could scientifically support what she claimed about herself while she was alive."

"This brain would be perfect," confirmed Nathan.

"What was special about this person?" asked Stewart.

"She was a psychic," said Ethan and Nathan at the same time.

"Really?" was all Stewart could say, while consulting his watch. "The bus is going to be here in five minutes! We've got to go!"

Ethan checked the door to make sure it was locked after the boys left the lab and ran to the elevator. Nathan pushed the "down" button and the elevator doors opened. Hustling into the elevator, the boys waited impatiently during the few seconds it took for the doors to close.

The elevator reached the first floor and the doors opened. The boys stepped out and saw Dr. Jenkins, the twins' father, using his key to open the entrance door.

"What do we do?" said Stewart in a shrill whisper.

"Get back in the elevator!" ordered Alex. He hit the "up" button and the doors opened. The boys jumped back in and Alex pushed the button for the second floor sending the elevator upwards.

The doors opened and the boys quickly stepped into the hall.

"Everyone calms down," said Alex, maintaining his composure. "Let's wait for your dad to get to his floor and we'll take the stairs." Stewart and the twins nodded their heads and looked up at the floor indicator above the elevator doors. They could see the light go from the second floor to the first floor, pause, then back to the second floor and stopping at the third floor. The boys ran to the end of the hall towards a door with a diagram of stairs stenciled on it, opened the door and entered the stairwell.

They exited the stairwell on the first floor and ran for the doors at the entrance. "We've got a minute!" yelled Stewart to the others, looking at his watch as they ran out of the building.

"No, we don't!" said Ethan pointing down the street as the bus drove closer and closer to their stop. The bus stop for the return trip was across the street and the boys stood on the curb, waiting for an opening in traffic on the busy street.

"We've got to catch this bus!" Stewart yelled frantically. "The next one won't be here for another half hour!"

Dr. Jenkins stepped into the office and set his briefcase on the table. Walking to the window, he opened the blinds to let more light into the room. Turning back to his desk, he stopped and looked out the window to the street below. That's odd, he thought. He had caught a glimpse of a group of boys running across the street just as the bus came to a stop. Two of the boys were in striped shirts and looked like his boys. Looking out the window, he watched the bus drive away. Were they his boys? He wasn't certain, so he pulled out his cell phone and dialed a number.

The boys found seats together near the back of the bus and sat down as Ethan's cell phone began ringing. "Hello," said Ethan into the phone.

"Hey son, it's me. Where are you and Nathan at this moment?"

"Uh, we're at the mall. Why?"

"I was just wondering. Is everything going okay?"

"Sure, everything is fine. Where are you?" Ethan found himself asking.

"At the office," replied Dr. Jenkins. "I have a little work to do. Okay, you boys behave yourselves."

"We will. See you later." Ethan put the phone back in his pocket. "Why do you think he called? Did he see us?"

"If he had, he wouldn't have called to ask where you are," said Stewart.

"He could be testing us. Our dad has this amazing ability to detect when we're getting in trouble," argued Nathan.

"We can't get away with anything around him," chimed in Ethan.

"There's nothing to worry about," said Stewart as confidently as he could, cradling the jar with the brain.

Annie went around her bedroom, organizing and rearranging the dolls and stuffed animals on her shelves. Though she always wanted to give the impression to everyone that she was grown up and wanted to be treated like an adult, she still cherished certain dolls and stuffed animals from her childhood and couldn't bear to think of putting them in a box and storing them away for the rest of her life. Besides, nobody came to her room, so she was free to decorate it however she pleased.

She adorned the walls of her room with pictures of places she dreamed of going to someday and of people she admired. Among the pictures of the Eiffel Tower, Notre Dame Cathedral, and the Louvre were pictures of prominent figures such as Albert Einstein, Madame Curie, Claude Monet and Stephen Hawking.

Hearing a car drive past, she looked out the window, and saw Nora driving the boys back to her house and park in the driveway. Everyone climbed out of the car and walked to the front door. She noticed Stewart walking faster than usual and carrying something in a bag. Looking at her wall, she imagined a picture of Stewart, holding a medal for discovering a new mathematical theorem that would revolutionize the world. If anyone could do it, she believed it would be him.

The boys stared at the brain in the jar placed on Stewart's desk. Alex leaned close to the jar. "This is too weird. I've never seen a human brain before today."

"We've seen tons of them," said Ethan.

"After you've seen a bunch of them, it's like looking at frogs in science class. You don't think anything about it," added Nathan.

"Now what are you going to do with it?" asked Alex.

"I'm going to put it in a different container and add a heating element and an electrode for an electrical supply. If this can stimulate the brain, we may be in business," explained Stewart.

Alex frowned. "How do you know if it's going to work?"

"I don't," answered Stewart. "It's going to take a lot of trial and error. I'll try different temperatures, different electrical charges, and chemicals to help conduct electrical currents. Whatever I can think of, I'll try it."

Stavros proudly lined up the boys for pictures while Eleni looked into her camera. Customers in the restaurant watched and complimented the boys on their costumes. In full Spartan gear, the boys looked very authentic and ready for battle. They posed for pictures last year and one of them was on display near the cash register. Eleni had sent copies to both her and Stavros' families in Sparta and they were such a hit, everyone asked her to send pictures again for this year.

Eleni snapped frame after frame, then stopped, satisfied she had taken enough to please the families. She motioned for Alex, standing off to the side with Nora, to join the other boys.

Alex wore a black Ninja outfit, complete with black martial arts slippers, and a mask. Everyone exclaimed how great he looked, which made him feel better, because his outfit didn't quite fit with the others. At least he was a warrior, just like them.

Eleni finished taking pictures and put away her camera. The boys went to the bathroom and put on flesh-colored thermal shirts and long underwear underneath their costumes. The days had been pleasant recently, though the nights had become chilly and the boys wouldn't last long wearing just a chest plate and skirt. The boys emerged from the bathroom and waved to everyone in the restaurant. Nora led them to the car, where she would drive them to their neighborhood for trick-or-treating. Dino barked orders for everyone to hurry up in a deep, booming voice with a thick accent that was a remarkable imitation of his dad. Everyone laughed as they piled into the car. Nora laughed along with them, wondering how such a big voice could come from such a small boy.

The night was going well, thought Stewart, after finishing another street. It wasn't too cold, and the treats he and his friends were getting from his neighbors seemed to be unusually good. They decided to go to Dr. Connelly's house just to see if he would hand out anything different to the kids this year. Dr. Connelly was a local dentist and was known for passing out toothbrushes and toothpaste to all of the kids who came to his house on Halloween. Stewart had grumbled about it years ago, but his dad told him to look on the bright side, he was getting a free toothbrush. It became sort of a game to Stewart over the years to see if community pressure would get to Dr. Connelly, who would finally come to his senses and give out the greatest treats ever to make up for all of the bad years. But no, every year the treat remained a toothbrush and toothpaste, and this year was not any different.

The boys kept up a good pace that evening, a pace better than in years past, and were getting close to covering all of the streets in the neighborhood. Stewart attributed this to the laps they ran in P.E. and was surprised to admit he was actually benefiting from Mr. Pike's methods. Along the way, they passed groups of their friends from school. They would stop to compare how much candy each of them had acquired and discuss which homes were passing out the best treats.

Another hour later and they reached the last street in the development. In the past, they wouldn't make it as far and always circled back down a street leading to Stewart's house. This year, the boys covered every home by the time they reached the last street and as late as it was getting to be, they had no choice but to walk the half mile back to Stewart's house, where they would spend the night.

Walking down the street towards Stewart's house, they noticed they weren't seeing other kids. Since Spartan soldiers didn't wear watches, Stewart guessed it was about nine o'clock, which explained why they hadn't seen the younger kids for over an hour. The older kids, like themselves, seemed to also be calling it a night.

The boys only had a couple of more streets to go before they would be at Stewart's house, where his mother would be making hot chocolate for them. Stewart looked forward to going inside where it would be warm. The air now seemed to be getting cooler by the minute and Stewart pulled his tunic around him like a blanket.

They turned the corner to the street that led to Stewart's house and found themselves walking straight towards Raymond, Damon, and Willie, all dressed as bikers. They wore bandanas around their heads and motorcycle t-shirts with sleeves that had been cut off. Instead of grocery bags, they carried pillowcases completely full of candy.

"Oh no!" exclaimed Ethan, coming to a stop upon seeing Raymond and his friends.

"Can we make a run for it?" asked Nathan quietly.

"We won't make it," said Stewart, fearing the worst.

Dino tightly gripped the handle of his sword with Raymond and the others approaching. He didn't care if it was made of plastic. If necessary, he was going to use it to defend himself.

Raymond smiled as he, Damon, and Willie stood shoulder to shoulder in front of Stewart and his friends.

"Look what we got here," he said to Damon and Willie. "Four Roman geeks."

"We're not Romans!" said Dino through gritted teeth. "We're SPARTANS!"

"Whatever." Raymond took a few steps over to Alex, whose face, except for his eyes, was covered by the Ninja mask. "I bet this is the new kid. Pull up your mask so I can see you."

"We're not looking for trouble," said Alex. "You go your way and we'll go ours."

"That's the problem," sneered Raymond. "We're always looking for trouble." Damon and Willie laughed with Raymond. Raymond stepped forward and forcefully shoved Alex in the chest.

Alex stumbled backwards a few steps and quickly regained his balance. "I'll only say this one more time. We don't want any trouble. You go your way and we'll go ours."

Charging forward, Raymond raised his hands to shove Alex. Alex quickly grabbed Raymond's hands, spun around and flipped him over his shoulder. Raymond landed with a thud on his back and gasped for air.

Alex crouched in a fighting position and turned to face Damon and Willie. Standing in momentary shock, they realized they needed to stand up for Raymond and ran to Alex. Alex took a step towards Damon, leaped high in the air and delivered a powerful kick to Damon's chest, sending him flying backwards.

Willie lowered his head and began throwing wild punches as he rushed to Alex. Alex blocked the first punch, ducked under the second punch and delivered a crushing blow to Willie's ribs. Clutching his side, Willie sank to his knees groaning loudly.

Raymond crawled to his feet, his face red with rage. He ran as fast as he could at Alex and dove into him, tackling him with every ounce of strength in his body. Alex landed on his back with Raymond on top of him. Alex brought his legs up high, wrapped them around Raymond's neck, and jerked Raymond off of him. Before Raymond could climb to his feet, Alex pounced on him and punched him flush on the nose. Blood gushed out of his nostrils and poured down his face. Raymond held his nose as Alex stood up and looked at Damon who had crawled to his knees and was frozen with fear.

"Get out of here and don't bother us again," ordered Alex, his eyes dark and narrow. He looked at his friends, whose mouths stood wide open. "Let's go."

The boys walked down the street, looking over their shoulders in disbelief as Damon helped Raymond and Willie to their feet.

"That was awesome!" said Ethan when they were far enough down the street. Ethan, Nathan, and Dino just keep looking at each other with the biggest smiles Stewart had ever seen from them. Alex just stared down the street, his jaw tight. He clearly did not fight for fun.

The events of the confrontation happened so quickly, Stewart tried to recall every second from beginning to end as they walked down the street. Rather than think about it right then and there, he decided he would replay the sequence of the confrontation later and enjoy this feeling for as long as he could. After all, this had just become the greatest night of his life.

Stewart, the twins, and Dino smiled all of the way to Stewart's house. Alex, still wearing a grim expression, stopped on the sidewalk just as the boys reached Stewart's driveway.

"I'll see y'all later," said Alex, his voice flat.

"You're not going to spend the night?" asked Stewart.

Alex shook his head. "Not tonight. I'm really tired." He took a few steps down the sidewalk, stopped and turned towards the boys. "I would appreciate it if none of you said anything about this."

The boys were surprised by this request and promised to keep it to themselves. Alex waved a quick goodbye and crossed the street to his house. The boys watched him leave and proceeded up the driveway to the front door.

"I can't believe he doesn't want us to tell anybody," said a disappointed Ethan. "I was going to post this on the internet as soon as I got to my computer."

"Maybe he'll get in trouble with his parents," suggested Nathan.

"That could be it," surmised Dino. "Or maybe he's a top karate master and it's illegal for him to get into fights."

"Is there such a thing?" wondered Nathan.

"I don't know. Could be," allowed Dino.

"It's too bad we can't tell anybody. He would be the hero of the school," said Ethan, full of admiration. "Everybody would talk about this for years."

"We can't tell anyone. We have to respect his wishes," intoned Stewart, the voice of reason.

The other boys sighed as they agreed with him and entered the house. Nora greeted them with a tray of hot chocolate.

"I hope you boys had a successful evening of trick-or-treating," she said cheerfully.

The boys looked at each other before Stewart held up his bag full of candy. "It was a huge success."

Alex entered his house and headed up the stairs to his bedroom. Alison and Annie walked out of Annie's room as Alex reached the top of the stairs.

"How did your night go?" asked Alison.

"It went okay," Alex replied while looking at the floor.

Alison folded her arms as she tried to read Alex's body language. "Is anything wrong?"

"Nothing's wrong," Alex assured her. "I'm tired. We went to a lot of houses and it's pretty cold out there. I just want to go to bed."

"Okay. Well, goodnight. See you tomorrow morning."

"Goodnight," said Alex, forcing himself to be more cheerful. He wished he had stayed home with Annie, who didn't want to go trick-or-treating anymore. At least he would be warm and not have gotten into it with those bullies.

Alex walked into his room and closed the door without turning on the lights. He dropped his bag of candy on the floor and went to his bed, where he settled on top of the covers. His arms folded under his head, he concentrated on relaxing his body. He had studied various forms of martial arts for years and his favorite instructor told him if he never had to use his skills in a fight, he should consider himself blessed. Fighting was only a last resort and only for self-defense. He felt badly he hadn't been able to prevent a confrontation with Raymond. After replaying the events of the evening over and over in his mind, Alex finally decided he had done everything possible to avoid it. Closing his eyes, he fell into a deep sleep.

Holding his blood-soaked bandana to his nose, Raymond walked alongside Damon down a dark street. Willie followed a few paces behind them, grimacing as he clutched his side. They arrived at Raymond's house, a small, dismal shack with peeling paint and a yard filled with weeds and trash. The boys walked across the driveway full of motorcycles and headed for the front door. Raymond grabbed the screen door, its hinges barely clinging to the frame and the top half of the screen torn and dangling over the handle. He flung it open, pushed on the wood door with a cracked window, and entered the house.

Beer bottles were everywhere. Tough men, many with beards and mustaches, lounged on the couch and chairs in the living room. Music boomed from the stereo. The men stopped talking to each other and loudly commented on Raymond's appearance as he entered the house, his eyes and nose purple and grotesquely swollen. Holding a beer, a mountain of a man emerged from the kitchen after hearing the commotion from the living room. Carl Burns stood six feet six inches tall and weighed close to three hundred pounds. He was the fearless leader of his friends and a man no one in his right mind wanted to tangle with, especially when Carl had too much to drink.

He crossed his beefy, tattoo-covered arms and waited for Raymond's explanation.

"We got jumped," said Raymond. "High school kids hanging out by the gas station. We got them good."

Pleased, Carl smiled. "Looks like they got you too. Go wash off." Carl's friends laughed and patted him on the back as Raymond headed for the bathroom.

Raymond learned long ago if he came home and told his dad he lost a fight, his dad would slap him around to show him if another kid ever got the better of him, he would get it worse at home. Raymond hadn't lost a fight since then until tonight. Damon and Willie knew exactly how it worked in this house and were quick to agree with Raymond's story of getting jumped, knowing it would help keep Raymond from getting beaten by his dad.

09

THE MAKING OF A MACHINE

THE NEXT MORNING, STEWART waved goodbye to Dino, who drove away with his mom. The boys slept late that morning after staying up well past midnight to eat their favorite candy and discuss every detail of Alex's battle with Raymond, Damon, and Willie. Nothing like that had ever happened to any of them before and it was so surreal, they all felt like they were in the middle of a martial arts movie, with bodies flying everywhere. Stewart knew it was going to take all of his willpower to not talk about it with anyone outside of their group to honor Alex's request. He was especially worried about the twins, knowing they didn't do a good job of keeping secrets.

With all of his friends now out of the house, Stewart raced upstairs, ran to his bedroom, and closed the door. He went to his closet, pulled out a box and brought it to his desk. From the box, Stewart pulled out a specimen jar and various pieces of equipment. He took off the lid to the specimen jar and placed it next to the jar containing the brain. Taking off the lid to the jar with the brain, he slowly poured the brain and preservation fluid into the other specimen jar.

Lying on the desk was a box with a control for speed from a model train set he had received as a birthday present. The control was a good way to gradually adjust the power transmitted from the box but Stewart wanted to have the option to be able to send electrical current in a pulsating manner. He also felt the settings marked on the box weren't sufficient for reading the power output. Nora had taken him to an electrical supply store the prior weekend, where he bought a digital power meter and a device for controlling the electrical pulses. She never understood the equipment Stewart bought from this store though the purchases seemed important and kept him busy, and that was fine with her.

Stewart wired the power meter and the pulse control device to the power box and was ready for the final piece of equipment. He attached a wire from an electrode to the power box and threaded it through a tiny hole he had drilled in the lid to the new specimen jar. Once the wire was threaded through the hole, Stewart reattached the end of the electrode to the wire. Taking the end of the electrode, Stewart carefully placed it on the frontal lobe of the brain. Lastly, to help aid the transmission of electricity in the preservation fluid, he poured electrolytes into the specimen jar and tightly screwed on the lid.

Standing up and pacing his room, Stewart took a moment to contemplate what he was about to do. If the brain could be electrically stimulated and receive his thoughts, and the stimulus was great enough for the brain to amplify his thoughts, he would be transmitting thoughts into the universe. Surely, someone or something was going to be the receiver of these thoughts. If only this contraption works, he thought. Wait, it's not a contraption, it's a machine. Think positive thoughts! Yes, and it's not just a machine, it's a brain machine!

Stewart walked back to the machine and reached for the on/off switch on the power box. As his finger touched the switch, he stopped. He went back to the closet and dragged out a heavy, medium-sized box. It was filled with rocks that used to be on the shelves in his room until he put them in the box to make room for his model spaceships. Most of the stones came from a store that sold only rocks and related accessories. The store was owned by a ninety-two-year-old man named Mr. Beal, who had worked as a geologist and knew everything there was to know about geology. Stewart was eight years old when he first visited the store and thought it was the greatest store on earth. There were countless shelves and bins filled to the brim with an amazing variety of minerals. Stewart asked Mr. Beal how many items were in the store and he said he honestly didn't know, as there were thousands of them. A couple of years later, Mr. Beal began having health problems and decided to close the store. Stewart pleaded with his parents to buy the store, but they told him they didn't know anything about running a store such as this and besides, Byron was too busy with his own business. With nobody interested in buying the store, all of the merchandise was sold at a steep discount before closing for good.

On the last day the store was open, Nora brought Stewart to say goodbye. As Nora and Stewart were about to leave, Mr. Beal opened a drawer under the cash register and took out a glass vial filled with dust in an odd silver-blue color. He told Stewart he got this dust from a crater where a comet had crashed into the earth in a remote corner of New Mexico. Since it came from the sky, he thought of it as magical stardust and wanted to give it to Stewart. Shortly after the store closed its doors, Mr. Beal passed away. Stewart and Nora went to his funeral and Stewart sat in the church with the vial of dust in his suit pocket, thinking of all of the kindness Mr. Beal had shown him over the years.

Stewart brought the vial to his desk and unfastened the lid to the machine. Opening the vial, he took a pinch of dust and sprinkled it into the fluid surrounding the brain, thinking it couldn't hurt to add a little magical stardust to the machine. He placed the lid back on top of the specimen jar and fastened it tightly. Confident he had the placed the correct ingredients in the machine, he sat down and turned on the power and watched the power meter. His plan was to begin with a low volume of electrical current and slowly increase it to see if it made a difference.

Pulling up a form he devised on his computer for logging in data, he typed in the setting shown on the meter and the time of day. Every modification and anything else he observed would be recorded in this log. Lying on his bed and closing his eyes, Stewart was now ready to transmit his thoughts. He concentrated on thinking of a sentence he had practiced speaking aloud in the bathroom mirror: *This is Starhawk Ranger from Mother Earth. Can anyone hear me?*

Jolted by the sound of Nora's voice, Stewart sat upright and tried to figure out what was happening. He had dozed off and now his mother was peering at the brain in the jar.

"Oh my!" she repeated, moving her head around the jar. "What is this?"

The fog in Stewart's head began to clear. "It's a cow brain. I'm doing an experiment for science class."

"What kind of experiment?"

"Uh, I'm trying to see if the brain responds to electrical stimulus," Stewart explained, hoping this would satisfy his mother.

"How do you know if it responds?" asked Nora.

"Well, a light bulb is supposed to light up and would you look at this? I forgot to hook up the bulb. Thanks, mom, you really helped me out," said Stewart, full of gratitude.

Nora beamed. "Anything to help my junior scientist." She looked out the window and saw Alex and his dad throwing a football back and forth to each other in the street. "Look, it's Alex and his father."

Stewart moved over to the window and watched Andrew throw a long pass to Alex, who sprinted down the street and caught the perfectly thrown ball. Smiling, he threw the ball back to his dad. Stewart found himself wishing it was he and his dad out there on the street throwing passes, even though he couldn't throw or catch any kind of ball. Still, seeing the two of them together made him think of how little time he spent with Byron.

Nora watched him for a moment, knowing exactly what he was thinking. Byron and Stewart would never bond over sports, though they could bond over something if Byron could ever find the time. It wasn't so bad when Stewart was younger, while over the last few years, Byron had gotten busier and busier with work. If only Byron had a hobby, then perhaps that could be something they could share together. She reminded herself to look into finding Byron a hobby as she left the room.

Stewart watched Alex throw the ball with his father for a little while longer. Suddenly inspired to see if he could get his father to take a break from working out of the house that day, Stewart headed downstairs.

Entering Byron's home office, Stewart stopped as he found himself looking at his dad, sound asleep on the couch. Not wanting to disturb him, Stewart quietly backed out of the office. His dad had been working very hard for the last few months and probably needed all of the sleep he could get, thought Stewart, as he silently walked away. Maybe Byron would be able to do something with him later in the day.

Stepping out of the house, Stewart closed the front door behind him and watched Alex run past his house while Andrew launched another pass that settled into Alex's outstretched arms. As Alex turned to throw the football back to Andrew, he saw Stewart and waved for him to come over and join him. Stewart wasn't sure what he meant, so he pointed at himself and Alex nodded.

Alex waited in the street as Stewart walked over to him and they headed to Andrew.

"How are you doing?" asked Stewart.

"Doing okay," answered Alex with no trace of anguish from the night before.

"That's good," said Stewart.

The boys approached Andrew.

"Dad, this is Stewart."

"Pleased to meet you," said Andrew pleasantly, shaking hands with Stewart, who looked Andrew in the eye and grasped his hand firmly, a lesson Byron had taught him on the importance of making a good first impression.

"Nice handshake," said Andrew as he pulled his hand away. "You two throw it around, I've got a little work to do." Andrew turned and headed towards his house.

"Do you want to throw a few passes?" asked Alex.

Embarrassed, Stewart looked at the ground.

"I can't throw and I can't catch," admitted Stewart.

"Really? Hmm. Okay, let me show you," offered Alex, backing up so there was ten feet of space between them. "Put your hands in front of you like this. When the ball comes, clamp your hands on it. Here goes." Alex gently flicked the football to Stewart, who closed his eyes as he turned his head and waved his arms as the football approached him.

Alex folded his arms for a moment. "Stewart, number one, you can't close your eyes. How are you going to catch the ball if you can't see it? Number two, you waved your hands like I was throwing a brick with spikes on it. Keep your eyes open and bring your hands together to catch the ball. Let's try it again." Alex walked within four feet of Stewart and gently tossed the ball to him. This time, Stewart kept his eyes open and his face lit up as he easily caught the ball. Alex smiled as he ran over and gave Stewart a high five. "To throw it back to me, put your fingers on the laces like this, then flick your arm towards me. Like this."

Backing up a few feet from his last toss, Alex lobbed another pass to Stewart, who again caught the ball. "Nice catch!" shouted Alex. Stewart grinned as he carefully placed his fingers on the ball as Alex had done. However, instead of flicking the ball, Stewart threw with a motion across his body causing the ball to spin sideways and miss Alex by a wide margin.

Unperturbed, Alex picked up the ball. "Make sure your arm goes forward towards the person you're throwing to. Like this." Alex gently threw another pass to Stewart. Determined, Stewart put his fingers on the laces, cocked his arm and imitating Alex's motion, threw a perfect spiral to Alex. Catching the ball, Alex let out a whoop and ran over to give Stewart another high five. "Now you're doing it! Let's throw a few more to make sure you got it." Stewart beamed as he continued to throw passes with only a few wobbles and caught most of the passes without too much difficulty as they increased the distance between them.

Watching all of this from the living room window, Nora couldn't stop smiling. This boy Alex is a gift from heaven, she thought. Why couldn't he teach P.E. instead of that arrogant Mr. Pike?

Sofie, Linh, and Debbie sat behind the counter in the convenience store located on the corner of a busy intersection near the school. Most Sunday afternoons, Sofie and Debbie spent a few hours with Linh and kept her company while she worked her shift at the family-owned store. Linh's family emigrated from Vietnam when she was barely old enough to walk and after many years of saving their money, her parents bought this corner gas station with a convenience store. As with Dino's family, Linh's parents relied on the family to help with the business. Sofie and Debbie met Linh in kindergarten and had been best friends ever since. They enjoyed hanging out at the store and after Linh's shift, they would go to her house, where Linh's mother would prepare a fabulous Vietnamese dinner for the girls.

A customer finished pumping gas and walked in to buy a soft drink and potato chips. Linh rang up the sale on the cash register and gave the customer change. The customer walked out of the door as Brittany, Shelby, and Courtney entered.

"What are they doing here?" wondered Linh in a soft voice.

Brittany and her friends acted like they didn't notice Linh, Sofie, and Debbie at the counter and strolled down the aisles, pretending to be interested in the items on the shelves. Brittany, walking down the middle aisle, reached the rear of the store and stuck a box of cookies in her purse. She could see Linh watching her and whispering to Sofie and Debbie in the reflection of a mirror placed high in the corner of the store.

On the aisle to Brittany's left, Shelby grabbed a bag of candy and put it in her purse, knowing she was also being watched. Courtney, on the aisle to Brittany's right, took a cleaning spray bottle and placed it in her purse.

From the mirrors, Linh, Sofie, and Debbie were able to see Brittany and the others stealing the merchandise. Shelby and Courtney joined Brittany at the back of the store and as they passed each other, unseen by Linh, took out the merchandise from their purses and stashed the items randomly on the shelves. They moved on to different aisles and continued to act like they were looking for items to purchase.

Brittany signaled to Shelby and Courtney and they headed for the door. Linh quickly stepped from behind the counter and stood at the door, blocking their exit.

"Please put back the items you stole," said Linh with a lump in her throat.

Brittany smirked as she looked at Linh, then Sofie and Debbie. "I don't know what you're talking about," she said innocently.

"I watched you steal things and put them in your purse. Please put them back."

Brittany loudly chewed her gum, while she enjoyed watching Linh stand nervously before her. "I told you, I don't know what you're talking about."

"Open your purse," Linh demanded.

"I don't have to do that," retorted Brittany.

"I saw all of you put something in your purses. I'm going to call the police." Linh took a step towards the counter.

"Okay, okay," said Brittany. "Look." Brittany, Shelby, and Courtney opened their purses. Linh peered in each purse and stepped back puzzled. The purses did not contain any stolen items. Brittany and the others laughed as they walked out of the store. Linh ran to the back and found the items Brittany and her friends appeared to have stolen. She gathered the items and returned them to their proper place.

"Those girls are terrible. I have to keep them out of the store from now on," muttered Linh angrily.

"Why would they do that?" wondered Debbie.

"They think it's funny." Sofie responded. "Too bad they're the only ones who think so."

Raymond, Damon and Willie sat on a wall in an alley behind a row of stores. Damon and Willie smoked cigarettes. Raymond didn't smoke because Mr. Pike told him it would affect his lungs and he didn't want anything affecting him when it came to football. Besides, sucking on a cigarette wouldn't have been any fun for Raymond because his head was pounding and his nose was throbbing. His eyes were almost completely swollen shut and the color around his nose and eyes had changed from purple to black. People looked at him in horror while he walked down the street with Willie and Damon. On one hand he liked how it made people feel uncomfortable, while on the other hand, his head hurt.

Raymond stared ahead as his friends smoked.

"You gonna get him back?" asked Willie, looking at Raymond's discolored face.

Raymond continued staring. "Yeah."

Willie threw his cigarette butt on the ground. "What are you gonna do?" Raymond continued staring, a faraway look in his eyes.

"Not sure. All I know is he's gonna get hurt."

Sitting at his desk with his head on his hands, Stewart stared at the brain in the jar. He checked the time and looked at the log on his computer. It had been hours since he activated the brain with the initial power setting. Should he change the setting or leave it alone? He tried to remind himself that it could be hours, days, weeks, months, even years before he might hear anything. Then again, who wants to wait? Patience is an overrated virtue he concluded after pondering this notion for several minutes.

Aw, what the heck, he finally decided, it couldn't hurt to change the setting for tonight. He upped the power setting, logged it into the computer, and headed for his dresser. Tomorrow is a new day and new days are always full of promise, Stewart mused, wondering if positive thinking would somehow help his cause. He changed into his pajamas and hopped into bed. Closing his eyes, he concentrated on his message... *Starhawk Ranger from Mother Earth... Starhawk Ranger from Mother Earth...* After a few minutes of concentration, he was sound asleep.

The room was completely dark for the next hour. Then, the brain began to glow ever so slightly, increasing in visibility and emitting a faint pink color.

10

EXPERIMENTS

THE NEXT MORNING, STEWART resisted awakening. He was having so much fun while in the middle of another flying dream, he didn't want it to end. In the past, when he didn't want to awaken, he would try to fool himself into thinking he was still asleep so the dream would continue. Surprisingly, this worked some of the time. Not today. The more he tried to tell himself he was still asleep, the more alert he became, so rather than fight it any longer, he opened his eyes. At first, he couldn't remember which day it was and hoped it was Sunday so he could go downstairs and ask his mom to make something special. If he was lucky, Nora would already have a plate of homemade waffles with strawberries and whipped cream waiting for him. As he pictured himself feasting on waffles, he looked at a calendar on his bulletin board and saw it was

Monday. Darn, he thought, and swung his feet over the side over the bed.

Nora poked her head in the room. "Good morning, sweetie. Hope you slept well," she said, cheerfully.

"Yup," replied Stewart. His throat felt a little dry and this one-word answer was all he could manage until he could get something to drink.

"No waffles today, but I'll have eggs for you and a glass of orange juice. That will help moisten your throat." Nora left the room and headed downstairs.

Stewart sat on the edge of his bed so he could give his mind a few more seconds to fully awaken. Once he stood up, he was committed to the day. No crawling back into bed and pulling the covers up to his chin on these increasingly chilly mornings. Standing up, Stewart took one step towards his dresser and froze, his eyes opening wider and wider. How did she know he was thinking about waffles!? How did she know he had a dry throat?? He ran the few steps to his dresser, jerked open the drawer and pulled out clothes as fast as he could. Stewart dressed quickly and ran downstairs.

Nora placed a couple of strips of bacon on a plate with two eggs, sunny side up, and handed it to Stewart as he entered the kitchen. He walked over to his chair and upon sitting down, picked up the glass of orange juice and drank half of it before setting it back on the table.

"Mom?" asked Stewart cautiously.

"Yes?" Nora replied from the sink as she poured water into the skillet used to cook the eggs.

"Why did you think I wanted waffles?"

Nora turned off the water, a puzzled expression on her face. "You asked for them...I think." She turned towards Stewart, who noticed that while his mom was looking at him, she wasn't really seeing him, her mind somewhere else and getting more confused by the second.

"Yes, you asked for them," she said with a quiet finality. Shaking her head, she turned back to the sink and resumed washing the skillet.

Stewart jumped up from his chair. "I'll be right back." He casually walked out of the kitchen as Nora washed the dishes. Once out of the kitchen, he ran up the stairs and into his room. Stewart rushed to the machine and let out a gasp, seeing the pink glow surrounding the brain. Taking a deep breath to calm himself, he carefully adjusted the power control to the original setting. It would be better to change the setting so his mom couldn't read his mind all day. Plus, it seemed like it was freaking her out a little bit and he didn't want her to go through that again.

Stewart watched the pink glow slowly fade and stared at the brain. He became more and more excited as he thought about what had just happened with his mom. She had read his mind in some way, like a voice talking to her, based on her reaction to his question. He was going to analyze this more completely after school, so he could determine exactly what was going on with her. Why hadn't he read her mind? The more he thought about it, the more questions he had. Regardless, this was incredible, he thought, as he looked at the brain. It worked. The machine worked!

"Stewart, come back and eat! We're going to be late!" yelled Nora from downstairs.

"Coming!" responded Stewart as he left his room. This was going to be one heck of a day.

Nora looked over at Stewart, fidgeting in his seat as she drove to school. She noticed he was a completely different person when he came back to the kitchen. He was full of energy and his eyes darted everywhere while he ate his breakfast as fast as humanly possible. Upon finishing, he asked if she could take him to school so he could get ready for a math quiz instead of going with the McKnights.

"Is everything okay?" she asked.

"Huh? Yeah, everything's okay," responded Stewart, losing the battle to contain his excitement.

"You seem quite antsy," observed Nora.

"I guess it's because of the quiz."

"You don't normally fret over a quiz," said Nora, as she pulled up to the curb and slowed down the car.

"It's not that I'm worried. I'm just excited. Thanks mom." Stewart quickly unbuckled his seatbelt, opened the door and hopped out as the car was slowing to a halt.

"Hey! Wait for the car to stop!" shouted Nora.

"Sorry!" yelled Stewart, closing the door behind him and running down the sidewalk.

Nora shook her head in exasperation, then drove away.

Anxious to see the twins before class, Stewart forgot to be on the lookout for Raymond and his friends until he was close to entering the building. He paused in alarm and swung his head back and forth until he saw them sitting on a concrete bench not far from the entrance. Raymond, Damon, and Willie all leaned back on the bench, casually watching the students enter the building instead of being at their usual position near the door.

Stewart gasped when he saw Raymond's swollen and bruised face. He had never seen a face that had been beaten like that before and it wasn't a pretty sight. Turning away from them, Stewart hustled inside the building and headed for the library. Before he left his house, he had sent the twins and Dino a text message to meet him in the library before school started. The library was a great place for them to gather because it had meeting rooms, and they knew it was one of the few places in the school Raymond and his friends would not likely visit. Stewart once joked that if Raymond were taken to the library, he would start screaming like the demon kid in the horror movie who was taken to church.

Mrs. Darby peered at Stewart, quickly entering the library. Stewart caught her gaze and immediately slowed down, realizing he was exceeding her library speed limit of somewhere in the neighborhood of one-eighth of a mile an hour and didn't want to give her a reason to detain him from meeting his friends. She was known to stop students for walking too quickly and had given Stewart a demonstration in walking at the appropriate speed at the beginning of last year. He felt like he was moving in slow motion and that Mrs. Darby surely must have been joking. He had looked at her, waiting for a smile or a twinkle in her eye that would tell him he was a victim of her prank. Her stern expression let him know she wasn't kidding.

Stewart entered the room and quietly closed the door. Dino and the twins stood in the room and looked at him with a combination of impatience and curiosity.

"So, what's the big news?" asked Dino.

"It works!" replied Stewart, surprised he was able to speak without shouting. "The machine works!"

"How is it working?" Ethan asked with a hint of skepticism.

"My mom read my mind this morning. I was thinking of what I wanted for breakfast and she came upstairs and told me I couldn't have it. How would she know that?"

"You're sure you didn't say anything to her?" asked Nathan.

"Not a word. Oh, and I had a dry throat and she told me she would have orange juice for me. She knew two things I was thinking about. Two things!"

"Okay," said Dino, "But aren't you trying to get aliens to read your thoughts?"

"Yes!" answered Stewart. "And having my mom read my thoughts proves it works. Now, I just need to keep sending thoughts on different settings and see if an alien responds."

"Can we see it work on your mom?" wondered Ethan.

Stewart nodded enthusiastically. "Let's go to my house after school."

The boys walked out of the room and past Mrs. Darby, who scrutinized them in case they were smuggling books out of the library. Stewart noticed her fall-themed sweater covered with images of pumpkins and ears of corn. He recognized this sweater from last year and remembered he had given it the name "Attack of the Killer Pumpkins."

They entered the hall and headed for math class. Approaching the main entrance, they saw Alex and Annie enter the building. Stewart observed that Annie was wearing a plain, beige sweater with her standard navy-blue beret. He was tempted to direct her to Mrs. Darby for tips on selecting sweaters with colorful patterns and decided against it.

"There he is," said Dino admiringly. "Alexander the Great." The twins nodded in agreement. Stewart wasn't paying attention to Dino. Instead, he had taken a good look at the shirt Alex was wearing, brightly colored with the silhouette of a skier on the back, similar to all of the other ones he had been wearing since he moved to the neighborhood. He looked at Dino and the twins, and noticed they were all wearing shirts similar to Alex's. Since when did Dino and the twins wear this style of clothing?

Annie walked alongside Stewart as they headed down the hall.

"Are you ready for the quiz?" she asked.

"Sure," said Stewart, who barely paid attention to her as he was still distracted by his friends' shirts. A small smile appeared on the corners of Annie's mouth as they continued walking. She had spent a good part of the prior day studying and couldn't wait to take the quiz. Though she was now smitten with Stewart, she was going to do her best to get a better score than him. Love was not going to get in the way of her being the best student in math class.

Sitting in his office, Mr. Pike hung up the telephone, leaned back in his chair, and put his feet on his desk. Why did he have to deal with a class at this moment? If it were summertime, he would be driving a boat around the lake and puffing on the largest cigar he could find. He had another successful weekend with his football picks. Betting with the credit he was granted had quadrupled his winnings to eighty thousand dollars. As he had done previously, he was not going to take any money and was going to continue betting all of his winnings and more credit given to him by the bookie. According to his calculations, his account would be up to a million dollars by the end of football season. Retiring from teaching would be the first thing he would do when he could get his hands on that million dollars. Mr. Pike glanced at the clock on his desk, grabbed his clipboard, a bag of balls, and walked out of the office.

Stewart stood uncomfortably in line next to Raymond, wondering if he would try to inflict some kind of pain upon him in retribution for being Alex's friend. Thankfully, Raymond seemed to be ignoring everyone, because they were all staring at Raymond's bruised face. Alex did his best to avoid Raymond, a tense situation that only Stewart was aware of among the boys.

Mr. Pike dropped the bag of balls and began to take roll. He stopped in front of Raymond, with a look of surprise.

"What happened to you?"

"I had an accident," Raymond replied.

"What kind of accident?" asked Mr. Pike.

This is going to be good, thought Stewart.

"I was riding my bike on Bear Mountain, hit a rock, fell over the handlebars, and landed on my face."

Mr. Pike shook his head. "Well, you could say it's an improvement." Mr. Pike smirked at his little joke and continued taking roll.

"Camby."

"Present and accounted for," responded Stewart.

Mr. Pike stopped and gave Stewart the stink eye. "Next time, just say 'here.'"

"Sorry, I wasn't trying to be funny," said Stewart sincerely.

"Good, because you aren't funny." Mr. Pike moved to the boy next to him and resumed calling names. Stewart breathed a sigh of relief. He was so wrapped up in Raymond's yarn about his "accident," he temporarily lost control of his senses and had no idea how those words came out of his mouth.

After calling out the last boy's name, Mr. Pike headed over to the bag of balls, opened it, and dumped basketballs onto the floor.

"Okay, listen up. We're going to be playing basketball for the rest of the semester. We'll cover the basics for the next few weeks and then I'll divide you into teams. I'm going to start by showing you the correct way to dribble. Everyone at half court."

The boys gathered on the court as Mr. Pike picked up a ball. Stewart was happy to leave football behind and move on to basketball. Although he was a terrible basketball player, at least they would be indoors where it was nice and warm.

Stewart felt tense during the entire class, wondering if Raymond would somehow try to get back at Alex. P.E. was their only class together and Raymond's best opportunity for revenge. Class ended and Stewart started feeling better the moment he and Alex left the locker room and headed up the stairs. Fortunately, Mr. Pike had placed them in separate groups for the basketball drills and afterwards, in the locker room, Raymond and Alex managed to avoid making eye contact with each other. While Stewart believed Raymond was a complete idiot, he hoped he was smart enough not to try anything in P.E. Though he believed Mr. Pike was also an idiot, he knew Mr. Pike wouldn't want to deal with fighting in his class and would put a quick stop to any kind of trouble. Regardless of this logic, Stewart wasn't entirely comforted, knowing anything could happen with Raymond.

Stewart and Alex reached the top of the stairs and headed down the large hallway towards study hall. Stewart looked forward to study hall because unlike most of his classmates who viewed study hall as a period to goof around, he tried to get as much homework done as possible. After study hall, he rarely had any homework left to do at home, giving him more time to play on his computer and shortwave radio.

On that day, he was completely caught up with his homework and would be able to spend most of the period thinking about his machine and daydreaming about Sofie, who was also in the room. With the excitement of the machine, he felt he had been neglecting his duties of admiration and needed to start planning how he may someday have an actual conversation with her, so she could see how dashing and daring he was.

Stewart and Alex had barely taken their seats, when Mr. Leiker stepped in the room. He spotted Alex and waved for him to come to the door. Stewart wondered what was going on as he watched Alex rise from his seat and leave the room. He turned his attention to Sofie, who was seated near the front of the class and was busy with her homework. He rested his head on his hands and gazed at her long golden locks pulled back with a yellow bow. Yellow is a lovely color, he thought, although the bow could have been any color and it would have looked sensational next to Sofie's golden hair. In fact, she could be wearing a burlap sack and still look wonderful. How would Sofie look in a burlap sack? Or a toga? Goddesses wore togas, didn't they? He closed his eyes and as he began imagining Sofie in a toga, his mind started drifting....

Having found Queen Sofie in chains in the dungeon of Raymond the Terrible, Captain Stewart Camby of the First Inter-Galactic Space Division now found himself face-to-face with his longtime adversary. He calmly pointed his electrolaser gun at Raymond the Terrible.

"Give me the keys to the chains," ordered Captain Camby.

"Never!" retorted the defiant Raymond the Terrible.

"Just the answer I was hoping for!" shouted Captain Camby. He pulled the trigger and instantly turned Raymond the Terrible into a column of vapor. Stewart threw a fist into the air as good finally tri-

umphed over evil, then rushed over to Queen Sofie's limp body and took a close look at the locks to the chains on her wrists. He pulled out his trusty Swiss Army knife, removed the plastic toothpick, and inserted it into the lock. After wiggling the toothpick in the lock for a few seconds, it sprang open and he quickly opened the other one.

Captain Camby picked up Queen Sofie, whose labored breathing told him he didn't have much time to get her medical treatment. It wasn't going to be easy, as the battle above ground continued with forces loyal to Raymond the Terrible, but if there was one person in the universe up to this challenge, it was him. Queen Sofie's eyes slightly opened and she smiled faintly at the reassuring sight of Captain Camby. Without a moment to spare, he began running up the stairs with the Queen in his arms....

"Stewart?" asked Mr. Leiker.

Stewart sat upright in his chair. "Huh?" he said, trying to figure out how Mr. Leiker could also be in the dungeon with him.

"Please come with me."

"Sure," Stewart responded, realizing he was in study hall back on earth and that Raymond had not been vaporized. He followed Mr. Leiker into an office where Alex was already seated. Closing the door, Mr. Leiker sat behind a desk and motioned for Stewart to sit down.

"Stewart, Alex has been struggling in our math class. It's clear he needs a little help catching up because we're covering an area different from what he was studying before he moved here. Since math is easy for you and you live close to each other, I'm wondering if you would consider helping Alex as a tutor?"

"Okay," replied Stewart. "What do I do?"

"It looks like you'll need to go back a couple of chapters and go over them with Alex until he is solid on the concepts. This will help him understand the material we are currently studying. Then, go over the current lessons until Alex is caught up. Sound like a plan?"

"Yes," acknowledged Stewart.

"Thank you for doing this, I know you'll be a great help to him," said Mr. Leiker, smiling appreciatively.

Stewart and Alex left the office and headed back to study hall.

"You sure you don't mind?" asked Alex.

"Not a problem. If you don't mind me asking, why isn't your sister also behind?"

"Well," said Alex somewhat painfully. "Annie is super smart and determined. She learns everything real easily and studies like crazy. She's already read the entire textbooks in most of her classes."

"Why doesn't she help you?

"Are you kidding? Sisters can't help. After two seconds she gets impatient and doesn't understand why I'm not like her. I have a slight case of dyslexia and it takes me five times as long as her to study something, but once I get it, I get it. I'm really glad you'll help me."

"Not a problem at all," said Stewart, more than happy to help the one person not afraid of Raymond.

Stewart and his friends ran up the stairs and into his bedroom. They followed him to his computer and after typing a few commands on the keyboard, the log appeared on the monitor. Stewart checked the power setting he entered for Nora and moved the control on the power box until her number appeared on the digital meter.

"Now what?" asked Dino.

"We have to wait. I'm not sure for how long," replied Stewart.

The boys anxiously stared at the brain, watching and waiting.

"How long do you think it will take?" asked Ethan impatiently.

"I don't know. I turned it to this setting last night and found out it worked when I woke up. Maybe it worked right away. Maybe it took all night. I don't know," responded Stewart, trying not to sound irritated as he looked at his friends standing together in their matching shirts. He wondered what was next for them. Going to an amusement park so they could buy caps with mouse ears and have their names embroidered in gold thread on the back? Wouldn't that be the obvious next step in the formation of Alex's fan club?

After a few minutes longer, the twins sat on the bed. Dino busied himself with looking at Stewart's latest spaceship model on the nearest shelf. Only Stewart and Alex continued to observe the brain. All of a sudden, the brain began to glow a faint pinkish glow.

"It's working!" shouted Stewart.

Thrilled, his friends ran to the desk and crowded around the machine.

"When can she read your mind?" asked Nathan.

"I don't know" replied Stewart.

Stewart covered his ears as everyone began shouting ideas at the same time.

"Quiet!" yelled Alex. Instantly, everyone stopped talking.

"Okay," said Stewart. "Let me think of something without all of you talking."

"Here, lay down on your bed. Get comfortable," suggested Dino. Everyone nodded their heads as Stewart lay on his bed. He closed his eyes and put his fingers to his temples. After a minute, he opened his eyes, stood up, and went to the machine, where he changed the power setting. His friends looked at him with great anticipation.

"What did you do?" asked Ethan.

"I thought of how great it would be if my mom would make chocolate chip cookies. I changed the setting so she won't be able to read any more thoughts. Let's see if it works…"

Stewart had barely finished his sentence when Nora called out to him from downstairs.

"Would you boys be interested in a fresh batch of chocolate chip cookies?"

The boys' faces brightened as they jumped up and down and looked at Stewart in amazement.

"Yes!" Stewart yelled down to his mother. "We're interested! Thank you!"

"This is INCREDIBLE!" Dino proclaimed. "Do it again."

"Do it again," seconded the twins in perfect unison.

"Let's see," Stewart said deliberately as he paced the room. "Okay, how's this – I will think about not going to school tomorrow. I'll think about telling her I'm sick so I don't have to go to school."

Everyone agreed it was a good plan, as Stewart went back to the power box and adjusted the setting. He ran back to his bed.

"Tell me when it's glowing." Stewart closed his eyes and concentrated. After just a minute, the brain resumed its faint pinkish glow.

"It's glowing!" Nathan exclaimed in a loud whisper.

Stewart put his fingers to his temples, with his eyes scrunched in deep concentration.

"Stewart!" yelled Nora from downstairs. "Please come here."

Leaping out of bed, Stewart raced to the machine and turned down the power. The boys covered their mouths as they tried not to laugh out loud. Stewart walked down the stairs and went to Nora, who was waiting for him in the kitchen with a look of displeasure.

"Are you going to tell me you can't go to school tomorrow?" demanded Nora.

"Uh, no?" whimpered Stewart.

"You are darn right you are not going to do that. If you aren't sick, you're going to school, do you hear me? I have half a mind not to make these cookies." A strange look immediately crossed Nora's face.

"Mom, are you all right?" asked Stewart.

Nora paused and blinked a couple of times. "I'm fine. Okay, go back to your friends. The cookies will be ready in fifteen minutes."

As Stewart left the kitchen, Nora leaned back against the counter and closed her eyes. What was going on here, she thought? Did Stewart tell me he wasn't going to school or am I hearing voices in my head? Maybe I'm too distracted. Maybe I need a nap.

Stewart turned the corner to the hallway and bumped into his friends, who had crept down the stairs to eavesdrop on Stewart's scolding.

"Ahhhh!" exclaimed Stewart, completely startled.

"What's wrong?" yelled Nora from the kitchen.

"Nothing! I, uh, just slipped on the floor," Stewart replied as his friends continued struggling to stop themselves from laughing.

"Be careful! Don't run!" shouted Nora.

The boys quietly hurried back to Stewart's room and closed the door behind them.

"Do you know what this MEANS?" asked Dino, who couldn't have been more excited if he had just discovered fire. "If you can send thoughts to your mom, you can send them to ANYBODY!"

"That makes sense," said Stewart. "But here's the problem. I just put my mom on a random setting. I got real lucky. If I change the settings, I won't know who is reading my thoughts."

"I see what you mean," said Ethan. "There's got to be a way to calculate the settings systematically."

"Automatically," added Nathan.

"Thematically," Ethan concluded as Nathan nodded approvingly.

Stewart sat in his chair and looked at the twins in exasperation. "Once I figure it out I'm going to give you two lobotomies."

11

IMAGES

BYRON CAREFULLY STUDIED A tax court case with circumstances similar to a situation facing one of his clients. He loved these projects where he could explore various facets of tax law and use his ingenuity to develop a plan that would save his client thousands if not tens of thousands of dollars in taxes. It was easy for Byron to become completely consumed by this kind of work and forget about everything else going on around him, including the time of day.

Charlie stopped at the door to Byron's office carrying his briefcase, having just returned from being at a client's office. He walked over to Byron's desk and made himself comfortable in one of the guest chairs. Byron finished making a note on a yellow legal pad and looked over at Charlie.

"How did it go today?" asked Charlie.

"Good. Looking into a little wrinkle in the Mountain Tech merger. Should have preliminary recommendations by tomorrow."

Charlie nodded his head. "Have you had a chance to think about our conversation last Friday about adding staff?"

Byron leaned back in his chair, took off his glasses and rubbed them on his shirt. He held them up to the light and, satisfied he had removed a smudge, put them back on his head.

"I have."

Charlie raised his eyebrows, waiting for the rest of Byron's response.

"I don't think we need to add staff for a while."

Charlie's shoulders slumped. Though he was expecting this answer, he somehow hoped Byron would finally see it his way.

"I thought of a way to add two hours of productivity to my day. Ten hours a week, forty hours a month."

"How are you going to do that?" wondered Charlie.

Byron leaned forward in his chair. "I'm going to rent an apartment two blocks from the office. Instead of commuting, I'll be working."

Charlie gulped. There was no way he could have anticipated Byron proposing to live in a nearby apartment to be a solution for his workload.

"Are you and Nora having difficulties?" asked Charlie, hoping he hadn't crossed the line by asking such a personal question.

"No, not at all," responded Byron. "This is a logical solution. It would actually be easier for me without the weekday commuting. I've heard many businessmen on the east coast have apartments near their office. I would spend the weekends at home."

"And Nora is okay with this?"

Byron sat back in his chair. "I haven't discussed it with her," he admitted.

Charlie shook his head. "Honestly, I don't see her going for this."

"I think she will. She has always supported me. She understands how our business is good for us. I want to send Stewart to the best college possible someday and you know how much that can cost. It's going to be much more in five years when he's ready to go. And I'm also trying to build up my retirement fund as much as possible. These are my golden years to make as much money as possible. I've got to do it while I still have the energy."

Charlie pondered Byron's thoughts for a few seconds. "I understand what you're saying. But living away from home during the week..." Charlie looked at the ground, a sad expression on his face. "I just don't think it will be good for you and Nora. And, you and Stewart." He sprang to his feet and managed a smile, realizing he was projecting an air of gloom. "Hey, I'm not you. Just make sure Nora is okay with it. Maybe think it over for a few more days before you talk to her."

Giving Byron a half-hearted wave, Charlie stepped into the hall. He couldn't stop shaking his head as he walked to his office, disappointed with Byron's decision.

Byron leaned back in his chair and stared out the window while absent-mindedly drumming his pencil on his desk, lost in thought. Yes, he convinced himself, this was the best possible solution to managing his workload. So, when would be the best time to discuss this with Nora?

Stewart and Nora quietly ate dinner in their usual places at the table in the kitchen. Suddenly, Stewart's eyes opened wide as if he had just been struck by a bolt of lightning. He quickly scooped up the rest of the food from his plate, shoveling it into his mouth and chewing as fast as he possibly could. Nora, who had been carefully cutting her meat, looked over at Stewart.

"Stewart, please slow down! What on earth is the big rush?"

"Sorry, mom," mumbled Stewart, barely able to speak, his checks filled with more food than a chipmunk preparing for the ice age. "Can we go to the mall?" Just as Stewart finished his question, a piece of meat flew out of his mouth and landed on the table right in front of Nora's plate. Appalled, Nora leaned forward and fixed Stewart with an even stare. Uh-oh, he thought, here it comes.

"First of all, you will not speak with food in your mouth, do you understand?" asked Nora in a firm voice. Stewart nodded with the nod he knew best conveyed remorse.

"Secondly, it's 'May we go to the mall,' not 'Can we go to the mall.' I know you understand the difference." Stewart nodded with even greater remorse.

Nora studied Stewart for a moment to make sure her point was getting through to him. Satisfied, she leaned back in her chair. "So, why do you want to go to the mall?"

"I need to get something at the electronic store for science class."

Nora folded her arms. "And when do you need this equipment?"

"Tonight?" Stewart replied weakly. Nora sighed. "Why do we have to do this at the last minute?" she asked.

"Sorry, I forgot all about it. I'll try to do a better job next time."

"I'm certain you will," said Nora skeptically as she rose from her chair. "Would you like a warm slice of homemade pecan pie for desert? With a scoop of vanilla ice cream?"

"You bet!" bellowed Stewart, momentarily forgetting why he wanted to go to the mall in such a hurry. As far as he was concerned, his mother's pecan pie was the best in the country.

Stewart and Nora entered the mall, which was unusually busy for a week night. Nora stopped as they walked past the fountain.

"I'll meet you right here. How much time do you need?"

"Half an hour," answered Stewart. "Where are you going?"

"The Bathroom and Kitchen Palace. I need to see what you can get me for Christmas." Smiling, she kissed Stewart on the forehead and walked away. Stewart looked around to see if anyone was watching. Kids his age don't get kissed on the forehead, do they? He didn't think so. He also couldn't understand why The Bathroom and Kitchen Palace was his mother's favorite store. There wasn't anything interesting in there, just scented soaps and kitchen items. Why anyone would pay extra for scented soap was a mystery to him.

Stewart walked to the other end of the mall and resisted the urge to stop at the cellphone kiosk and analyze the latest models. He was on a mission and needed to keep his focus. Arriving at the electronic store, he was happy to see only a couple of customers. He needed to speak with someone and didn't have time to wait. Brian, the young night manager who had helped him before, was on duty and recognized Stewart as he approached him.

"Hi, Stewart." greeted Brian.

"Do you have thermal imaging cameras?" Stewart inquired.

"We do, but you're not going to like what I'm about to tell you," replied Brian.

A look of concern crossed Stewart's face "Why not?"

"They're very expensive."

"How expensive?" asked Stewart, afraid to hear the answer.

"Our least expensive model goes for a thousand dollars, and our most expensive one goes for twenty-five thousand dollars." Stewart's heart sank.

Brian put his hand to his chin. "So, how much money were you planning on spending?"

Stewart pulled a roll of bills out of his pocket. "I have sixty dollars." He reached back into his pocket and pulled out a small handful of change. "And fifty-five cents."

"Well, it looks like you're a little short today," said Brian gently. "If you hit it big with Christmas money, come back and see us."

"That would be nice," said Stewart dejectedly, and walked away. Just as Stewart reached the door, Brian called out to him.

"Hey! Wait! Come back." Puzzled, Stewart turned and walked back to Brian.

"I just thought of something. We have one that was returned. It's broken and since it's a discontinued model, the manufacturer gave the customer a new one. Nobody can fix it. It's just sitting in the back. One minute, I'll be right back." Brian walked briskly to the back room, leaving Stewart with his mouth wide open.

Brian returned with a box and handed it to Stewart. "Here you go."

Stewart cradled the box as if it contained the crown jewels. "How much does it cost?"

"Nothing," said Brian, smiling. "We were going to throw it away. It would be a great camera if it worked. The least expensive one in the store has 4,800 pixels. This one has 307,200, the same as the top model. So, what are you going to do with it?"

"Take pictures!" exclaimed Stewart, as he walked away. He stopped and turned at the door. "Oh, thank you!"

The next thing Stewart knew, he was standing at the fountain. He looked back, wondering how he got there. For a moment, he thought he had broken the time continuum, but decided he must have been preoccupied. While in the store, he had wanted to correct Brian when he said nobody could fix it though he decided to keep his ego in check. He just couldn't believe he was holding the device that would take his machine to the next level.

Nora walked up to him holding a decorated paper sack. She pulled out a small package of soap and held it under Stewart's nose. "Look what I bought. Smell it. It's lilac. Isn't that wonderful?"

Wonderful? To Stewart, it smelled like overpowering flowers. Why did soap have to smell like that? Why couldn't it smell like something good, like fresh-baked doughnuts? If that package of soap smelled like doughnuts, he would actually consider buying it.

Nora looked at the box in Stewart's hands. "What did you buy?"

"A camera."

Nora looked at him quizzically. "You already have a nice camera. The one you took to France."

"Yes, but this one takes thermal images."

"Oh," said Nora, realizing she had no idea what that meant, though it did sound like something someone would need for a science class.

Laying the camera on his desk, Stewart turned on his computer and desk lamp, and sat down, ready to get to work. He had read the instructions on the way home from the mall and couldn't believe all of the features that came with it. One of the best features was the wireless capability, allowing images to be sent directly to a computer. This was exactly what he needed.

For the rest of the evening, Stewart examined the camera and, using his electrical test equipment, tried to figure out why it wouldn't work. He glanced at the clock and saw that it was close to his bedtime and he would have to stop for the night. Dejected, he started to shut down his computer, when an idea struck him. He found it humorous when ideas like this popped into his brain; it could actually feel like getting tapped on the head, like the time he went outside last spring during a hailstorm and got hit by a hailstone the size of a pea. However, it felt, he was happy ideas popped into his head, mostly at random, and he would always welcome their appearance.

Stewart pulled up the program code for the camera and scrolled down to a certain area, searching for a bug in the code. He kept scrolling and stopped, a huge smile spreading across his face. He changed the commands in the code, then saved it and exited the program. The problem was similar to a situation he encountered on a computer a year ago. The error message was misleading and after many days, he found the problem to be something other than what the error message was showing. When he saw this same error message, he knew to look elsewhere, and sure enough, he was able to find the problem and fix it.

Disconnecting the camera from the computer, he wiped his hands dry and reached for the start button. Pushing it slowly, he held his breath. Nothing happened. Then, after a couple of seconds, the power light turned on. Stewart stood up from his chair and began jumping around the room. "It works!" he shouted to the heavens.

Stewart tossed and turned under the covers in the darkness of his room. His mind was racing, making it difficult to turn off the switch in his brain so he could go to sleep.

He heard Byron enter the house and imagined him setting down his briefcase in his office and looking at the mail. In a few minutes he would quietly walk up the stairs so he wouldn't disturb Stewart and enter the master bedroom. Stewart had been so wrapped up in his machine, he was beginning to forget his dad lived with them.

Byron turned on the lights in his home office and set his briefcase on the floor next to his desk. He flopped in his chair, tired by the long day. He went through the envelopes Nora had left for him, as she did every day. He threw the junk mail in the trash and put the remaining envelopes of bills to be paid in a tray labelled "Pay Bills." He appreciated Nora taking care of household chores and paying bills, which left him free to work. Taking off his glasses and rubbing his eyes, he realized he needed to get to sleep soon, as he had another important day ahead of him. Nora would be sound asleep, as she always was, when he came home this late. He would have to tell her about his decision to rent a downtown apartment another day.

Stewart opened his eyes and looked around the room, seeing it was morning. He jumped out of bed, grabbed his cell phone, and called Ethan. The phone rang and rang, and finally went to voicemail. Exasperated, Stewart held the phone to his mouth, ready to leave a message. "Hey! I need you and Nathan to come over right after school! Please! Don't go anywhere else. My house. After school!" Stewart turned off the phone and headed for his dresser.

Nora pulled up to the curb, and Stewart, Alex, and Annie stepped out of the car. They closed their doors and headed up the sidewalk towards the main entrance. Out of habit, Stewart looked for Raymond and his friends near the front doors, and to his relief, saw them standing with a group of boys at the end of the building. As those boys chatted with each other, Stewart noticed Raymond carefully watching Alex as he entered the building. To anyone else, there was nothing unusual going on though Stewart knew Raymond was keeping a safe distance from Alex. For now.

Stewart and his friends walked into math class and went to their seats. Sofie was already in her seat, looking radiant as ever. She was smiling, which made Stewart wonder why animated birds weren't following her around, singing and doing chores for her. While walking to his seat, he noticed she seemed to gaze at Alex and brighten her smile as he passed by her. Did this really happen, or was he just seeing things? Was it possible for Sofie's smile to become even more radiant? He wasn't sure.

Mr. Leiker stood up from his desk and passed out the quizzes he had graded the night before. The twins turned to Stewart and waved their quizzes towards him, to show him they both scored a 98, while Dino scored a 95. Thrilled, Annie saw her score was a perfect 100 and turned to Alex who, with a blank face, showed her his quiz with a score of 82. Annie couldn't resist and snuck a peek at Stewart's quiz as she turned away from Alex. She let out a sigh when she saw he had also scored a 100. She didn't find much consolation in tying for best score on the quiz. Besides, it had taken her most of the class to work on it and Stewart had breezed through it in less than fifteen minutes.

After taking roll, Mr. Pike divided the boys into teams of five and announced which four teams would begin playing. The gym was designed so two games could be played simultaneously, while two teams had to wait on the sideline. Mr. Pike wasn't happy about having boys standing idle, though with the large number of kids in the class, it was the best he could do. After a certain number of points, the losers would leave the court and the two teams that had been waiting would take their places.

Stewart's role was to run up and down the court and not get in anyone's way. He also prayed no one would throw the ball to him. Last year, when the ball was thrown his way, he took one dribble, bounced the ball off of his foot and watched it go out of bounds. His teammates were not amused, and frankly, neither was he.

Alex was on the team opposing Stewart, and after tipping the ball to a teammate, ran down the court waving his arm. His teammate threw the ball back to him, and after taking one dribble to the basket, Alex launched himself into the air and ferociously dunked the ball over a hapless defender. Everyone in the entire gym stopped playing and spontaneously began cheering as Alex casually ran back to the other end of the court.

Mr. Pike's whistle dropped out of his mouth. Alex's dunk was something he would expect from a college player or even a professional, but a kid, of what - thirteen years old? Mr. Pike tried to think of when he had seen anyone with this kind of athleticism. There was a teammate in college who was supremely talented and ended up playing professional football, but he was 22 years old at the time. He couldn't help but look at Alex in amazement. This kid, he thoroughly believed, could play any sport he wanted, and one day, be able to play at the highest professional level for that sport. Kids like this come along once in a generation and here he was, in his class.

Mr. Pike watched the last boy leave the locker room, sat at his desk, and picked up his phone. He took a couple of deep breaths before dialing the number of his bookie. The bookie had increased his credit and with the games he won on Sunday, he was going to bet it all on the Thursday night game. Despite knowing it could be foolish to bet everything on one game, he was so sure of the outcome, he was willing to take the risk. If his pick was correct, he would be sitting on two-hundred and fifty thousand dollars. Then, he would roll the money he made from those bets into the next weekend's games. With a couple of months left in the season including the playoffs, he calculated that his bets would end up being in the millions.

Stewart entered the house and ran up the stairs to his bedroom. He grabbed his camera and ran down to the kitchen where Nora was busy preparing dinner. Stewart had so much to do before the twins came over. They weren't able to come after school as he had hoped, because their chess club was getting ready for a tournament and the twins could not miss practice or their club wouldn't let them compete in the tournament.

"Mom, can you turn around?" Nora turned away from the stove and seeing Stewart holding a camera, smiled as he took her picture. He walked to her and showed her the display. It was her image in bright colors ranging from yellow, to green, to blue, to red. Nora arched her eyebrows in astonishment.

"Oh my! I have never seen anything like this. What is this?"

"Thermal image pictures, mom. It's a picture of your body heat."

"This is wonderful. The colors are beautiful. I hope it helps you in science class."

"Huh?" Stewart responded, then remembering, "Oh yeah, it will. Thanks."

Stewart ran upstairs and looked at the image of his mother that had been transmitted to his computer. He began pointing the cursor at areas around Nora's head and typing on the keyboard. He was hoping to finish his project before the twins arrived.

Stewart sat at his desk and busily typed on the keyboard. A wire ran from the computer to the container holding the brain. The door to his bedroom opened and Ethan and Nathan walked in and flopped on the bed.

"Okay, we're here. What's going on?" asked Ethan.

Stewart spun around in his chair and faced the twins.

"I'm going to find your wavelengths."

"How?" said Nathan.

"I set up a way to increase the power sent to the brain in tiny increments. I'm going to start with the setting right after my mom's, then keep adjusting it until I find your setting."

"So, your systematic way of finding our wavelengths is trial-and-error?" observed Ethan, not too impressed. Stewart looked momentarily defeated.

"Yes," he admitted. "But, I do have a plan."

"What is it?" demanded Nathan.

"Well…finding the setting for your wavelength is trial-and-error," Stewart began, as Ethan and Nathan rolled their eyes. "Once I get the setting for you guys, I'll have more reference points. Mom, and you two."

"Then what?" asked Ethan, ever the skeptic.

"I have a camera that loads thermal image data into my computer. I'm writing a program to assign values to key indicators based on the heat reading. With the number of pixels in this camera, the computer can evaluate the image in more detail. The program will take this information and calculate a value for that person. I'm starting with my mom. Look."

Stewart moved the monitor so the twins could see the thermal image of Nora's head on the screen. The twins jumped to their feet and peered closely at the monitor.

"This is really cool," said an impressed Nathan.

"How did you get this picture?" asked Ethan.

"With this thermal imaging camera I got last night."

"So, let me get this straight," said Ethan. "You're using a thermal imaging camera to take a picture of someone and will come up with a method to assign a value to that picture?"

"Yes," said Stewart. "I think there's a relationship between the heat emanating from around a head to the wavelengths from a brain. I can't measure wavelengths directly because they are weak and you have to attach electrodes to a person's head to read any kind of brain activity. Your dad does that with his EEG machine. I can't hook everybody up to an EEG machine, especially because I don't have an EEG machine."

"Makes sense. And what will you do with this value?" wondered Nathan.

"I set up a table with one column that will show the power setting on the brain machine and another column that will show the value for that person. Once I figure out your wavelength and power setting, I'll correspond that to your value. Don't let me forget to take your pictures before you go home. Then, based on your data and my mom's, I'll come up with an algorithm that calculates power settings relative to a person's value. After that, all I'll need to do is take someone's picture with the camera, let my program figure out the value for that person and it will tell me what their power setting should be."

Ethan and Nathan both sat on the bed at the same time. Ethan looked at Stewart with a hint of admiration. "Dude, I don't know how else to say it, but that's pure genius. If it works."

"I agree," said Nathan. "If it works."

"So, what do you want us to do?" asked Ethan.

Stewart beamed. "Lie down on my bed. Make yourselves comfortable and close your eyes. He ran over to the switch on the wall and turned off the light as the twins took off their shoes and positioned themselves on the bed.

Sliding into his chair, Stewart typed on the keyboard and turned to face the twins.

"I'm going to think of something and if you sense my thoughts, let me know. If I don't hear anything from either one of you after a couple of seconds, I'll bump up the setting by one unit. I'll keep doing this until we find your setting. You guys ready?"

"Ready," replied the twins at the same time.

Stewart closed his eyes and concentrated. After a few seconds, he opened his eyes and turned his head to look at the twins. They remained motionless on his bed with their eyes closed. Turning back to the computer, he typed a few commands, closed his eyes and concentrated. Hearing nothing from the twins, he typed a few more commands and closed his eyes. No response. Stewart again typed a few commands, closed his eyes, and found himself thinking this might be a long evening.

After three hours of adjusting settings and concentrating on his thoughts, Stewart had nothing to show for it. He and the twins were getting tired despite a couple of bathroom breaks and an intrusion by his mother bringing in bowls of ice cream. Normally, he welcomed her food service, but was afraid it would distract the twins from helping him. He remembered reading how important it was to feed the troops, so he tried to remain patient as the twins devoured their chocolate ice cream with chunks of chocolate chips. The twins resumed lying on the bed, and as Stewart turned out the lights, Ethan's cell phone beeped. Ethan looked at his phone and saw that his mom had texted him a message that it was time to come home. He stood up and held the phone out to Stewart so he could see the message.

"We've got to go."

"Please just a little longer. We're almost there," begged Stewart.

"We've been 'almost there' for the last hour," complained Nathan.

"Just a little longer. Please." Stewart put on his best puppy-dog-lost-in-the-rain look. Ethan and Nathan knew this look and couldn't bring themselves to leave.

"Okay," said Ethan, firmly, "Just a little longer." The twins laid down and Stewart resumed operating the machine.

After fifteen more minutes, Ethan's phone beeped again. Ethan and Nathan sat up. "Okay, we've got to go now."

"One more time, please! Just one more time!" pleaded Stewart. Ethan and Nathan looked at each and sighed. "One more time," said Nathan.

Stewart adjusted the setting and closed his eyes and concentrated as hard as he could. Ethan and Nathan both stood up, instantly angry.

"What do you mean?" Ethan demanded.

"We're not a bunch of crybaby mama's boys," chimed in Nathan. They stopped, looked at each other and began laughing.

"Dude, I can't believe that's what you were thinking!" said Ethan.

"You did it! You found our wavelength!" marveled Nathan.

Stewart breathed a huge sigh of relief. "Thanks a million," he said as he picked up the camera and pointed it at Ethan. "Say cheese."

12

DISCOVERY

ALONE IN HIS ROOM, Stewart stared at the pictures on his monitor. On one half of the screen was a thermal image labeled "Ethan" and on the other was an image labeled "Nathan." He clicked his cursor on Nathan's image and dragged it on top of Ethan's. Leaning forward, he noticed that every color, every shade, every nuance in the overlapped pictures was an exact match, which is what he expected.

As Stewart was about to close Nathan's picture, he thought about how Ethan always seemed to get a slight preference, being the older twin. He decided to keep Nathan's picture on the monitor, thinking he would be pleased to know he was placed first for a change. He then brought up his mother's picture and placed it next to Nathan's. After studying their pictures for a moment, he moved his mother's image over Nathan's, and was surprised at the large number of subtle differences. The trick would be to identify which areas around the head to include as key points in his mapping program.

Working diligently, Stewart lost track of time and was surprised when his mother entered his room and reminded him it was getting late. It felt like he had just had dinner and now she was telling him it was time to go to bed. Maybe this was how it was for his dad, who was so involved in his work, that he frequently lost track of time.

Stewart went to his bathroom and brushed his teeth. He went to his mother's room and peeked inside.

"Goodnight, mom," said Stewart.

"Goodnight, Honey. Sweet dreams," Nora responded.

He headed back to his room, closed the door, and turned off the light. Stewart walked quietly to the computer and in the darkness of his room with only the light of the monitor illuminating the keyboard, sat down and continued working on his program.

Stifling a yawn, Stewart popped a reed in his mouth and assembled the pieces of his clarinet. He worked on his program late into the night and came up with a valuation system and a formula for the power setting. His goal this morning was to just make it through the day and it was fortunate he didn't have tests in any of his classes. Dino would be going home with him and be his first test subject. Getting through band class would be easy enough and finishing the day with French wouldn't be a problem, because he was banking on Annie raising her hand for every question, allowing him to not be too involved and have to think too much.

Stewart watched Mr. Stimple enter the room with a stack of music sheets and handed a small portion to Kevin, the first chair trumpet. Kevin kept one and passed the rest to Alex, who had proven his talent and was now sitting in second chair. Alex passed the remaining sheets to the boy next to him, while Mr. Stimple proceeded to pass out the rest of the music to the remaining instrument sections of the class. "This is what we are going to be working on from now until our concert at the end of the semester. It's a collection of classic symphonies from Beethoven."

Stewart sighed in great frustration. That's just great, he thought. Our entire concert will be playing music over 200 years old.

Please drive faster, mom, please, thought Stewart as Nora drove home from school. He was anxious to get to his room and take a thermal image of Dino and Alex, who were in the car along with Annie. It was obvious to Stewart that he should put the brain in a case that would allow it to be transported so in instances like this, he could send thoughts to his mother. He imagined seeing her race through the streets at top speed, turning corners so fast, the car would be on only two wheels, then, accelerating with such force, everyone's head would slam back against their seats. With images of his mother hot-rodding it through the streets filling his mind, Stewart was surprised to find his mother pulling into their driveway in no time at all. Stewart and the boys jumped out of the car and ran inside. Annie thanked Nora for the drive and headed to her house.

The boys burst into Stewart's room and dropped their backpacks to the floor. Stewart turned on his computer and opened the thermal image program. He picked up the camera and pointed it at Dino. "Say cheese." "Tee-ree!" said Dino. Stewart rolled his eyes, guessing it was the Greek word for cheese. He turned and pointed the camera at Alex. "Smile," Stewart requested as he snapped Alex's picture. They huddled around the monitor and looked at the images that had been transmitted to Stewart's computer.

"That is so COOL!" exclaimed Dino. The smile disappeared from his face, and he stood back and looked at Stewart.

"Hey, we need to talk about this," said Dino, as serious as Stewart had ever seen him.

"What about?" asked Stewart, rising from his chair.

"With this information, you are going to be able to send thoughts to us, right?"

"Right," replied Stewart, confused as to where Dino was headed with his questions.

"Don't you realize what this MEANS?" asked Dino almost incredulously.

"It means I'm sending thoughts to you," replied Stewart.

Dino placed both hands on Stewart's shoulders and looked him in the eye. "Yes, and it means you might be able to CON-TROL our thoughts."

Stewart's eyes slowly widened at the impact of Dino's words. "I hadn't thought of it that way."

"THINK about it," Dino continued. "If you can control someone's thoughts, you are going to have UNBELIEVABLE power."

Stewart sat down. He was so caught up in making his machine function, he hadn't considered the consequences of its abilities.

"I'm okay with this as long as you PROMISE you won't send any thoughts to me without my permission. Alex, what do you think?" asked Dino, as serious as Stewart had ever seen him.

Alex nodded his head vigorously. "Dino's right. You have to promise you won't use this machine on us without our permission."

Standing straight as possible, Stewart stood and held up his hand. "I promise I won't use this machine on you without your permission." He looked at both Dino and Alex with as much sincerity as he could summon. He sat back down and typed in a few commands on the keyboard. Dots appeared in scattered areas on Dino's image. "The program is evaluating key points in your image," Stewart explained. A series of numbers flashed across the screen and two numbers remained. "The first number is the value of your image and the second number is the power setting. Let's see if it works!"

Stewart typed in the power setting and looked at the brain. After a few seconds, the brain began to glow. Closing his eyes, Stewart held his fingers to his temples and concentrated for half a minute. He opened his eyes and looked at Dino, who stared at Stewart with a blank expression on his face. "Anything?" asked Stewart expectantly. Dino shook his head.

"Okay, let's try Alex." Stewart pulled up Alex's image, typed in commands and watched the dots appear on the image and numbers flash across the screen. Once the two numbers appeared on the screen, Stewart typed a few commands and looked over at the brain, which remained glowing. Stewart closed his eyes and concentrated for the next minute. Opening his eyes, he looked up at Alex, who also stared at Stewart with a blank expression.

"Nothing, huh?" asked Stewart, who already knew the answer as Alex shook his head.

"Looks like you have more work to do," said Dino as he patted Stewart on the shoulders. "Don't give up, you'll make it work. I've got to get to the restaurant." Dino grabbed his backpack and stopped as he reached the door. "When you make this work, you will have the most powerful machine in the WORLD."

Stewart reflected on Dino's words as he left the room. Alex sat in a chair next to Stewart. "Are you still up for the math lesson?" asked Alex, hopefully.

"Yeah. I've got to be honest, I'm really bummed about this," said a glum Stewart.

"I understand. This doesn't mean it's over, it just means you've got to try again."

A look of determination came over Stewart's face. "That's what I'll do, after I help you with math."

Stewart spent the next three days working on his program every chance he had. He stared at the thermal images over and over until he felt he didn't know which direction to go. Everything he did was based on an assumption or a theory, and nothing he tried worked. Frustrated, he was getting to the point where he wanted to pick up his computer and throw it out the window. Seeing it smashed into a million pieces would have given him a tremendous amount of joy. For the moment. Then where would he be? He would have to get a new one and start all over. He looked at his computer and thought of how he had just granted it a stay of execution. At least it could show him some kind of gratitude. But, if things didn't work out soon…

Stewart glanced at the clock and saw it was getting close to his bedtime. Though he didn't have much time, he wanted to give it another try for the day. Stewart cleared the screen and brought up Nathan's picture. Tapping on the zoom feature,

Stewart enlarged the image as he had done before and continued zooming, wondering how far he could go before the details became distorted.

The picture grew and grew with no apparent distortion. Stewart was again grateful for the capabilities of this camera with the large number of pixels allowing for such enlargement. Now, only the top of Nathan's head was on the screen. The enlargement could go beyond his monitor. Would a larger monitor make a difference? And then, he saw it. Or, to be more accurate, it's what he did not see. At the top of Nathan's head was a very tiny void, the size of a speck of dust. No color, no anything. There was color above and around the void. How could this be? He brought up Ethan's picture and placed it over Nathan's. Ethan's image also had a void and it was exactly the same as Nathan's.

Stewart closed the twins' pictures, brought up his mother's image, and enlarged it until he saw the void above her head. He jumped out his chair with excitement, then sat back down and brought up Nathan's image. Overlapping it with Nora's, he observed that her void was in the same area as Nathan's, only slightly smaller and with a different shape. He outlined her void with his cursor and had the computer calculate the area of her void. Stewart repeated outlining the voids for the twins', Dino's, and last of all, Alex's images. The area in everyone's void was different, except for the twins, and each person's area in their void, he decided, would be their value. He would call this value their void area calculation, or VAC.

Stewart brought up the program that calculated the power setting for the twins and for Nora and replaced their values with the newly calculated VAC. Then, he inserted Dino's and Alex's VAC, and after a few seconds, the results for their power setting appeared. His hands trembling with anticipation, Stewart keyed in the power setting for Dino. He looked over at the brain as it began to glow. Holding his fingers to his temples, he closed his eyes and concentrated. After twenty seconds, he opened his eyes, believing he had another failed attempt. Greatly disappointed, he reached for his keyboard to close out the program and get ready for bed. Stewart flinched, startled from the ringing of his cell phone.

Picking up the phone, he saw the call was from Dino. What a coincidence, he thought.

"Hello," said Stewart.

"The Roman Empire was NOT the greatest empire in the world!!" bellowed Dino into the phone. Stewart began laughing as hard as he could.

"It works!" responded Stewart, full of joy.

"Wow, this is CRAZY!" said Dino. "It felt like you just told me this. You figured out the setting for me? That's GREAT! Okay, no more messages to me tonight, I've got to go to bed. Now remember, don't use it on me without my permission."

"Don't worry, I'll remember," responded Stewart. He hung up the phone and laughed. He had purposely sent a thought to Dino that he knew would cause an instant reaction. Stewart adjusted the power setting for Alex's VAC. Closing his eyes, he concentrated on his message. Sure enough, his phone rang.

"Hello," said Stewart, innocently.

"Texas is not full of illiterate people driving pickup trucks!" shouted Alex, full of indignation. Stewart could not help laughing.

"Oh boy," said Alex. "What just happened? Did you plant that in my head?"

"I sure did!" exclaimed Stewart.

"Unbelievable. Well, congratulations. This is amazing."

"Thanks," said Stewart. "Okay, I'll turn off the machine now. I just want you to know I won't use it on you again."

"Good. See you tomorrow."

Stewart stood and ran around his room, leaping for joy.

Mr. Pike jumped to his feet as the football game came to an end. His team had won and he was now sitting on a quarter of a million dollars of winnings. He wanted to watch the game in a sports bar, but with so much riding on this game, he didn't want to make a fool of himself in public, especially if the unthinkable happened and his team was to lose. Celebrating in the comfort of his apartment was just fine with him. He sunk back in his recliner and propped his feet on the coffee table. Besides, he had to turn his attention to the next game on Sunday. These upcoming games were going to determine his future, and the way it was going, it was going to be great. If he hit on his picks the rest of the season, he was going to retire from teaching for good. At that point, he wouldn't have to work another day in his life.

The next morning, Stewart entered the school and instead of heading towards his first period math class, he walked quickly to his English class on the other side of the school. He didn't want to wait until later in the day to speak to Mrs. O'Brien, his English teacher, and thought he had enough time to see her before school started.

Rounding the corner, Stewart weaved around students filling the hall on their way to class. He reached his English classroom and found Mrs. O'Brien seated at her desk, reviewing her lesson plan for the day.

"Good morning, Mrs. O'Brien," said Stewart cheerfully.

"Good morning, Stewart," replied Mrs. O'Brien. "What can I do for you?"

"Because you're in charge of the school yearbook, I was wondering if I can join the staff of students working on it? I have a real nice camera and I could take pictures."

"We would love for you to join us. We are always looking for students who want to become involved. You would need to start attending our meetings, which are every other Wednesday in this classroom after school. Are you sure you can make this commitment?"

Stewart hadn't planned on being this involved and hesitated for a moment. "Yes, I can make the commitment," Stewart confirmed, while ignoring an urge to immediately run out of the room.

"Wonderful," said Mrs. O'Brien. "See you next Wednesday. And see you later today."

"Thank you," murmured Stewart as he left the room. Darn, he didn't plan on having to attend regular meetings, though he needed an excuse to take pictures of students. He was going to take a thermal image of everyone in the school, students and teachers, so he could have a database of everyone's VAC. Being a member of the yearbook staff gave him free reign to take pictures of everyone without raising any suspicion. He thought it could turn out to be fun and it would be something his mother would approve of, especially because he had ignored her previous efforts to get him to participate in school activities.

Stewart couldn't believe his good fortune. Mr. Pike had regrouped the boys into different basketball teams after watching them play for the last week. The teams would begin playing each other and by the end of the semester, the best team would be the champion. With Alex dominating everybody and every team, Mr. Pike decided to place Alex on a team with the worst boys in the class, and Stewart was the first one moved to Alex's new team.

Alex didn't mind because he knew his team would still do well and he was eager to face the challenge of trying to win with teammates that weren't very skilled. Winning as an underdog had always been more satisfying to him than being on a team loaded with good players. For Stewart, he was happy to not only play with his friend but have a close view of all the highlights Alex was sure to provide in the upcoming weeks.

Stewart's mood soured when he saw Raymond was on the first team they would be facing. Rather than use his skills, which were pretty good, Raymond preferred to throw his body around, especially under the basket, where his size gave him a huge advantage.

The game started as expected, with the bad players unable to do anything with the ball and the other team racing to the other end for what seemed to be a sure easy basket, only to have Alex arrive to save the day by constantly blocking their shots. Raymond became increasingly frustrated with Alex's heroics and tried to slam his body into him any chance he could. Alex's quick feet allowed him to step away from Raymond and not take a direct hit.

On their next possession, one of Stewart's teammates missed a shot and the ball careened off the rim towards Stewart, who put his hands up in a protective manner. Raymond appeared out of nowhere and snatched the ball out of the air. As he landed, he swung his arms and caught Stewart with an elbow to the jaw. Stewart felt like he had been hit with a hammer and dropped to his knees. The boys stopped playing and Alex ran to him.

Concerned, Alex leaned over Stewart. "Are you okay?" Stewart rubbed his jaw and finding everything where it should be, especially his teeth, nodded his head and stood up. Alex walked to within inches of Raymond.

"That was a cheap shot."

Raymond's jaw tightened. "Nothing cheap about it. Tell that spaz to stay out of my way."

Alex glared at Raymond, then walked with his team to the other end of the court and waited for Raymond's team. One of the boys passed the ball to Raymond and as he muscled his way up for a basket, Alex leapt high in the air and instead of blocking the shot, he trapped the ball with both hands. His eyes burning with an intensity Stewart had not seen before, Alex dribbled down the court at full speed. Raymond chased him as fast as he could and as Alex leaped for what was going to be his best dunk ever, Raymond, with no real chance of defending the play, jumped on Alex's back. With the weight of Raymond, Alex flew forward and crashed to the floor.

Instantly, Alex grabbed his right leg above his ankle. The boys, including Mr. Pike, ran over to him.

"Okay everybody, step back, give him some room. What happened?" asked Mr. Pike.

"My leg...I think it's broken," stammered Alex, his teeth clenched.

Stewart took a few steps over to Raymond and pointed a finger in his face.

"It's his fault!" yelled Stewart. "He hurt him on purpose!"

Raymond clenched his fist as his face turned red. "I was just trying to make a play!"

"That's a lie and you know it!" retorted Stewart. Mr. Pike jumped up and forced himself between Stewart and Raymond.

"Everybody, class is over. Hit the showers." Mr. Pike leaned over Alex who remained in great pain. "I'm going to call the paramedics. Just hang tight, it's going to be okay." Mr. Pike jogged to his office as the boys headed for the locker room. He was hoping Alex was correct in believing he had a broken leg. Broken bones heal better than torn ligaments.

Stewart kneeled by Alex and glared at Raymond as he followed the others. Raymond turned to them and paused as he reached the door, flashing a quick grin before disappearing into the locker room. Instantly filled with anger, Stewart resisted the urge to go after him, knowing it would give Raymond an excuse to beat him to a pulp. He let himself calm down and felt a warm sense of satisfaction spread over him. Let's see if Raymond smiles after we get his VAC.

Carrying a picnic basket, Nora stepped off the elevator and walked down the hall to Byron's suite of offices. She opened the door and stepped inside just as Byron and Charlie were escorting Angelo Moretti and Bruno Russo to the door, having just finished a meeting. Nora smiled cheerfully at the men who stopped to greet her.

Byron gestured to Nora as he looked at Angelo and Bruno. "This is my wife Nora, and this is Angelo Moretti and Bruno Russo." The silver-haired Angelo smiled his charming smile. He pleasantly shook Nora's hand and turned to Byron.

"Such a lovely lady. You are a lucky man."

"I am," responded Byron.

"You will have to try my gelato some time," said Angelo, clasping Nora's hand.

Nora's face brightened. "Oh, I have and it was absolutely delicious."

Pleased, Angelo chuckled. "We use my grandmother's recipes. From the old country." He released Nora's hand and looked at his watch. "We must be going. Nice to have met you," said Angelo, slightly bowing to Nora before turning for the door.

"I'll go down the elevator with you," said Charlie, as he followed Angelo and Bruno. "I have a meeting on the other side of town." Charlie waved at Byron and Nora as he left the suite. Nora headed for Byron's office and began clearing the coffee table so she could set up for lunch.

Byron sat on a chair and clasped his hands in front of his mouth. Nora noticed his silence and stopped to look at him. "Is everything okay?" she asked.

Though Byron looked towards Nora, he avoided making eye contact. "Yes, everything is fine. There is something I want to run by you, something I have been thinking about." Nora felt a chill on her spine and sat on the couch. Byron was acting very unusual.

"What is it you want to tell me?" she asked uncertainly.

"Well, I've been thinking," said Byron slowly, as the words seemed to have thickened in his mouth and had trouble escaping. "You know how busy I have been. I used to be swamped January through April. Now, it's all the time. We have so much going on, I can't seem to get caught up."

"You should hire more people," said Nora.

"It's not that easy. I don't want to train people and spend time reviewing their work and correcting their mistakes. We have too much at stake. If I can just be a little more efficient, I can get through all of this work and assuming this much work keeps coming to our office, we will be in great shape financially for years to come."

"How can you be more efficient?" wondered Nora.

Byron looked at the floor as he paused for a moment, and then raised his eyes to Nora. "I'm thinking of getting an apartment near the office. I'll spend weekdays here, which will eliminate the commuting."

Nora looked away as a wave of emotion swept over her. "I...I don't know what to say. This is an unusual arrangement."

"Not really," offered Byron.

Her knees felt shaky which Nora found odd as she was sitting down. "I just don't know what to say right now. I guess you could say it feels like...like we're getting a divorce."

"We're not," said Byron as reassuring as he could be. "Lately, as it is, I'm only coming home to sleep. I get home after you have gone to bed and leave before anyone is awake."

"What about Stewart?"

Byron sighed. "He'll be fine. I'll make more time for him on the weekends."

Nora stared straight ahead, trying to process the entire situation. Finally, she decided to put on a brave smile and continued taking items out of the picnic basket. "Well, if this is what is best for our family, then there is nothing I can say."

13

SAY CHEESE

HALFWAY THROUGH STUDY HALL, Stewart entered the classroom and handed Mr. Walls, the teacher assigned to his study hall period, a pass from the front office. Stewart insisted on waiting with Alex until the paramedics arrived. Once they arrived, the paramedics immobilized Alex's leg and lifted him onto a stretcher. All of the attention embarrassed Alex while Mr. Pike told him he had to follow the required school policy for injuries. The paramedics placed straps over Alex to secure him to the stretcher, lifted him, and headed to the ambulance. Alex looked at Stewart and gave him a "thumbs up." Stewart followed them to the main entrance and turned to go to the office to get a late pass.

Stewart sat at his desk and didn't bother taking any homework out of his backpack. He rested his chin on his hands and began plotting Raymond's demise. The first order of business would be to take Raymond's picture with the thermal imaging camera and calculate his VAC. This was not going to be an easy task, because Raymond would never pose for a picture. He would probably end up taking the camera and that would be a total disaster. Though the camera was able to take quality pictures from at least forty feet away, it was still too close, as Raymond would notice him taking his picture. He would have to come up with something clever.

After he calculated Raymond's VAC, he would find the power setting for the brain and would begin transmitting thoughts to him. What kind of thoughts? The thoughts would have to be stronger than calling Raymond a mama's boy or an illiterate Texan. Could he actually make Raymond do something he wouldn't normally do? Like make him dive into a pit of molten lava? Or make him throw himself in front of an oncoming train? Perhaps he wouldn't mind jumping off the roof of a five-hundred-foot building. Stewart felt his eyes turning watery and bile rise in his throat as he thought back to that horrible afternoon when Raymond jumped him after he got off the bus. There wasn't a punishment too extreme for him.

Stewart spent the next ten minutes dreaming of one horrible outcome after another for Raymond. It began to occur to Stewart that he was thinking of purely evil thoughts. He tried to justify it by thinking of all of the bullying he had suffered and how seriously Raymond hurt Alex. At first, it felt good to think of something as elaborate as inventing a time machine, so he could manipulate Raymond into agreeing to be transported back to 17th century France, where he could suffer a beheading. However, he came to realize it was doing something to him, something he wasn't quite sure of what it was, and it didn't feel good. Is this what power feels like? Could he make

Raymond do such things? Dino was right, this could be the most powerful machine on earth.

He was going to have to develop a set of rules for himself for using the machine, so he wouldn't be corrupted by its power. Before he did anything, he needed to get Raymond's picture. Another interesting problem he would surely solve.

Stewart and his friends carried their trays of food to their usual table in the cafeteria and sat down. While in line to get lunch, their entire conversation had been about Alex's injury at the hands of Raymond. They all agreed that Raymond should suffer an appropriate punishment, something that would fit his crime and hopefully, the machine could help them.

Annie approached the table with her tray and sat down at the end of the table by herself. She always sat with them, but without Alex, she seemed alone and sad. Stewart leaned towards her from a few seats away.

"Annie, why don't you sit by us?"

Annie stopped in the middle of a bite, surprised Stewart spoke to her. He never spoke to her. "Uh, that's okay," she responded. "Thank you anyway."

Stewart moved to the seat next to her.

"I'm really sorry about your brother. The paramedics think he'll be okay."

Annie looked at Stewart and found herself gazing at his eyes. What interesting eyes, she thought. His eyes seemed brown from a distance though they were actually green. A lovely shade of green. Annie lowered her head as she realized she was beginning to blush.

"I just talked to my mom," she said. "They put his leg in a cast. The doctor said he would have to wear it for eight weeks and it would heal as strong as ever."

"That's great news," said Stewart, very relieved. "Well, I'm going back to my seat."

"Okay. Goodbye," said Annie. Why did I say "goodbye?" she asked herself. Did that sound stupid? I may as well have said "au revoir," or, "adios," or, "see you later, alligator." Anything would have sounded better than "goodbye."

Stewart slid back to his seat just in time to hear Sofie and her friends at the next table talking about the Sadie Hawkins dance that would take place at the end of next week. Stewart did his best to listen to their conversation, while pretending to listen to Dino and the twins. He had been so busy thinking about his machine, he found he was losing touch with what was going on around him. His first exposure to the Sadie Hawkins dance was last year. He thought the concept for this dance was one of the greatest ideas ever, where a girl asked a boy to go to the dance with her. Seeing how he still couldn't say much to Sofie without fighting to control his bodily functions, a Sadie Hawkins dance would take all of the pressure off him, and others like him. However, he had not been asked by anyone to the dance and decided to chalk it up to it being his first year in middle school. This year, as a seasoned veteran, surely, he would be asked to the dance by someone special. A special someone named Sofie. Would she ask him? Perhaps he ought to try and make eye contact with her, even though it meant risking all of the blood immediately rushing out of his head. Maybe he should lie down before making eye contact. That way, if he fainted, he would already be on the ground.

Stewart finished eating and was prepared to spend the remaining few minutes of his lunch hour sitting at the table, talking about important topics such as the latest computer game.

Suddenly, he realized he was wasting a golden opportunity. He opened his backpack and took out the thermal imaging camera and his other camera. His plan was to take pictures of the students with the thermal imaging camera and a few pictures with the other camera, pictures that he could submit to the yearbook staff for consideration that were worthwhile and would make him seem like a legitimate photographer.

Pointing the thermal imaging camera at Annie, he asked her to smile. Much to his surprise, she smiled a sweet smile. He couldn't recall seeing much more than a small grin from her. After he snapped the picture, he held up his other camera and asked her to smile again. Something about her smile would make a nice picture and he wanted to see how it would look on the other camera.

"Why do you have two cameras?" asked Annie.

"This one takes regular pictures. The other is for, uh, artsy pictures. Look." He showed Annie the display, and she gasped in astonishment. "This is beautiful. The colors really stand out. Thank you for taking a picture of me." She smiled, which again seemed to catch Stewart off guard. Was her smile that pretty or was it because he wasn't used to seeing her smile like this? He turned his attention back to taking pictures, knowing the bell would be ringing soon.

He walked to the POP sister's table and took a deep breath before he looked at Brittany. She looked at him with utter disdain, wondering why he had bothered to come to her table.

"I'm taking pictures for the yearbook. Can I take your picture?" Instantly, Brittany's face came alive.

"Of course." She smiled a large, fake smile, while Stewart took pictures of her with both cameras. Finished with Brittany, he took pictures of Shelby and Courtney. "Thank you," said Stewart graciously. He checked their pictures on the display, wondering if their images would appear with devil horns, fangs and blood-shot eyes. The pictures did not turn out as he thought they may, and disappointed, he headed to Sofie's table.

Sofie turned to him just as he approached her and for a moment, Stewart felt unable to move a single muscle in his body. Though he could feel the blood draining from his head, he managed to move his mouth and much to his surprise, was able to form complete sentences.

"I'm with the yearbook staff. Do you mind helping me take a few pictures?"

A smile so gorgeous spread across Sofie's face, he found himself wondering if he should stare or just start weeping out of pure joy. "Sure, I can help," replied Sofie "but I don't know anything about cameras."

Stewart suddenly felt emboldened, as if having an ounce of knowledge on a subject she knew nothing about made him more masculine by the second. "It's really easy," he said with a confidence he had never before experienced. "You just point it at the person and push a button." He dug into his backpack and pulled out the thermal imaging camera. Pressing the power button, he handed it to Sofie just as Raymond entered the cafeteria. The stars must be aligned for me, thought Stewart. "Why don't you take a picture of Raymond?"

Sofie smiled, thrilled to be holding such a valuable piece of equipment. Stewart practically skipped towards his friends, who were in awe as they watched his interaction with Sofie.

"Raymond, please come here," asked Sofie in a voice sounding like it had come from a harp in heaven. Raymond walked over to her and stopped a couple of feet away from her. Sofie raised the camera. "Smile." Raymond smiled and Sofie snapped his picture. She lowered the camera and looked at the display, puzzled. Instead of the normal picture, she saw the thermal image of Raymond's head. Raymond leaned over to the camera and also looked at the image. "That's weird," he said. "Do you need another picture?"

"No, I'm not sure the camera is working. Thank you." She walked over to Stewart and handed the camera to him. "Did I do something wrong?" she asked. Stewart looked at the image and smiled. "No," he assured her. "It's perfect. The picture will be just fine."

"Oh, okay," said Sofie, greatly relieved. "See you in class."

"Thanks for helping," said Stewart.

"Any time," offered Sofie as she left the cafeteria with her friends.

Raymond, who had gone to the line for food, watched Sofie leave, and turned his gaze to Stewart, wondering why Sofie took the picture and handed the camera to him. Stewart happened to glance at Raymond at that moment and realizing Raymond's dim brain was trying to figure out what was going on, he decided to leave the cafeteria as quickly as possible. He found himself thinking of Sofie's comment about seeing him in class. He didn't realize she was aware he was in any of her classes. Maybe she was more aware of him than he had thought. Maybe she was thinking of asking him to the Sadie Hawkins dance. Wow, would that be something.

Stewart didn't notice that his mother seemed unusually quiet while she drove him, the twins, and Annie from school. She did express her sympathies concerning Alex's broken leg, but other than that, she didn't say much of anything the rest of the way home. She had barely come to a stop when Stewart leaped out of the car, followed by the twins, and sprinted to the house.

"Why are they always in such a rush?" Nora wondered aloud.

Stewart flung the door open, ran into the house, and started up the stairs. He tripped on the first step and Ethan and Nathan, following too closely, fell on top of him, stacked like pancakes.

"Get...off!" gasped Stewart, barely able to breathe. The boys untangled themselves and continued up the stairs.

Stewart removed the thermal imaging camera from his backpack after he and the twins entered his bedroom. They crowded around the desk and Stewart turned on the computer. Though Stewart had a very fast computer, the few seconds it took for the computer to spring into action felt like hours. Stewart pulled up the program and immediately sent Raymond's thermal image to the computer. With a few clicks of the mouse, Stewart was able to define the void in Raymond's image and clicked on the calculate function. Raymond's VAC and corresponding power setting appeared. Stewart looked up at Ethan and Nathan, smiled, and keyed in the power setting for the brain.

A few seconds later, the brain began to glow.

"Wait!" shouted Ethan. "Turn it off!"

"Why?" said Stewart, completely shocked by Ethan's outburst.

"You haven't figured out what you want to do with Raymond, right?" asked Ethan.

Stewart thought for a moment, then turned down the power setting and the glow of the brain began to fade.

"We need to think about this," said Nathan. "We shouldn't be messing with Raymond until we have a plan."

"Let's test it first," suggested Ethan.

"We have tested it. We know it works," said Stewart.

"Yeah, but you haven't tested sending thoughts that make people do crazy things."

"You're right," Stewart allowed. "I could test you guys."

Nathan shook his head. "That wouldn't be a good test. We'd be expecting it."

Ethan pointed out the window. "There's our test. Right there."

Stewart and Nathan went to the window and saw Zack riding his bicycle down the street.

"Oh, this will be great. Let's do this," said Stewart, recalling a recent apple plunking to his skull, courtesy of Zack. Stewart picked up the camera and handed it to Ethan. "I'll stand in my driveway like I'm hanging out. You guys go across the street with the camera. Zack will see me and ride slowly on the other side of the street and yell at me. Act like you're talking to each other and you don't see him. When he rides by, take his picture."

Stewart sat at the end of his driveway while the twins crossed the street. They decided to take a position near a large group of bushes along the street, making them less visible. They were careful not to step on the yard owned by Mr. Lester. He was a crotchety old man, who spent his afternoons looking out the window to make sure none of the neighborhood kids stepped on his lawn. A minute later, Zack rode back down the street. He looked at Stewart, who was innocently gazing at the clouds while sitting cross-legged at the end of his driveway, and as predicted, steered his bicycle to the other side of the street.

"What's the matter, you too fat to stand up?" Zack sneered. As he rode past, Ethan and Nathan jumped out from behind the bushes. "Smile!" said Ethan. Zack instinctively turned towards Ethan, who snapped a perfect picture, sending Zack pedaling as fast as he could to get out of harm's way. When he was a safe distance down the street, he circled back.

"What a bunch of losers, taking pictures! Why don't you try to get me?"

"Don't worry, we will," retorted Nathan smugly. The twins crossed the street and followed Stewart back into the house.

After Zack's image was loaded and his VAC and power setting was calculated, Stewart keyed in the power setting. "Is he still out there?" asked Stewart to Nathan, sitting by the window.

"Yeah, he just rode past. He's looking towards the house, probably hoping you'll come back outside."

"Good." Stewart watched the brain as it glowed, then leaned back in his chair and closed his eyes. "Let me know if you see him do anything." Stewart concentrated on sending his thoughts to Zack.

"He's back!" reported Ethan. "Now he's stopping across the street. He's parking his bike. He's got a goofy look on his face like he's sleep walking with his eyes open. He's on Mr. Lester's yard. Oh, Mr. Lester isn't going to like that. Zack's on his knees. Now he's crawling. He's opened his mouth. I can't hear him." Ethan opened the window. Ethan and Nathan laughed, hearing Zack barking loudly. Zack crawled over to an empty flower bed and dug in the dirt with his hands. Ethan and Nathan fought to control their laughter, afraid it would interfere with Stewart.

Mr. Lester burst out of his front door and marched over to Zack.

"What in the world are you doing?" demanded Mr. Lester. "Get off of my yard!"

Zack looked up at Mr. Lester and began growling. Mr. Lester took a step backwards, wondering what was wrong with this kid. Could he have rabies? Mr. Lester continued to step back as Zack growled with a crazed look in his eyes.

"All right young man, I'm calling the police!" Mr. Lester hobbled into his house and slammed the door behind him.

"He's calling the police," said Ethan. "Maybe you better call it off." Ethan and Nathan watched as Zack stood on his feet. An odd look passed over his face. He blinked his eyes and looked at the dirt on his hands. He wiped his hands on his pants and realizing he was in Mr. Lester's yard, ran to his bicycle, hopped on, and rode away, as quickly as his legs could pedal. Ethan and Nathan laughed and laughed.

"Okay, he's gone," said Nathan. Stewart opened his eyes and turned down the power setting on the machine.

"How was that?" he asked.

"That," said Ethan and Nathan simultaneously, "was great!"

The twins had just left and Stewart sat at his desk, thinking about how he was able to affect Zack's actions. Hearing footsteps, he turned to see Nora appear in the doorway.

"Hi, mom. What's for dinner?"

Nora sighed. "How about I order a pizza? I don't feel like cooking."

"Pizza!" exclaimed Stewart. He loved pizza, especially topped with Canadian bacon and pineapple. His excitement over the thought of eating pizza quickly subsided as he realized Nora seemed sad.

"Mom, are you all right?" asked a concerned Stewart.

Nora paused for a moment, then entered the room and sat on Stewart's bed.

"I had lunch with your father today…" Nora hesitated, trying to find the right words. Alarmed, Stewart's mind immediately began racing. The various possibilities did not seem good.

Nora cleared her throat. "Your father is going to get an apartment near his office…"

"Are you getting a divorce?" blurted Stewart, surprised how the words seemed to just shoot out of his mouth. He felt his lower jaw slightly tremble.

"No, Honey, we are not getting a divorce. Your father thinks this will help him get through all of the work he has in his office. He will only stay there during the weekdays and come home on the weekends," said Nora, as reassuring as she could be.

"Why can't other people do his work?" asked Stewart. "All he does is work, work, work. He never spends any time with us anymore."

"His job has become busier and busier. Your father is very good at what he does and people are realizing it and coming to him for help. We need to be proud of his success."

Stewart slumped in his chair, trying to process everything Nora had just told him. "I don't understand why he can't have people help him."

Nora thought for a long moment before looking at Stewart. "Honey, your father is a wonderful, intelligent man. But, he isn't comfortable working around other people. What I mean is, he is extremely uncomfortable around other people."

"Why? People like him, don't they?" asked Stewart.

"Everybody likes him. To be honest, I don't understand it completely. He's tried to explain it to me, but I'm not sure he understands it himself. It's just how he is. He has trouble speaking in front of others. Haven't you noticed how he will only say a few words if someone tries to talk to him? He's been this way his entire life."

Stewart's eyes narrowed. "So, is he going to stay in the apartment forever?"

Nora shrugged her shoulders. "Not forever. I honestly can't say for how long."

"Mom, be honest. Does he like working better than being with us?"

"Oh no, that isn't true. He's just trying to make a good living to support us and make sure we have the money for you to go to a good college. Then someday, he can retire."

Nora stood up. "He does love us, you don't have to worry about that." She put on a brave smile for Stewart as she left the room. Stewart wasn't sure he believed her.

Stewart peered at the monitor and typed on the keyboard. After lunch, he had taken pictures before and after each class of as many teachers and students as possible. When the twins left for dinner, he began the process of loading the images for each person into the computer and calculating their VAC. After each person's VAC was obtained, he typed their information into a database he devised so he could click on a person's name and the power setting for the brain would automatically adjust to that person's setting.

Bringing up each person's image, highlighting the void and calculating the VAC was taking longer than Stewart had originally anticipated. He was thankful it was Friday and he would have the entire weekend to analyze the one hundred pictures he had taken that day. Realizing it would be difficult to go to sleep once he started this project, he prepared himself to work late into the evening and would have to make it appear to Nora that he had gone to sleep at his regular time.

Around the time Nora called up to Stewart to remind him to start getting ready for bed, Byron walked into the house. Stewart had been so immersed with his work, he didn't hear him drive into the garage.

After a short while, Byron walked up the stairs and entered Stewart's bedroom. Stewart quickly clicked on a computer game that filled the screen and obscured the VAC program. Byron sat on the bed, something Stewart found unusual. He never sat on his bed or even took the time to hang out in his room.

"What do you have on the computer?" asked Byron.

"Just a computer game," Stewart replied coolly. He was still upset from hearing about the apartment and didn't want Byron to see exactly how upset he was.

"I see," said Byron. "Your mom told you about me renting an apartment downtown?"

"Yeah," replied Stewart, trying not to show any emotion.

"And she explained why I'm considering this?"

"She did," said Stewart robotically.

"And you understand the reasoning?"

Stewart paused, and then looked his father straight in the eye. "No, I don't understand. I'm sorry. I don't understand."

Byron was surprised, yet proud of Stewart. He wished he could have been that direct with his father. "As you can see, I've been swamped for a long, long time. It's amazing how much work has come our way. I have to take advantage of this while I can."

"How long will you need to have this apartment?" asked Stewart sadly.

Byron looked up at the ceiling, as if staring at a giant calendar. "I really couldn't tell you. I can get a short-term lease at one of the buildings near the office, so if I can see the work load decreasing, I won't be locked in long-term. I can honestly tell you I wouldn't be doing this if I didn't think there was an upside. By being more efficient during the week, I won't have to work as long on the weekends when I'm back here with you and mom. That way, I can start spending more time with you."

Stewart felt his jaw tighten. Byron had mentioned spending more time with him before and never seemed to follow through. Work always came first. I'll believe it when I see it, thought Stewart.

"That would be great," said Stewart half-heartedly. Maybe it would be different this time.

"Well, get some rest. I'm sure you had a busy week," said Byron.

"I sure did," muttered Stewart. "Dad?"

"Yes?"

"Can I take your picture?" asked Stewart.

"Of course," said Byron obligingly.

Stewart reached for the thermal imaging camera and pointed it at his father. "Smile."

14

REVENGE

MR. PIKE PULLED INTO his usual space in the furthest corner of the teacher's parking lot and turned off the engine. Before stepping out of his truck, he took a few seconds to reflect on the surroundings of the school and how, if everything went as planned, his teaching career at this school would be over in a month. He had hit on every pick the day before and was now sitting on a half-million dollars of winnings. Analyzing the games for the upcoming weekend, he identified the picks he believed were sure bets and if successful, would double his winnings to one million dollars. He let the thought of those numbers roll around in his brain for a few seconds. Having a million dollars would make him a millionaire. How many teachers become millionaires on a teacher's salary? Zero?

He wasn't going to stop at a million, not the way he was going. All he had to do was get through this week and the Sadie Hawkins dance Friday night, and he would be ready to assume the role of America's newest millionaire. He wasn't looking forward to being a chaperone at the dance. Mr. Turley, the school principal, asked him to work at the dances only because he served unofficially as school security. No one in their right mind would mess with him, especially a kid. The positive side to the Sadie Hawkins dance, he decided, was that it would be the last school dance he would ever have to attend.

Stewart fidgeted in his seat, trying to pay attention to Mr. Leiker, standing at the chalkboard and explaining a formula. Mr. Leiker was known for writing clearly and carefully, making it easy for the students to take notes. The formula was the most complex and lengthy formula the class had studied so far this year and as Mr. Leiker completed it, he paused for a moment. An odd expression came over his face.

"Okay, class, this formula looks lonely, don't you think?" he asked, looking out at the students. "Don't you think it needs some company? How about a nice, white, fluffy bunny?" Mr. Leiker drew a very nice illustration of a bunny. He took a step back, surveyed his drawing and moved back to the chalkboard. Meanwhile, the students looked at one another, trying to make sense of Mr. Leiker's behavior. Stewart heard a giggle from across the room.

"I think this bunny looks lonely as well, so I'm going to draw this bunny's family. How about a Mr. Bunny, and three little baby bunnies?" Mr. Leiker continued drawing the bunnies, all in a row. When he finished, he looked at the class.

"Your homework assignment for tomorrow is to draw bunnies. One bunny for each member in your family."

The bell rang and the students filed out of the room. No one said a word, though every student did a good job of suppressing smiles. Mr. Leiker sat at his desk and blankly stared at the chalkboard. Stewart stopped as he passed by Mr. Leiker.

"That was a nice lesson today, Mr. Leiker. Thank you." Mr. Leiker's expression returned to normal as Stewart walked away. Mr. Leiker found himself wondering what had just happened. It sure felt odd.

Ethan, Nathan, and Dino waited for Stewart in the hallway as he stepped out of the classroom.

"Did you do that?" asked Ethan.

Stewart answered with a grin.

"How did you make him do that?" pressed Nathan.

"I spent the weekend coming up with thoughts and sending them to a lot of people in the school. I told them to do things based on a certain cue, then stop doing it at another cue. That way, they won't be like zombies all day. It looks like it worked with Mr. Leiker, don't you think?"

"It sure did," said Dino. "But, I'm going to have to draw the MOST bunnies in the class tonight. Thanks a lot." The boys laughed as they headed down the hall.

Alex would be spending P.E. in the library until his cast was removed. It didn't make sense for him to trudge down the stairs to the gym where he could only sit and watch the class. Without Alex's presence, Raymond was up to his usual tricks and had given Stewart a quick elbow to the ribs as they lined up for roll call.

Stewart tolerated the temporary pain from Raymond's elbow as this was the moment he had been waiting for all morning. Mr. Pike strutted out of the locker room holding his clipboard and a bag of basketballs. He blew his whistle to get everyone's attention. Immediately, Raymond ran around the gym and gracefully flapped his arms. The boys looked at Mr. Pike, who at first seemed dumbfounded, then increasingly irritated.

"Burns, get over here!" shouted Mr. Pike. Rather than run directly to Mr. Pike, Raymond began a series of loops while continuing to flap his arms. After a couple of loops, Raymond stopped in front of Mr. Pike.

"Burns! What is your problem?" barked a flustered Mr. Pike.

"My problem? My problem?" asked Raymond, a dazed smile crossing his face. "My problem is I'm an orange monarch butterfly! I wanna be a beautiful pink unicorn!"

Clenching his right hand in a fist, Raymond held it to his forehead and extended his index finger so it stuck out like a tiny horn. With a large, happy smile, he began galloping around the gym with his tiny horn while the boys laughed uncontrollably. Mr. Pike stood and watched, unable to make sense of the situation. In all of his years of teaching, he had never seen anything like this.

With great satisfaction, Stewart watched his classmates enjoy the spectacle taking place in the gym. He figured Raymond had bullied all of them at some time and humiliating him in front of them was proving to be a great deal of fun.

Mr. Pike clenched his jaw as he tried to make sense of the situation. He momentarily turned towards the boys and saw them all convulsed with laughter. Except for Stewart, who just stood there with a satisfied grin. Mr. Pike found that very strange.

Stewart and his friends finished eating and rose from their seats. It was a warm day for that time of year and the students liked to spend the rest of their lunch period outdoors on days such as this. The most popular place to congregate was the area at the back of the school where there were benches scattered around the lawn. Stewart noticed that everyone in the lunch room was headed for the back of the school. With Alex slowed by his crutches, Stewart and his friends were at the back of the crowd. Stepping outside, Stewart gave his friends a sly nod.

Brittany, Shelby, and Courtney walked to the bench closest to the doors and sat down. They liked this particular bench because they could easily make snide comments to everyone walking past them on their way to the other benches. As Stewart walked past them, he looked at Brittany. "Nice day isn't it?" he said to her, nonchalantly. Instantly, Brittany's eyes grew blank, as did her friends. The girls put down their purses, walked a couple of steps onto the lawn, and got down on their hands and knees.

Brittany turned to Stewart. "Baaaaa," bleated Brittany.

"Baaaaa," responded Shelby and Courtney. Together, the girls put their faces on the lawn and began to chew the grass. Brittany raised her head, chewing the grass as if an entire pack of gum was in her mouth. "Baaaaa," bleated all of the girls simultaneously. The rest of the students laughed and pointed at them as they continued grazing.

Taking a walk around the school to get a little fresh air during the lunch hour, Mr. Turley rounded the corner and came upon the students, who had formed a small crowd around the POP Sisters.

"What is going on here?" demanded Mr. Turley, as he forced his way through the crowd, only to find three girls grazing on the lawn. "Okay girls, stop that!" shouted Mr. Turley. The girls continued to graze. This did not sit well with him at all. He had spent years building a sparkling reputation at the school and was hoping to be promoted to a nearby high school next year when the principal retired. If word got out that he could not control middle school students, it would most likely ruin his chances for a promotion.

Mr. Turley reached down and grabbed Brittany's arm, helping her to her feet.

"What has gotten into you?" he asked.

Brittany leaned towards Mr. Turley and spat the clump of grass out of her mouth. The grass landed on Mr. Turley's nicely polished shoes. "Baaaaa," bleated Brittany. Mr. Turley's face turned red as he reached for Shelby and Courtney, trying to pull them to their feet.

"Okay, this is enough. We're all going to my office for a little chat." Mr. Turley led the girls into the school, all of them now sporting matching grass stains on their knees.

"Mr. Turley should be one of the shepherds in the Christmas play," observed Ethan.

"He's a natural," said Nathan.

The students assembled their instruments and warmed up, creating a chaotic din with every person playing random notes at the same time. Mr. Stimple appeared in front of the class. A strange expression crossed over his face.

"I want everyone to pass the Beethoven music back to me." Confused, the students looked at Mr. Stimple, who picked up another stack of music and walked towards them.

"I have decided we are going to play different music for our concert. Our concert is now going to be a collection of theme songs from science fiction movies. The first song we will be working on is the greatest theme song ever, the score from 'Star Wars,' written by the legendary John Williams."

Everyone's expressions immediately changed with this announcement, observed Stewart, as he looked around the room, now filled with excitement. The students eagerly took the music from Mr. Stimple and practically threw the Beethoven sheet music back to him.

Stewart couldn't stop smiling as his friends looked at him with great appreciation. This was going to be the greatest concert in the history of the school.

Walking down the hall on his way to French class, Stewart and his friends came upon a large cluster of students. The boys moved around the edge of the crowd until they were able to see the reason for the gathering. On his hands and knees, Raymond was crawling down the hallway while making engine noises. Crawling quickly, he sounded just like a race car changing into high gear. The crowd of students moved with him and when Raymond came upon a couple of students slow to get out of his way, he looked up at them.

"Honk, honk!" beeped Raymond impatiently.

Laughter echoed through the hallway until Mr. Turley burst onto the scene. Not another one, he thought, pushing his way through the students. Mr. Turley bent down to grab Raymond's arm and as he did so, Raymond crawled away at an amazing rate of speed while continuing to sound like an engine. Mr. Turley was forced to run after him and comically kept trying to reach for him, only to have Raymond crawl away in a different direction. This went on until another teacher helped corner Raymond, who did a nice job of slowing his engine noise as he came to a stop. Taking Raymond's arm, Mr. Turley led him through the laughing crowd.

"All right everyone, that's enough. Go to your classes. Please." With that, Mr. Turley escorted Raymond down the hall to his office. *What has gotten into these kids?* Mr. Turley had dealt with Raymond on more than one occasion in the past for the typical bullying incidents. *Was there something else going on here?* He could not detect the presence of alcohol on Raymond. *Was he under the influence of some kind of drug?* The girls convinced him they did not take any kind of drugs but were unable to explain why they had suddenly taken a liking to the school lawn. *So, what would cause this strange behavior?* He was going to have to get to the bottom of these episodes of bizarre behavior.

Mr. Turley led Raymond down the hall and into the suite of offices. At the end of the corridor was Mr. Turley's large office. He escorted Raymond inside and shut the door behind them before motioning for Raymond to take a seat. Mr. Turley sat down behind his desk.

"So," Mr. Turley began, "would you please explain to me what you were doing in the hall?"

Raymond, with a slight groggy expression, looked at the floor. "I'm not sure."

"What do you mean you don't know?"

Raymond looked up at Mr. Turley. "It's hard to explain. It's like I'm watching myself doing these things. I don't know why I'm doing it."

Mr. Turley clasped his hands on the desk, leaned forward, and cleared his throat. "I have to ask you these questions and I need an honest answer. Are you under the influence of alcohol?"

Raymond shook his head. Mr. Turley looked at him for a moment. "Are you under the influence of any drug?" Raymond again shook his head. Mr. Turley stared at Raymond.

"I've never taken drugs," said Raymond firmly. Mr. Turley stared at Raymond for what seemed like an eternity before leaning back in his chair. In his years of dealing with students, if a kid was lying, his eyes would have given him away by now. Raymond appeared to be telling the truth and Raymond's answers to his questions were the same as the answers from the three girls he had brought in earlier. So, if the kids weren't under the influence of alcohol or drugs, what was going on? He was stumped.

Mr. Leiker entered the suite of offices and stopped in the room designated as the infirmary. Louise Sanders, the long-time school nurse, sat at her desk and made notes in a file. She closed the file as Mr. Leiker entered.

"Hello, Louise," said Mr. Leiker, somewhat subdued. "Do you have a few minutes?"

"I do," responded Louise. "What can I help you with?"

Mr. Leiker sat in the chair beside her desk. "Can you give me a quick checkup? Look into my eyes, take my temperature, check my blood pressure, that sort of thing."

"Are you not feeling well?" asked Louise with the appropriate amount of concern.

"Uh…I'm not sure. I'm not sure how I'm feeling." Mr. Leiker looked up at her, slightly bewildered. "Is that odd? I can't honestly say how I am doing."

"Well, we can take a look and see if anything is abnormal. Sometimes a person is coming down with something and can't tell if they are sick or not. It happens all of the time. Let me get my thermometer." As Louise reached into a drawer for the thermometer, she thought it wasn't odd how Mr. Leiker was feeling. What was odd was that Mr. Stimple had been in her office just a short while ago and had made the same comments as Mr. Leiker.

Alison pulled into her driveway and turned off the engine. Alex opened his door and swung his legs out of the car. Propping himself on his crutches, he slowly moved to the house. Alison walked ahead of him and opened the front door. Annie and Stewart stepped out of the back seat and Stewart began to head across the street to his house.

"Stewart!" shouted Annie as she ran to him.

Stewart turned around, wondering what she would want from him. "Yeah?"

Annie pulled nervously on her dull, gray sweater. Hasn't she learned anything from Mrs. Darby by now, wondered Stewart?

"Would you go with me to the Sadie Hawkins dance?" asked Annie, her voice slightly trembling.

Stewart stood with his mouth hanging open, completely unprepared for this request. His mind raced at full speed. If he said "yes" to her, what would he say if Sofie asked him? The dance was at the end of the week and time was running out. He quickly tried to sort out the possibilities.

"We can go with Alex and Sofie," offered Annie, hoping that would help convince Stewart to go with her. Stewart looked at her, unable to speak for a moment.

"Alex and Sofie?" he finally blurted, feeling as if he had just been hit on the side of the head with a frying pan.

"Yes. Sofie asked Alex to the dance just before we came home today. She is so nice. It really cheered him up."

Stewart's mind went numb, much like when he sat on his leg too long and couldn't walk for a minute. Thinking, which always came easy for him, suddenly seemed incredibly difficult. He looked at Annie, whose eyes were filled with anticipation.

"Yes...I'll go to the dance with you," responded Stewart. Did he actually utter those words or had an alien taken possession of his body?

Annie's face immediately expressed joy, and then turned blank as she tried not to show too much emotion. "Oh, good. Thank you," said Annie. Did I just say "thank you," she wondered? Are you supposed to thank someone for accepting an invitation for a dance? Do they say that in movies? Is he going to change his mind? I better go before he does, thought Annie. She gave Stewart a quick smile and ran to her house.

Reaching the door, she turned to watch Stewart walk across the street. Would he consider wearing a beret to the dance? How would he look with a pencil-thin mustache? Would he be able to grow one in time for the dance? Can he grow facial hair? Annie pondered these questions as she stepped inside the house and closed the door behind her.

Stewart trudged up his driveway, his mind reeling. How could Sofie ask Alex to the dance? Couldn't she somehow have sensed his devotion to her as he spent hours staring at the back of her head? He stepped onto the front porch and paused. Maybe she asked Alex out of sympathy for his broken leg. Even so, how would he be able to do anything at a dance? Don't you have to dance at a dance? Wouldn't she risk humiliating him by asking him to a dance when he would only be able to sit in a chair and watch everyone else having all of the fun? What was she thinking? Trying to figure out Sofie's reason was going to be an exercise in futility, he concluded, as he reached for the door.

Stewart dropped is backpack on his desk and lay on his bed. His head was still spinning from his conversation with Annie. Why couldn't he have heard about Sofie asking Alex to the dance the next day? This news basically ruined the best day of school he had ever had. Everything went as planned, especially with Raymond and the POP Sisters. Despite how well it went, he decided he would need to take everything more slowly, maybe one incident every day or two. If there were too many more days like today, he could see Raymond and the POP Sisters being expelled from school or committed to an insane asylum. What fun would it be if he wasn't around to see them make fools of themselves?

His next order of business would be to deal with his dad. Just as Stewart anticipated, Byron ended up working most of the weekend and was not available to spend any time with him. He asked his mom if his dad was going to be moving into the apartment soon and Nora said she wasn't sure. She assumed he would be moving that coming week. We'll see about that, thought Stewart.

Byron reached for a stack of documents sitting on his printer. He felt a strong sense of satisfaction because these documents represented weeks of planning a complicated merger strategy. After a few hours of proofreading, he would be ready to present the plan to the client. Actually, Charlie would be making the presentation after Byron walked him through it. This arrangement suited him perfectly. Charlie was very good at presentations and Byron didn't mind if the clients thought Charlie had devised the strategy. As long as he didn't have to say more than a few words, everything would be all right.

After reading the first page, Byron felt a strange sensation, similar to the time he felt light-headed in an overheated church as a boy. It wasn't really that warm in the office. Maybe he was getting dehydrated. He found it helpful to constantly keep his water glass full. A trip to the water cooler would help clear his head. Byron picked up his glass and walked out of his office.

Normally, he would turn right as he left his office and head to the end of the hall where the small kitchen with the water cooler was located. Instead, he turned left and went towards the front of the office suite.

Bernie peered intently at her monitor as Byron approached. She looked at him pleasantly, wondering what small task he was going to assign to her.

"Well, 'ello love," said Byron in a perfect Cockney accent.

Bernie stared at Byron as if he had just grown three heads and his skin turned green.

"I...beg your pardon?" stammered Bernie.

"I've got a treat for you, love," continued Byron in his newly acquired Cockney accent. He stood straight in front of her and inhaled deeply.

"Jack and Jill went up the hill to fetch a pail of water. Jack fell down and broke his crown and Jill came tumbling after."

Byron gave Bernie a quick salute. Bernie stared at him in disbelief, unable to move a muscle.

"Cheerio," said Byron as he headed down the hall with his water glass. After filling his glass in the kitchen, Byron strode to his office, shut the door and sat down on the couch.

What the heck just happened out there? What did he do? Byron stretched out on the couch. Am I losing my mind? What is Bernie going to think? Maybe I'm pushing it too hard. Byron closed his eyes and soon heard a knock on the door.

The door opened gently and Bernie poked her head through the opening.

"Byron?"

"Yes?"

"Is everything okay?"

Byron thought for a moment. "I…don't know."

"Is there anything I can get for you?"

"No, I'm…okay."

Bernie looked at him for a moment, and slowly began closing the door.

"Bernie?"

"Yes?"

"Whatever happened out there, I'm sorry. It won't happen again," said Byron.

"Do you want my honest opinion?" asked Bernie.

Byron sat up. "Of course, I do."

"Well," Bernie began as she stepped into the doorway, "that was the most entertaining thing I have ever seen from you. You made my day. I wouldn't mind seeing that side of you more often." Bernie closed the door behind her.

Byron reclined back on the coach and closed his eyes. Entertaining? How can acting like a lunatic be entertaining? I need to do a better job of taking breaks. I'm definitely working too hard.

15

THE DANCE

THE STUDENTS SMILED AT Mr. Leiker as they entered the classroom and filed past him, each one placing their drawing of bunnies on his desk. Mr. Leiker had a vague recollection of assigning the drawing as homework and spent most of that day trying to figure out what had come over him. All he could think of was that he just had one of those random days when a person loses their mind. This must happen to everyone at some point, so it wasn't worth dwelling on it. He returned each student's smile good-naturedly and commented on drawings that were particularly well done. Mr. Leiker picked up Dino's drawing and let out a soft whistle as he looked at the family of six bunnies, all of them wearing Greek dance costumes.

"This one is definitely an A plus," remarked Mr. Leiker admiringly.

Sofie had already taken her seat when Stewart walked in and made his way to his desk. Keeping his eyes focused on the floor, Stewart managed to avoid making eye contact with her while taking his seat. He hadn't decided if he was mad at her for asking Alex to the dance and needed more time to sort it out. His plan was to pay attention to Mr. Leiker and ignore Sofie's golden locks flowing over her shoulders. Despite his intentions, Stewart soon found himself absent-mindedly gazing at her.

While analyzing the curls in Sofie's hair, Stewart continued the debate with himself of whether he should use the machine on Sofie, so she would change her mind and ask him to the dance instead. Though tempted to use the machine, he was sure all of his friends would strongly object. Reluctantly, he knew it would be best for him to accept the fact she would be going to the dance with Alex. Accepting a fact is one thing he realized, liking it is another.

From the corner of his eye, Stewart thought he saw Annie glancing his way. Had she been looking at him often? Did she look at him the way he looked at Sofie? He didn't think so, since he considered Sofie a goddess and he was just a mere mortal. What should he make of this unfamiliar attention?

He began thinking of Annie's sweater of the day, another dull, uninspired article of clothing. Would she wear one of those dowdy items to the dance? Would she ask him to wear matching sweaters? Stewart made a mental checklist of all of his clothing and tried to remember if he had anything similar to Annie's clothing. If anything, figuring out what they might wear to the dance was a welcome distraction to thinking of Sofie.

Raymond walked across the basketball court to his place in line, aware that all eyes were on him. He gave one boy a stern look and instantly, everyone's heads turned away, because none of them wanted to incur his wrath. Reaching his place in line, Raymond managed to shove a quick elbow into Stewart's ribs and as usual, acted like nothing happened. He looked at Stewart and to his surprise, Stewart locked eyes with him. The look of fear Stewart normally had when facing Raymond was replaced with something different. A look of confidence. Maybe he needed to hit Stewart harder next time. Nobody was going to look at him like that and get away with it.

Mr. Pike walked into the gym and dropped the bag of balls in the center of the court. He motioned for Raymond to come over to him. Raymond jogged over and stopped in front of Mr. Pike, who placed his hand on Raymond's shoulder and turned him so their backs were to the boys in line.

"I want to know if there's going to be a problem with you today," growled Mr. Pike in a low voice.

"No problem today," replied Raymond.

"There better not be. Okay, get back in line." Mr. Pike followed Raymond to the beginning of the line and looked at his clipboard. "Arnett."

"Here," said Arnett.

"Burns."

"Ribbit," croaked Raymond.

Mr. Pike put his hands on his hips and stared at Raymond. "What did you say?" asked Mr. Pike, whose mood worsened in the blink of an eye.

"Ribbit!" Raymond hunched down on the floor and sprang forward like a frog. "Ribbit!" shouted Raymond gleefully, hopping across the gym while the boys held their sides, bursting with laughter.

Mr. Pike dropped his clipboard and ran over to Raymond, who managed to hop away from Mr. Pike's outstretched hands. After a couple of failed attempts, Mr. Pike faked as if he was going to his right and cutting back quickly to his left, timed it perfectly and caught Raymond in mid-air. Throwing Raymond over his shoulder like a sack of potatoes, Mr. Pike hustled him out of the gym and into the locker room. Breathing hard from exertion, he set Raymond down and with both hands, pinned him against the wall.

"What is going on with you?" demanded Mr. Pike. Looking into his eyes, he saw that the lights were on, and no one was home. He shook Raymond, who suddenly recoiled in Mr. Pike's grasp. His eyes came to life as he looked at Mr. Pike.

"What're you doing?" asked Raymond somewhat fearfully.

"That's what I'm asking you!" Mr. Pike retorted. "What has gotten into you the last few days? You're acting like some kind of maniac. Are you trying to get suspended?"

"No!" replied Raymond emphatically.

"So, what is going on with you?"

Raymond stopped resisting and almost became entirely limp. He put his face in his hands as he slid down the wall and sat on the floor. "I don't know. I really don't know. It's like there's an alien in my body."

Mr. Pike stepped back and folded his arms as he pondered the situation.

"Look Raymond, I'm just trying to figure out what is going on here. What you're doing isn't normal. If this happens again, I'm going to have to send you to the front office. Maybe the school nurse should take a look at you."

"I've already been in Mr. Turley's office."

"What did he say?" asked Mr. Pike.

"He wanted to know if I was on drugs."

Mr. Pike's eyes narrowed. "Are you?"

"No, I'm not!" Raymond replied angrily. Mr. Pike looked at him for a long moment.

"Okay, just do a better job of controlling yourself. Go back to the gym."

Raymond crawled to his feet and left the locker room. Mr. Pike followed, shaking his head in exasperation. He sincerely hoped Raymond wasn't on drugs. He had seen too many athletes ruin their lives from terrible addictions.

Byron felt his head growing heavy as he read through documents in preparation for a meeting later that afternoon. He would normally keep reading and fight off any fatigue, having become an expert in pushing himself well beyond normal limits. However, after his little scene in front of Bernie that morning, he thought it would be best to take a break. Looking at his watch, he realized it was lunchtime, and since Nora wouldn't be coming to the office for lunch that day, it was a perfect time to head down the street for a sandwich.

Walking out of the office, he was relieved to see Bernie had already left for lunch. He had managed to avoid her the rest of the morning and was somehow hoping she would forget all about his performance. He approached the elevators and pushed the button.

Stepping out of the building, Byron felt very comfortable in his suit coat on this beautiful fall day. He stopped at the corner along with a large number of people on lunch break and waited for the light to change. Just as the light turned green, Byron felt a strange sensation pass through his head. Holding his elbows to the sides of his chest, he raised his hands in front of him and began hopping across the intersection with very long hops.

Everyone around the intersection couldn't help but notice Byron in a nice business suit hopping to the other side of the street. He reached the other side of the street and paused to wait for a group of men to get out of his way so he could resume hopping. The men moved slowly away as they stared at him. Byron smiled happily at the men.

"Haven't you seen a kangaroo before, mate?" asked Byron in a perfect Australian accent. He hopped down the sidewalk until he reached the sandwich shop. Byron shook his head as if he had just awakened and looked around, puzzled as to why everyone in every direction was looking at him. He entered the sandwich shop, wondering what was going on with all of them. Byron looked at the menu posted above the cash register and thought about which of the delicious sandwiches he would order. He was definitely hungry and a large corned beef sandwich sounded perfect. For a reason he couldn't understand, his legs were extremely tired.

The cafeteria was filled with students by the time Stewart arrived with Alex. They had spent extra time in study hall going over the math homework, which worked out well, as Alex did not have to worry about maneuvering around crowds of students in the hall between classes. Alex could move around quite well, though he found his armpits were being rubbed raw, making the crutches increasingly uncomfortable for him. He wished someone had told him how hard it would be on his armpits, which bothered him more than his broken leg.

With Alex on crutches, it was necessary for someone to carry Alex's tray of food from the lunch line to the table. Ethan climbed out of his seat and accompanied them to where the food was served. Stewart and Ethan emerged with trays while Alex followed and proceeded to their table. Stewart smiled with satisfaction while looking at the empty table next to where Sofie and her friends ate lunch. All of the POP sisters had called in sick that day, with the rumor being that they were dealing with some kind of mysterious illness. Stewart wanted to tell everyone the mysterious illness was called 'humiliation' and there would be more of that to come.

Debbie nudged Sofie's foot with her foot to catch her attention. "Here comes your McKnight in shining armor," said Debbie with a teasing smile.

Sofie smiled and turned just enough to see Alex sinking down into his seat. Stewart heard Debbie and instantly lost his appetite. Why couldn't she have said "Here comes your Camby in shining armor?" Or, how about "McCamby?" Stewart realized it didn't have quite the same gusto as Alex's last name. How about "Here comes Captain Stewart Camby of the First Inter-Galactic Space Division?" That would be an announcement impossible to top.

Ethan, Nathan, and Dino finished eating while Stewart pushed his food around the tray with his fork.

"Aren't you going to eat?" asked Dino.

"I'm not hungry. You guys want to go outside?"

"Sure," replied Ethan. Stewart picked up his tray and followed the twins and Dino while Alex and Annie continued eating together.

Byron exited the sandwich shop, completely satisfied with a sandwich stacked high with beef, and walked back to his office. He passed a couple of stores and stopped to peer into a window, where a mannequin wearing a loud suit was prominently displayed. Byron stroked his chin as he admired the suit and entered the store.

Stewart and his friends sat on a bench in the back area close to the teacher's parking lot. Unzipping his backpack, Stewart took out his laptop and a container.

"Guess what's in here?" asked Stewart, holding up the container. None of the boys could think of a good guess, so they all shrugged their shoulders. "It's the brain," answered Stewart.

"You're kidding me. You brought it to school?" asked Ethan.

"I made a new container so I can bring it with me. This one is sturdier than the old one and will do a better job of protecting it. I also attached a battery pack for power. Now, let's see who can be the next subject." Stewart connected it to his laptop and flipped a switch on the battery before returning the container to his backpack. He turned on the laptop and the boys waited for the computer to warm up. Once it was running, Stewart brought up the program with the VAC's for everyone.

"How about her?" remarked Dino as he pointed to Ms. Robitaille, who had just climbed out of her car and was heading towards the building.

"Perfect," said Stewart, pulling up the VAC for Ms. Robitaille and keying in the power setting for the brain. Stewart closed his eyes and put his fingers to his temple, something he found helped him do a better job of concentrating.

A glazed look spread across Ms. Robitaille's face and she stopped, raised herself on her toes, and executed an elegant pirouette. She walked to the building on her toes, executed another pirouette and continued walking on her toes. She repeated this sequence halfway to the building before stopping. Her eyes fluttered and looking around, she found the boys smiling at her with large grins. Flustered, she quickly made her way to the building and stepped inside.

"That was great!" laughed Ethan.

"Did you know she could do ballet?" asked Nathan.

Stewart nodded his head. "I heard her talking about it with one of the girls before class. I guess she studied it for years before becoming a teacher."

Sitting in his truck, Mr. Pike observed the entire scene from the moment the boys came outside and sat on the bench. On nice days such as this, he would return from lunch at his favorite Mexican restaurant and sit in his car for a few minutes, listening to the radio before going back to his little office in the locker room.

He watched with interest as Stewart had taken the laptop and container out of his backpack and noticed how shortly after Stewart had closed his eyes, Ms. Robitaille began spinning around and walking on her toes. Could there be a connection between Raymond's crazy behavior in the gym and what he had just seen with Ms. Robitaille's little dance? If so, was that Camby kid part of this connection? He remembered how Stewart's reaction to Raymond's wild gallop around the gym was much different than his classmates, something he found strange at the time. What could Stewart possibly be doing to cause this behavior? It would be worth keeping a careful eye on this kid from now on he noted, as Stewart put his laptop in the backpack and joined the boys walking back to the building.

Throwing the door open to his office suite, Byron strutted inside wearing a bright orange suit, orange tie, orange shoes, orange fedora, and sunglasses. Bernie looked up from her computer and stared in complete shock at Byron.

"What's up girlfriend?" asked Byron.

After staring at Byron for a few moments, Bernie attempted to speak.

"I…uh…huh?" stammered Bernie.

"Is Big C back from lunch?" asked Byron as he adjusted his fedora.

"Uh, no, not yet," replied Bernie.

"Okay, tell him Fly Tax Dog is ready for the meeting. I'll be in my office." Byron walked with a cool, casual swagger to his office.

Byron laid down on the couch, putting his feet on the coffee table and his arms behind his head. Shortly after, Charlie walked into Byron's office with an expression of great concern.

"Hey Big C," said Byron smoothly.

"Byron, are you okay?" asked Charlie.

"I'm great. Just kickin' it, waiting for you."

"You don't seem to be yourself…" began Charlie.

"Of course, I'm myself. Who else would I be?" interrupted Byron.

"Uh, that's not what I mean. Byron, we have an important meeting in an hour. How can we do this if you are not acting like yourself?"

Byron rose from the couch and smiling, gave Charlie a little pinch on the cheek. "Don't worry, my man. Fly's gonna take care of everything. Now go back to your office and chill."

Byron reclined back on the couch, tilted the fedora over his face and looked out the window. Flabbergasted, Charlie left

Byron's office and returned to his office. He sat behind his desk, picked up the telephone and dialed a number.

"Nora? Hi, it's Charlie. Are you busy? I think it would be a good idea if you came to the office and took Byron home. He's acting very strange. Not like himself at all. Okay, see you soon."

Charlie hung up and leaned back in his chair. It's happened, he thought. Byron has finally gone over the edge. Hopefully, all he needs is a little rest.

Stewart couldn't believe how quickly the week had gone by as he picked up the dress shirt his mom had placed on the bed for him. It was now time for him to get ready for the Sadie Hawkins dance and he found himself thinking of all of the uproar he had caused that week. Mr. Turley, who was rarely seen outside of the offices, now seemed to be everywhere, looking around as if his head was on a swivel, hoping he could catch whoever was behind the recent deluge of strange behavior. Though he decided to reduce the number of antics for at least a little while, Stewart thought he should send thoughts to Mr. Turley that would cause him to let Stewart do whatever he wanted, without any kind of punishment.

Despite the slowdown of incidents the rest of the week, Stewart was not about to let Raymond off the hook. Instead of outlandish behavior, Stewart changed his approach to Raymond by sending thoughts of odd, subtle behavior. A few days earlier, Raymond spent the entire day, except during P.E. class, sucking his thumb. Stewart decided not to have Raymond act unusual for a while in P.E., fearing Mr. Pike would start pushing for a suspension.

Willie and Damon grew more and more tired of Raymond's actions as the week went by. At first, they thought Raymond was being funny, as Raymond always liked doing the opposite of what was expected from him by people in a position of authority. After a few days, though, Willie and Damon became annoyed and increasingly embarrassed by Raymond's behavior and avoided being with him. Raymond noticed their increasing distance and didn't understand why they seemed to always have an excuse for why they couldn't hang around. He realized they were deliberately avoiding him when they told him that they couldn't have lunch with him because they had to study in the library. Willie and Damon never studied. Anywhere.

Stewart also backed away from sending thoughts to his dad the day Nora brought him home in a bright orange suit. Nora was near tears that afternoon and pleaded with Byron to see a doctor. Byron seemed confused and stubbornly refused to see a doctor, thinking he only needed to take the night off from working. Announcing he was tired, he went to their bedroom and took a long nap.

While Nora prepared dinner that evening, she told Stewart she was afraid something was very wrong with Byron and suggested he may have a brain tumor. Nora sobbed as she uttered the word "tumor," and Stewart tried to console her. Though he tried his best to persuade her that Byron was fine, Nora was not convinced. Seeing his mother this upset made Stewart feel awful and he resolved to find another way to have his father work less and spend more time with them.

Buttoning his shirt, the idea of handling his dad came to him. A simple solution that he thought should have come to him in the first place. Perhaps, in a way, he wanted to get back at his dad for all of the months, even years, that Byron was too preoccupied with work to spend much time with him. Once he finished getting dressed, he would turn on the machine and send the following thought to his dad: Byron would become more comfortable being around and talking to people; he would hire people to help him; he would work less hours; and; he would spend time with Stewart every day, starting on Monday. Stewart would let Byron work his normal long hours over the weekend, which would help him catch up from missing time during the week, but starting Monday, it was going to be different for the entire family.

Stewart descended the stairs and entered the living room, where Nora was reading a book. She covered her mouth as she stood, afraid she might start crying as she looked at her son, dressed so handsomely in his suit and tie. Recognizing the significance of what could be considered Stewart's first date, she was ready with her camera. Despite Stewart's protests, Nora stepped over to him, straightened his tie, brushed a few wayward hairs into place with her fingers, then backed away to snap his picture.

"Okay, let's go to the McKnight's house," directed Nora as she headed to the front door. Stewart followed Nora out of the house and across the street, where Alison was already taking pictures of Alex and Sofie in their front yard.

"Oh, what a beautiful couple," gushed Nora to Stewart, who didn't respond. He was too busy trying not to feel angry with Alex, while marveling at how wonderful Sofie looked in her dress. Stewart was hoping he wouldn't have to fight these conflicting feelings the entire evening.

Nora joined Alison in taking pictures of Alex and Sofie. Stewart stood to the side, wondering how long he would have to wait for Annie. He thought it was going to be an interesting sight, with Sofie looking like one of the top models in the world, and Annie wearing a frumpy sweater with her navy-blue beret.

The door opened and Annie stepped out of the house. Everyone turned her way as she stood in the doorway, momentarily embarrassed by having all eyes set on her. Stewart froze and felt his heart skip a beat. Annie's hair was slightly curled and completely visible since she wasn't wearing her beret. Her dark hair fell on her pale shoulders and her blue eyes were outlined with just the right amount of make-up. Stewart noticed she wasn't wearing glasses.

"My, don't you look beautiful!" exclaimed Nora, breaking the momentary silence. "Don't you think so?" she said directly to Stewart. Still in a minor state of shock, Stewart could only nod his head.

"Let's get you two together for some pictures," said Alison, and led Annie over to Stewart, who felt as if he were a marble statue. Alison placed Annie next to Stewart like an expert photographer and took a few steps back alongside Nora, where they both readied their cameras.

"Honey, smile," Nora requested from a still frozen Stewart as she raised her camera. Stewart managed a smile, while concentrating on trying to breathe. How could Annie look like this, he wondered? He would never have bet in a million years that she could be so pretty.

"Annie, please stop blinking so much," asked Alison, lowering her camera.

"Sorry," said Annie who then opened her eyes wide as if she had just been poked with a cattle prod.

"Okay, maybe blink a little," suggested Alison.

Alison leaned over to Nora. "She just got contacts today and is having a little trouble getting used to them." Nora and Alison quietly chuckled as they continued taking pictures.

Rather than stuff everyone into one car, Nora volunteered to drive Stewart and Annie to the dance. She followed Alison, Alex, and Sofie as they made their way out of the neighborhood. Nora insisted Stewart sit with Annie in the back seat, and Stewart found himself wondering what he should say to her. He felt like he was sitting with someone he had just met and as usual, struggled to think of something to talk about that wouldn't sound stupid, but would be interesting or even make him look heroic.

"So," said Stewart, "do you like scented soap?" He couldn't believe that was the best he could do and wondered why he even opened his mouth.

Annie turned to him and smiled. "I do. My favorite is lilac."

"Mine as well!" said Nora, pleased to find someone who shared her interest in soap. Instead of being annoyed at his mom's eavesdropping, he was happy to let his mom and Annie talk about soap the rest of the way to school. He didn't want to think for a few minutes due to feeling like his head was swimming with a strange variety of emotions.

The cafeteria was unrecognizable, having been transformed into a dazzling nightclub. Hanging from the ceiling was a revolving disco ball reflecting colorful light over the entire room. A DJ was stationed near the dance floor and played music that boomed from the speakers placed around the cafeteria. The bench style tables had been replaced with round ones covered with shiny material and balloon centerpieces.

Stewart, Annie, Alex and Sofie sat at a table with the twins, who were with Sofie's friends Debbie and Linh. Dino and his date, Amber Marquez, a girl as feisty as he was, were dancing up a storm on the dance floor. Stewart admired how Dino was able to dance without feeling self-conscious and thought nothing of being the only couple on the dance floor. Of course, Dino had been Greek dancing since he was a toddler, so it was second nature to him.

Mr. Pike stood near the main entrance and surveyed the scene before him. His job was to make sure everything went smoothly, as it always did. There had never been an instance where there was trouble in any of the previous dances he had attended, so this one shouldn't be any different. Normally, Mr. Pike would be looking at the clock every five minutes to see if it was time to end the festivities, though tonight, he kept thinking about his bets for the weekend and how his life was going to be changed. Tolerating one more dance was not going to be a problem.

Stewart spent most of the evening going to the refreshment table and drinking red punch from a punch bowl. His friends and their dates soon joined Dino and Amber and seemed to be having a great time out on the dance floor. He couldn't help but be impressed with how Alex was able to easily move around while on crutches. Annie, seated alone at the table, had told him she didn't mind if they danced at all, which was fine with him. Stewart practiced his moves in the mirror at home that day and decided he looked like a robot with bad wiring and no sense of timing. Better not to get out there and embarrass himself, he concluded.

After downing a couple more glasses of fruit punch, he brought a glass to Annie and told her he would be right back. Leaving the cafeteria, Stewart went down the hall and into the restroom. Returning to the cafeteria minutes later, he caught a glimpse of a couple behind a row of lockers. As he passed, he looked over to see who it was and saw Sofie place her hands upon Alex's face. Pulling him gently towards her, she tilted her head and gave him a long kiss.

Stewart almost tripped over himself as he continued walking. Approaching the cafeteria door, he felt nauseated and bent over with his hands on his knees. After a few deep breaths, Stewart straightened up, only to find he was sweating profusely and his hands were shaking. He decided it would be impossible to have a good time from that point forward, so there was no reason to stay at the dance. Stewart reached into his pocket and pulled out his phone.

"Mom, come and get me. I'm sick." Stewart put his phone in his pocket and went inside the cafeteria to tell Annie he would be going home. If she wanted to stay, that was fine with him.

16

REDEMPTION

STEWART BURST INTO HIS bedroom and dropped his suit coat on the floor. He wrenched his tie off with a little difficulty, further aggravating his frustration with life, and threw it on the floor next to his coat. He sat on the bed with his face in his hands, wondering how everything in his world could have gone so wrong so quickly.

The ride home from the dance was awful, with his mom asking him what seemed like a thousand questions on how he was feeling. Annie came home as well, not wanting to stay at the dance by herself. She looked out the window the entire way home without saying a word. When Nora stopped at their house to drop her off, Annie thanked her for the ride, told Stewart she hoped he would be feeling better soon, and hurried away. Nora felt a lump in her throat as she watched Annie enter her house, remembering how it was for her to go with a boy to a social event when she was that age.

She sensed something had gone wrong at the dance for Stewart, but until he decided to tell her, she could only guess what it was and tried not to think about it, though her mind was racing with possibilities. Had anyone made fun of Stewart's dancing? Had Annie made fun of Stewart? She knew he wasn't comfortable around girls, not having any sisters or close cousins. It probably wasn't anything Annie did, Nora assumed, because Annie didn't seem the type to hurt someone's feelings. No, it would be best not to think of anything until Stewart decided to tell her, which would probably take a day or two.

Annie entered her bedroom and kicked off her shoes as she sat on her bed. She felt like a fool. Stewart had not seemed sick to her shortly before they left the dance. It didn't make sense, unless a person can get sick that quickly from drinking too much punch. Seeing a reflection of herself in a mirror on the wall, she told herself it was probably her fault Stewart did not have a good time and used being sick as an excuse. Maybe if she was as pretty as Sofie, Stewart wouldn't have wanted to go home. Or, if she had been more willing to dance, maybe Stewart would have had more fun. The thought of dancing in front of people terrified her. However, he didn't seem like he wanted to dance, either. It then occurred to her that he may have told her he didn't want to dance to make her feel better. Maybe Stewart was an incredible dancer and she had ruined his fun. She pictured Stewart wearing black clothing and holding a red rose in his teeth while dancing the Tango with an older Latin woman. Lying on her bed, Annie wiped her eyes as they filled with tears, and went through each moment of the evening, trying to figure out where she blew it.

The next morning, Alex stared at the text message he had just received on his cell phone. Sofie had sent the message, which read: *I never want to see you again.*

Completely confused, Alex called her, wondering if this was some kind of a joke. Sofie's phone rang and rang and finally went to her voicemail. Alex left a message asking her to call him. Moments later, he received another message, which read: *Stop calling me.*

This could only be a joke, he thought. It was a strange joke. Could it be something else? He didn't know Sofie all that well, so maybe this was her sense of humor, though, it really didn't seem like her. It had to be a joke, he kept telling himself, as he called her number. Sofie did not answer and the call again went to voicemail. Alex left her another message, this time asking if she was joking. Sofie sent back another message which read: *I'm not joking. Please leave me alone.*

Alex put down the phone and put his hands behind his head and tried to figure out what was going on with Sofie. Last night had been one of the best nights of his life, even better than when his team won the league championship in football. Sofie was not only the most beautiful girl he had ever seen, she was also the nicest girl he had ever met. Maybe it was the kiss. But she kissed him. Was that wrong? It sure didn't feel like it was wrong. Maybe she wanted him to kiss her more. Would she be mad at him for not kissing her more? He would ask her if only she would talk to him. If she wouldn't talk to him on the phone, he was going to make sure she talked to him in person.

Alex reached for his crutches and just as he was about to approach his mom and ask her to take him to Sofie's house, a thought crossed his mind. Stewart. Yes, this is something Stewart had been doing with his machine all week. But why would he use it on Sofie? The more he thought about it, the more it bothered Alex. He picked up his phone and called Stewart. His call went straight to voicemail. Leaving voice messages is sure frustrating when you want to talk with someone, thought Alex. He asked Stewart to call him and put down his phone.

Stewart, sitting at his desk, looked up from his computer when he heard the phone ring. He had been expecting a call from Alex and planned on letting it ring. He wasn't even going to listen to his voicemail. He knew Alex would want to talk to him and ask him about Sofie. What was he going to say to him? Sending thoughts to Sofie through the machine was an accident? He didn't have any excuses that would make sense to Alex, so what was the point of talking to him?

Minutes later, the doorbell rang. Nora answered the door and called up to Stewart.

"Stewart, Alex is here to see you."

Stewart bolted upright in his chair. He didn't think Alex would come over to his house. It was too late to hide. He slowly rose from his chair and went downstairs. Nora smiled at Stewart as she left Alex in the doorway and returned to the kitchen. Stewart suddenly felt sweaty as Alex's expression intensified the moment Nora left the room.

"Did you use your machine on Sofie?" demanded Alex.

"Well...I...uh...um...yes," Stewart finally admitted.

"Why?" asked Alex.

"Because I like Sofie," blurted Stewart. "I've liked her for a long time. She should have asked me to the dance."

"Well, she asked me and you should have been okay with that," said Alex, greatly disappointed. "If she asked you, I would have been okay. And you used your machine on her to make her not want to talk to me. What kind of person would do that? I don't see how I can be your friend anymore."

Alex turned on his crutches and left the house. No big deal, thought Stewart as he closed the door. He had plenty of good friends who wouldn't kiss Sofie.

Late Sunday afternoon, Mr. Pike stood in the living room of his apartment watching the horror of the day unfold. He had made four bets on games that day, all of them based on the method that brought him five hundred thousand dollars going into the weekend. On this day, however, his method was an epic failure. Two of his bets were on morning games and they were a disaster. Both of the teams he felt most confident in winning had played miserably and were soundly beaten. He was reduced to praying for both of the afternoon games to come through for him so he could at least break even. Somehow, in an incredible stroke of bad luck, both of those teams played just as miserably as the morning teams. It was so unusual for all of these teams to play so badly on the same day, even the television commentators made mention of this fact. It did little to console Mr. Pike as he watched the final seconds tick away for the last game to be played. As the gun sounded after the final play, Mr. Pike threw his beer mug at the wall as hard as he could. The mug shattered into tiny pieces and left a large hole, with beer dripping from the edges. Every one of his picks had lost and had lost badly. His entire bet was gone. All of his months of hard work gone in a single day. And to add insult to injury, two hundred thousand dollars of the five hundred thousand was from credit the bookies extended to him. He would have to repay those funds.

Mr. Pike felt his chest tighten and his breaths grow short as he paced the living room. Two hundred thousand dollars. He did not have that kind of money just sitting around, and he couldn't imagine the bookie would let him pay it back in installments. On a teacher's salary, that would probably take him at least twenty years. Mr. Pike didn't think the bookies would want to wait twenty years to get paid. He needed to think of a way to come up with the money. And he was going to have to come up with it right away.

Stewart had never been as miserable in a class as he was in math on Monday morning. He already had to deal with making excuses to his mom as to why Alex and Annie would no longer be riding with them to school and now he had to sit directly behind the very person who had shattered his world beyond repair. Stewart tried not to think of the countless hours he had spent dreaming about Sofie, as well as a recent class when he had spent the entire period envisioning his wedding ceremony with her, which of course, would have had to wait until at least after high school. All of his friends would have been in the wedding and the wedding cake would not be a traditional cake. It would be layers of his mother's cinnamon rolls, something he thought should already be common practice at all weddings. He sadly acknowledged that his image of the perfect wedding was condemned to the recycle bin of broken dreams.

To make matters worse, he was surrounded by Alex, a partner in the crime, and his sister Annie, an innocent victim of this debacle. Before class, Stewart tried to talk to the twins and

Dino, who all coldly told him sending thoughts to Sofie to affect how she felt about Alex was the most uncool thing someone could do to a friend and walked away from him. Feeling like the world was against him, Stewart's mind battled one dark thought after another. It was extremely difficult to pay attention to Mr. Leiker, whose voice sounded like a muffled trumpet the entire time he was in class.

Mr. Pike ignored his cell phone as it rang. He spent the morning avoiding the phone, knowing the calls were coming from his bookie. Turning it off would be the best course of action for now so he wouldn't have to feel his heart racing every time it rang. He needed more time to come up with a plan, something he wasn't able to do yesterday. He tossed and turned all night with his thoughts racing from one crazy idea to another. One thought that went through his mind was to leave the country. Mr. Pike had read about men who had fleeced people in investment schemes and fled the country, though they always seemed to get caught. Besides, where would he go? He had never been out of the country and had no idea where he would be able to start a new life and not get caught. Living a life where he would be constantly looking over his shoulder did not seem like a good idea to him.

Stewart entered the cafeteria by himself and was met with a strange sight. Alex and Annie sat by themselves at a far corner of the room and Sofie and her friends were at a different table at the opposite corner of the room. The POP Sisters, who had returned to school near the end of last week, also sat at a different table and ate quietly without their typical constant chatter revolving around making fun of other students. Dino and the twins sat in their usual seats and avoided eye contact with Stewart when he sat down with them. None of them said a word during the entire meal. In fact, it seemed to Stewart that hardly anyone in the entire cafeteria said much of anything during the lunch period. It had to be a coincidence. Whatever it was, it made Stewart feel like he was eating lunch inside a tomb. When Dino and the twins finished their meals, they abruptly left the table without saying a word to Stewart and walked out of the cafeteria, leaving Stewart alone to finish his lunch.

- - - -

Nora entered the office with her picnic basket just as Bernie stepped away from her desk.

"Hi Bernie," said Nora cheerfully. "Going to lunch?"

"I am," she replied.

Nora nodded her head in the direction of Byron's office. "Is everything going…okay?" asked Nora hopefully.

Bernie smiled. "So far, so good," she said, making her way to the door. "He isn't wearing an orange suit." Both of them laughed politely as Bernie left the office.

Nora took a deep breath before walking into Byron's office. Upon hearing her enter, Byron, seated at his desk, looked up from his work. Nora set the basket on the coffee table, walked over to the desk and faced Byron. She softly cleared her throat and looked at him with as much determination as she could muster.

"I want to talk to you about the apartment," she said, suddenly feeling like her confidence was leaving her body like the outgoing tide of the Pacific Ocean.

Byron leaned back in his chair. "Okay."

"I think," said Nora, stopping herself. She cleared her throat one more time, and deciding she had nothing to lose, looked squarely at Byron. "I think," she continued, "that getting an apartment is a bad idea and will not be good for our family. I don't agree with this decision. I would rather sell everything we own and live in an apartment and take the bus if it meant you working less and spending more time with Stewart and me."

Byron considered her comments for a few moments and looked up at her with a new appreciation, proud of how she would fight to keep her family together. Byron stood up from his desk and went over to her. Putting his arms around her, he gave her a passionate kiss. Nora's face felt flushed as he pulled back from her.

"You are so right. I couldn't agree with you more." Byron kissed her again.

"Would you mind if we changed plans?" asked Byron.

"What do you mean?" replied Nora, suddenly fearful that Byron was about to embark on another episode of lunacy.

"I know you went through a lot of trouble to make our lunch today, but would it be okay if we went to a restaurant? A very nice restaurant. And a movie afterwards. I'll take the rest of the day off."

Nora stared at Byron. For Byron to say he was taking the afternoon off was a sentence she was positive she had never heard him utter before in all of their years together. Had she heard him correctly? Perhaps he had actually just spoken Chinese to her? She also couldn't remember the last time they went to a movie together. It had to be a few years. After a moment of collecting her wits, she squeezed him in a big hug. "Yes! Yes! Yes!" shouted Nora.

With his chin resting on his hands, Stewart sat in his room and stared at his monitor. He had been in this position since returning home from school on the bus. During the lunch hour, he received a text from his mother saying she was with his dad and wouldn't be home until later. Getting a ride home with Alex and Annie was out of the question, so he took the bus home, something he hadn't done since that fateful afternoon when Raymond jumped him. Though he had transmitted thoughts to Raymond to stay away from him, he felt extremely nervous as he stepped onto the bus and checked every seat to make sure Raymond wasn't on board before he sat down.

Entering his empty house, Stewart realized how lonely the day had been and let it sink in. The only thing he could think of doing was to go to his computer and find something to improve his spirits. After sitting at his desk for an hour, all he had managed to do was make himself feel worse, thinking of one negative thought after another. Was this how it was going to be the rest of his life? No thanks, just a few days were enough of the silent treatment. Stewart turned on his machine and, pulling up the VAC program, keyed in Sofie's name. Closing his eyes, he concentrated on correcting a major mistake.

Mr. Pike pulled his truck into the parking lot of his apartment building and turned off the engine. Instead of getting out, he leaned back and thought about his predicament with the bookie.

Lost in thought, he flinched when he heard a knock on the window next to him. Startled, he turned his head to the sound, only to look into the chest of an extremely massive person. The man outside of the driver's window bent down so Mr. Pike could see his menacing face and motioned for him to step out of the vehicle. He quickly looked across his seat to the other window and could only see the chest of another extremely large person. With nowhere to go, he climbed out and found himself looking up at a man that was a good eight inches taller than him and at least one hundred and fifty pounds heavier. The fellow on the other side of the truck walked over to them and was the same size as the first person. In all of his years of playing college football, he hadn't seen any player close to the size of one of these men, let alone two of them. He realized his best move would be to cooperate with these giants.

"Come with us," said the first man in a deep, rumbling voice. Flanked on both sides by these behemoths, Mr. Pike walked with them towards a black luxury sedan with dark tinted windows parked across the street. The first man opened the back door and motioned for him to get inside the car. His mind raced frantically, wondering what was going to happen to him. Would they take him to a deserted part of town and beat him senseless? Or worse?

The first man closed the door behind Mr. Pike as he climbed into the back seat of the luxury sedan. He found himself looking at someone he had never seen before. Definitely a no-nonsense type of guy, he observed. The person facing him was Bruno Russo, Angelo Moretti's right-hand business associate.

"You haven't been returning our calls," stated Bruno flatly.

"My phone's dead. Sorry," said Mr. Pike apologetically.

"Is that so?" said Bruno. "Give me your phone." Mr. Pike's stomach tightened as he handed his phone to Bruno. Pushing a button to illuminate the screen, Bruno saw that his phone was fully charged. "Seems to be working just fine," observed Bruno as he handed the phone back to him. Bruno said nothing as he watched Mr. Pike grow increasingly uncomfortable.

"You owe my boss a lot of money."

Mr. Pike nodded his head. "I know."

"He is going to want that money."

"I'll pay it back. I just have to work it out." Mr. Pike could feel perspiration gathering on the back of his neck. Bruno's eyes seemed like two lasers boring holes in his head.

"You're going to have to work it out soon."

"I will," said Mr. Pike with a tone of determination that he hoped would convince Bruno he was going to make good on his debt.

"Good. You have twenty-four hours."

Mr. Pike looked at Bruno in complete shock. Twenty-four hours? Where was he going to get that kind of money in twenty-four hours? Deadly serious, Bruno's expression remained unchanged.

Bruno tapped on the window and the first large man opened the door and motioned for Mr. Pike to get out of the car. Mr. Pike, his mind in a fog, managed to step out of the car with his legs feeling like they were made out of rubber. He walked to his apartment, with Bruno's words of "twenty-four hours" echoing in his head.

Stewart peered at his French dictionary and, finding the word he was looking for, continued writing a letter. He stopped and reviewed what he had just written. Frowning, he drew a line through a few words and resumed writing. Finishing the letter, Stewart read his rough-draft, and satisfied, tore another page out of his spiral notebook and began to carefully copy the letter onto the new page in his best handwriting.

As Stewart copied the last words of the letter, he heard his parents enter the house. Signing his name with a flourish that belonged on the Declaration of Independence, Stewart folded the letter, stuffed it into an envelope, and ran out of his bedroom.

Bounding down the stairs, Stewart leaped past the last few steps, landed on both feet, and ran into the kitchen. Nora and Byron greeted Stewart with the happiest expressions he had ever seen from them.

"Where have you been?" he asked them both.

"At the movies," answered Byron, and walked up to Stewart. He danced around him like a boxer, and, after a couple of fake punches, landed a soft jab to Stewart's chin.

"Didn't know I had a few moves, did you?" asked Byron as he threw a few more jabs. "Do you want to do something right now?"

"Dinner won't be ready for at least an hour," volunteered Nora.

Stewart's face broke into a smile. "Can you take me to the mall?"

"Absolutely! Let's go!" said Byron, putting an arm around Stewart's shoulder and steering him towards the garage door. He stopped to kiss Nora goodbye.

Reaching the car, Stewart jumped in and fastened his seatbelt. His cell phone sounded the arrival of a text message, so he quickly pulled the phone out of his pocket and checked the message. It was from Alex and read: *Just talked to Sofie. She sounds normal. Good job.*

Stewart felt a terrific sense of relief. His miserable day was getting better and better. Now he had just one more mission to accomplish.

Driving down the street, Byron told Stewart about the movie he and Nora had seen that afternoon. Halfway to the mall, Stewart abruptly pointed to a store.

"There! Go to that store!"

Byron slammed his breaks and shot diagonally across the lanes, narrowly missing traffic. He pulled into the parking lot of a flower store.

"I thought we were going to the mall," said Byron.

"We are, but I need to get something first."

Confused, Byron squinted at the store. "Flowers?"

"Dad," said Stewart confidently, "I'm going to show you how to treat a lady."

Stewart and his dad walked through the crowded mall. Passing the various stores and kiosks, they came upon the Bathroom and Kitchen Palace.

"Why are we here?" asked Byron.

"Dad, women like scented soap. Soap that smells like lilacs. Don't ask me why." Byron shrugged his shoulders and followed his son into the store.

Byron eased the car to a stop in the garage. He reached over to Stewart, who was holding two bouquets of red roses, and took one of the bouquets. Stewart handed him a gift-wrapped box, then stepped out of the car. He, too, was holding a bouquet and nicely wrapped box. They entered the house, and Byron went directly to Nora, handing her the flowers and gift. She put her hands to her face in amazement.

"They're lovely!" she exclaimed, as she admired the roses. "I'll have to find a vase for them. They're so pretty! Thank you!" She hugged Byron and gave him a kiss.

Stewart ran up the stairs and into his room. He picked up the envelope with the letter he had written earlier and ran down the stairs. Walking quickly, he left his house and made his way across the street. He approached the McKnight's front door and rang the doorbell.

Alison opened the door and her face brightened as she saw Stewart holding flowers.

"These are for Annie," said Stewart, handing Alison the flowers.

"They're beautiful!" Alison exclaimed.

Stewart handed her the gift-wrapped box and envelope. "These are also for Annie."

"I'll make sure she gets this right away," Alison assured him.

"Thank you." Stewart walked away, hoping Annie would appreciate his gesture. It was the least he could do.

Though Annie heard Stewart from upstairs, she was reluctant to see him at the door. As soon as Stewart left, she skipped down the stairs. Alison handed Annie the flowers.

"Aren't they beautiful?" asked Alison.

"They are!" beamed Annie as she leaned in to smell their wonderful fragrance.

Alison reached for the flowers. "Here, I'll find something to put them in, and these are for you, too." Alison held the box and envelope out to Annie, who took them, and ran to her bedroom. Upon entering, she immediately unwrapped the box, took out the soap, and held it to her nose, sniffing the essence of the pleasant lilac. Placing the box on her desk, she sat on her bed and opened the envelope. Her hands trembled slightly as she unfolded the letter. She admired Stewart's careful penmanship and the fact it was written in French, before reading softly to herself: *Dear Annie, I want to tell you how sorry I am that I got sick and ruined the dance for you. You were so beautiful and deserved to have a great time. You could have picked anyone to go to the dance with you and I am honored you picked me. I would like to go to the next dance with you if you are willing. If my mom and I go to Paris again, I would like for you to come with us. Stewart*

Annie sprang to her feet and ran out of her room.

Holding a plate with a thick slice of apple pie and a large scoop of ice cream, Stewart walked out of the kitchen and was about to head to his bedroom when the doorbell rang. He walked over to the door, peeked through the window, and saw Annie. Setting down his plate on a nearby table, he answered the door.

"Hi, Annie," said Stewart. Annie stepped forward, pulled his face towards her, and planted a kiss on his lips. She stepped back, covered her mouth with her hand, shocked by her own boldness, turned, and ran down the driveway. Stewart watched Annie run to her house, with a huge, silly grin plastered across his face.

Carl and his friends gathered at his house for the weekly professional football game. The men loudly discussed that night's upcoming game as they drank vast amounts of beer and devoured buckets of chicken wings. Carl held court in the middle of the room and chastised those foolish enough to disagree with his ideas about which team would win the game that evening.

Opening the front door, Raymond made his way into the crowded house. Why did everyone always have to watch the game at their house? It was fun at first, but after a while, he became tired of the mess they made with beer bottles and food strewn all over the house and how his dad made him clean up after them. As Raymond looked at his dad, a strange feeling came over him. He walked to the television, turned down the sound and clapped his hands to get everyone's attention.

"Before the game starts, I want to recite this old English nursery rhyme for all of you," he announced. The men looked at each other with puzzled expressions, and then at Carl, who was as puzzled as they were.

"Diddle, diddle, dumpling, my son John, went to bed with his trousers on; one shoe off,

and one shoe on, diddle, diddle, dumpling, my son John!" Raymond clapped and jumped up and down like he was on a pogo stick after he finished reciting the nursery rhyme.

"It reminds me of my dad after he gets drunk every night! Passing out with his clothes on! Huh, dad?"

Carl's eyes filled with rage as the men broke out laughing. Carl grabbed Raymond by his neck and jerked him down the hall into his bedroom. Carl closed the door, took a step towards Raymond, and slapped him forcefully across the face. Raymond flew backwards and landed on the floor against the wall. Foaming at the mouth, Carl leaned over him.

"Don't you EVER embarrass me like that again!"

Carl stormed out of the room. Woozy, Raymond remained on the floor and slowly moved his jaw, wondering if it had been dislocated. He crawled across the room and pulled himself onto his bed, trying to ignore the nonstop ringing in his left ear from the blow to his head.

17

ACTIONS AND CONSEQUENCES

IT WAS UNBELIEVABLE HOW much could change in one day, thought Stewart, taking his seat in math class the next morning. The day began when he got a text from Alex asking him to come to his house for a ride to school. With his leg in a cast, Alex sat in the front seat for the extra leg room, leaving Stewart sitting in the back seat with Annie. The new and improved Annie. Stewart was amazed at how she managed to upgrade her wardrobe overnight. Gone were the frumpy sweater, skirt, beret, and glasses. Annie looked like a young fashion model, wearing trendy jeans and a cute shirt. She wore just enough makeup to accent her beautiful blue eyes, though Stewart noticed she continued to blink a little more than normal, while still getting used to her contacts. From the corner of his eye,

Stewart could see her glancing at him adoringly the entire way to school and hoped his blushing wasn't too noticeable.

Stewart watched with mild interest as Sofie took her seat in class. After analyzing his feelings for her, he realized he couldn't force Sofie to be attracted to him, just as he couldn't be forced to be attracted to another person. The attraction is either there or it's not, and if not, accept it, and move on to another person. And for him, that other person was Annie. He turned to Annie, smiled at her, and watched her face break into a gorgeous smile, making him feel nice and warm all over. What a great feeling.

Stewart waited in line as Mr. Pike began taking roll.

"Arnett."

"Here," said Arnett.

Mr. Pike looked up from his clipboard and noticed Raymond was not in class. Stewart hadn't seen him all day, thankfully, which meant a reprieve from the routine elbow to the ribs.

"Burns, absent," said Mr. Pike as he checked the absent box for Burns on his clipboard.

"Camby."

"Here," replied Stewart, as Mr. Pike passed by. Stewart actually looked forward to basketball that day. Without Raymond around to terrorize the class, Stewart thought it was going to be fun for all of them.

The boys filed into the locker room, dripping with sweat after an intense period of basketball. Stewart's team continued to be beaten soundly by every other team in the class, as they sorely needed Alex, though he didn't mind. Winning didn't matter to him, he just wanted to avoid making mistakes, and the few times he actually touched the ball, he made good passes to his teammates. He thought if he kept it up, he was going to be a force to be reckoned with some day.

Stopping at his locker, Stewart dialed the combination and opened the door. He sat down to take his shoes off when he noticed something was amiss and jumped back to his feet. Panicking, he pushed his clothing aside in the tiny locker and stopped, frozen. His backpack was missing. The voice inside his head screamed "*How could this be?*"

Stewart ran over to Mr. Pike's office. Sitting at his desk, Mr. Pike looked up at Stewart as he entered.

"Mr. Pike, I think somebody took my backpack!"

"Are you sure?" asked Mr. Pike.

"Yes, I'm sure. I had it when I came to class and now it's not in my locker."

"Let's have a look," said Mr. Pike as he stepped out from behind his desk and followed Stewart to his locker.

"See? It's not there," fumed Stewart.

"Are you sure the door was closed before you opened it?" asked Mr. Pike.

"Yes, it was closed," said Stewart adamantly.

Mr. Pike thought for a moment. "I don't see how it could be missing. Maybe you should check the lost and found in the office."

Stewart felt the blood pumping harder in his temples. "I'm sure I put it in the locker before class."

Mr. Pike shook his head sympathetically. "It should turn up. Who would want a backpack?" He turned and headed for his office. Stewart stared at his locker. This is a disaster, he thought. The machine was in the backpack.

Stewart sat glumly with his friends as they ate lunch. He told them of the missing backpack as soon as he left the gym and had already made three futile trips to the office, asking if anyone had turned it in to the lost and found.

"So, if you know you put your backpack in the locker, and it's not there at the end of class, it can only mean ONE thing. Mr. Pike TOOK it," said Dino, ace private investigator, in between bites.

"I thought of that, but it doesn't make sense. Why would he take it?" moaned Stewart.

"Maybe he knows about the machine," suggested Ethan.

"How could he know about it?" asked Stewart.

"Maybe he saw you use it on someone," said Nathan.

"Quiet, here comes Annie," warned Dino as Annie made her way over to the table. The boys stopped talking about the machine and continued eating while Stewart looked sadly at his food.

Inside his office, Mr. Pike locked his door and closed the blinds to the window. He opened a file cabinet, took out Stewart's backpack and placed it on his desk. He removed the laptop and container. He looked at the attached battery pack and power setting device. Holding the machine next to his ear, he shook it vigorously to see if he could hear anything rattling.

Placing it on his desk, he tried to remove the lid and saw that it was screwed in place. He opened a desk drawer, took out a screwdriver and loosened the screws. Removing the lid and gasket, he peered into the container and recoiled in horror. What was that? It looked like a brain! Why would there be a brain hooked up to all of these gadgets? How could this be a device Camby used to make Ms. Robitaille twirl around in the parking lot? If he hadn't seen it with his own eyes, he wouldn't give this gizmo another thought, but he knew what he saw, and that was Camby fiddling with this device and typing something into his laptop.

Mr. Pike set the container aside and opened the laptop. He pushed the power button and waited for the computer to come to life. As soon as it warmed up, a box for a password appeared. Mr. Pike let out a loud groan. He wasn't going to be able to figure this out and glancing at a clock on the wall, he was running out of time. There was less than four hours remaining before the goons would be coming for their money. If this machine could do what he believed it could do, he knew it would be worth a fortune, and his gambling debts would completely go away. He was going to have to figure out how this device worked so he could prove its value to the bookie.

Stewart's head suddenly felt like it was going to explode as a surge of activity flashed across his brain. Sentences, words, thoughts raced through his mind like a pack of wild dogs running through the forest. It felt like a crowd of people shouting to him at the same time. He put his hands to his head and closed his eyes.

"Is something wrong?" asked Ethan with a mouthful of food.

"I...don't...know," replied Stewart He tried to think of a simple thought, hoping it would calm his mind. Soon, his thoughts became sentences that he could understand, though they were still flashing quickly, one after another. He thought he heard Nathan say "Now what's wrong with him?" When he quickly looked over at Nathan, he saw Nathan chewing a mouthful of food. He looked at Ethan, who was also eating. How could they speak if they were both eating?

Stewart thought he heard Dino say "This gyro sandwich is great. If mom was the cook at this school, everybody would buy lunch." Stewart quickly turned his head to look at Dino, who was also quietly eating. What was going on here? Stewart thought about this for a moment, and it occurred to him what was happening. He was reading their minds. How was this possible? Until now, he was only able to send thoughts. Something must have happened to the brain. He was going to have to find it before it was too late.

Raymond, almost comatose, lay still on top of his bed, wearing the same clothing as the day before. His eyes were open, but he was not seeing anything before him, his mind in another place. The left side of his face was swollen, his jaw ached whenever he opened his mouth, and his ear would not stop ringing. He hadn't slept that night as he thought about his life and how miserable it was. There was no way he was going to school that day. He found himself thinking of the day his mom left five years ago without telling anyone she was leaving or saying goodbye. How could she leave like that? Was she sick of Carl? He could understand that. Was she sick of him? Why would she be sick of him? Maybe she was sick of both of them. No matter what, everything seemed to go downhill after she left. Carl drank more and more. The house started falling apart. Carl constantly changed jobs, hating all of them, and nothing could make him happy. For years, he had directed his anger at Raymond.

The more Raymond thought of his situation, the worse he felt. He could feel a pain in his heart as if someone was standing on his chest. His throat began to swell, making it difficult to swallow, and tears collected in his eyes.

Carl's slap to the face was the last straw. Raymond sat up, swung his feet to the floor, and walked to the kitchen. He rummaged through a pile of trash on the counter, and unable to find a piece of paper, picked up a pen and an empty envelope. On the envelope he wrote:

YOU ARE THE WORST DAD EVER. I HATE YOU!!! I'M JUMPING OFF THE RADIO TOWER ON BEAR MOUNTAIN.

His eyes had a look of cold determination while he set down the pen and headed for the front door. He threw the door open, and, not bothering to close it, walked out of the house and jumped on his bicycle. Without looking back, Raymond pedaled quickly away from the house.

The last bell of the school day rang and the students filed out of their classrooms. Stewart and the rest of the Four Musketeers walked out of French class and joined the rest of the students in the crowded hallway, heading for the front doors of the school.

Just as Stewart reached the front door, he felt a hand on his shoulder, and looked back to see Mr. Pike.

"I might have found your backpack. I'll need you to come to my office to see if it's yours."

A bolt of joy shot through Stewart's body. "That's great, thank you!" said Stewart, greatly relieved. He followed Mr. Pike down the stairs to the gym. Stewart was sure it was going to be his backpack. How many of them could be lost in the locker room in one day? He was trying to figure out the best way to thank Mr. Pike as they entered his office.

"Sit down," said Mr. Pike gruffly, as he shut the door and clicked the lock.

Puzzled at Mr. Pike's sudden change in demeanor, Stewart sat in the chair next to the desk. Mr. Pike opened the bottom drawer of his file cabinet and took out the backpack.

"That's it!" shouted Stewart, leaping to his feet as if he had just won the lottery.

"Sit down!" ordered Mr. Pike. Stewart recoiled at the sharp tone in Mr. Pike's voice and sat back in the chair.

Mr. Pike dumped the laptop and container on his desk. "Tell me how this thing works," he snarled at Stewart.

Stewart looked up at Mr. Pike, trying to understand what was happening. He told Mr. Pike it was his backpack. Why was he asking him to show how the machine worked?

"I said show me how it works!" demanded Mr. Pike, trying to not sound desperate.

"I don't know what you mean," stammered Stewart, shaken by Mr. Pike's temper.

"SHOW ME HOW IT WORKS!" yelled Mr. Pike at the top of his lungs and pounding the desk with his fist. Stewart cringed at this outburst. "I know what you do with this...this gizmo! You can make people do crazy things! I want to know how it works!" shouted Mr. Pike, the veins in his forehead and neck ready to burst.

Frightened, Stewart flinched back in his seat, having never seen Mr. Pike this crazed. He slowly moved forward and reluctantly opened his laptop. After pushing the power button, he flipped the switch on the battery connected to the container.

"Don't try anything stupid!" said Mr. Pike as he hovered over Stewart's shoulder. Stewart tried to keep his hands from shaking as he typed on the keyboard. The VAC program came up and Stewart took a deep breath. He pulled up Mr. Pike's name from his database.

"What's my name doing there?" Mr. Pike asked accusingly.

"Everybody in the school is on the list," said Stewart, quickly selecting Mr. Pike's name. He closed his eyes to concentrate.

Mr. Pike bent over and grabbed his stomach.

"What the…" said Mr. Pike, grimacing as he clutched his stomach. "I told you not to do anything stupid!" Mr. Pike bent over and gasped for air. "Make…this…stop!" wheezed Mr. Pike. Stewart concentrated as much as he could. Suddenly, Mr. Pike lunged at Stewart and grabbed him by the collar.

"Make it stop!" hissed Mr. Pike through clenched teeth. Hunched in fear, Stewart tightly squeezed his eyes. Mr. Pike looked at his hand clutching Stewart's shirt and began to moan. He dropped to his knees, his hand shaking violently. Fighting the pain in his hand and stomach was finally too much for Mr. Pike. He struggled to his feet and with both hands clutching his stomach, leaned over the desk, his face inches from Stewart's.

"Don't go anywhere! Don't leave this office! You understand me?!" wheezing, Mr. Pike staggered to the restroom, dropped to his knees and began vomiting.

Stewart quickly stuffed the laptop and container into his backpack and ran out of the office as fast as he had ever run in his life.

Bounding up the steps, Stewart reached the main floor of the school and headed for the front doors. Bursting through the doors, Stewart ran to the pick-up zone, where he found his parents waiting in the car. Though he was running and panicking, he found himself thinking that this must be the first time his dad had ever picked him up from school. He decided he was going to have to reflect on this milestone event later and dove into the back seat, where Annie and Nora were seated.

"We've got to go!" Stewart yelled to his dad, who was behind the wheel. Alex turned from the passenger seat, wondering what was going on.

"Honey, what's the matter?" asked Nora.

"Go, please!" pleaded Stewart fearfully.

"Okay," said Byron, pulling away from the curb, "But you're going to have to tell us what is going on with you."

A sharp pain shot across Stewart's forehead. He pushed his fingers against both sides of his head.

Nora put her hand on Stewart's shoulder. "Honey, please tell us what is wrong. Do we need to go to the doctor?"

His head pounding, Stewart clenched his teeth.

"I don't need to go to the doctor. We have to go to Bear Mountain right now! As fast as you can!"

Byron looked back at Nora, confused along with everyone else in the car.

"Dad, please! Someone is going to kill themselves if we don't get there!"

"Shouldn't we call the police?" asked Nora, her face filled with concern.

"We don't have time! Drive as fast as you can!" shouted Stewart, nearing tears.

Byron drove away, just as Mr. Pike ran out of the school. He looked towards the parking lot and then the street, where he saw Stewart in the car. Mr. Pike ran to his truck, jumped in, gunned his engine, and sped off after them.

Byron drove quickly through the streets near the school and turned west onto Lakewood Boulevard, which would take them directly to Bear Mountain, an extremely large hill near the base of the mountains.

"Faster!" Stewart pleaded.

"I'm two miles over the speed limit!" replied Byron.

"The speed limit doesn't matter, dad! It's life or death!"

Realizing Stewart was right, Byron stepped on the gas. The acceleration threw everyone's heads back and the car flew down the street.

Mr. Pike saw Byron turn onto Lakewood Boulevard and continued to follow him. Surprised at the acceleration of Byron's car, Mr. Pike floored the gas pedal, trying to catch up to them.

Byron reached Bear Mountain and Stewart pointed to the radio tower at the top of this large hill.

"We need to get to the top."

"I can't drive up there," said Byron.

"Yes, you can," Stewart replied, pointing further down the street. "There's a road over there that goes to the top. I've taken it on my bike."

Byron headed down the street and stopped at the entrance to a rarely used utility road that was poorly maintained. He looked at a sign which read: *No motor vehicles allowed.* Byron hesitated for a second, then drove over the curb and began climbing the hill.

Mr. Pike closed the gap on them and smiled while Byron drove up the utility road. He reached the entrance and shifted into four-wheel drive. There's no way they can get away from me now, he thought.

Byron kept up a good pace despite driving over large bumps, potholes, and sharp hairpin curves. Unfortunately, Mr. Pike's truck was built for this kind of terrain and he kept gaining on them.

"Go to the radio tower!" ordered Stewart as they reached the top of the large hill. They sped to the tower and Byron slammed on the brakes. Stewart was the first one out of the car and the others climbed out after him.

Still wearing his backpack, Stewart reached the base of the tower and looking upwards, saw Raymond climbing the rungs attached to the structure. Without hesitating, Stewart climbed over the chain link fence surrounding the tower. He ran to the metal ladder and climbed up the rungs like he had never climbed before.

"Stewart Lewis Camby! What are you doing?" shrieked Nora.

Mr. Pike's truck spun to a stop in a cloud of dust. He stumbled out of his truck and ran to the radio tower.

"Don't let him up here!" shouted Stewart.

Byron ran to the tower, right behind Mr. Pike. As Mr. Pike reached the chain link fence, he was shoved aside by Byron. Startled, Mr. Pike regained his balance, turned, picked up Byron, and threw him against the fence. Mr. Pike reached for the fence and as he began to climb, Byron lunged at him and grabbed his leg.

Mr. Pike shook his leg as hard as he could while Byron held on with all of his strength. Mr. Pike dropped to the ground and grabbing Byron by the neck, lifted him off of the ground. Just as he pulled his fist back to punch Byron in the face, Mr. Pike's eyes rolled back and he sunk to the ground. Standing behind him was Nora, holding a rock the size of a softball she used to thump him on the back of the head. She dropped the rock and stepped backwards and put her hands to her face in complete shock. Byron ran over and wrapped his arms around her. Together, they looked up at Stewart, who continued to climb up the ladder.

Frantically climbing after Raymond, Stewart paused for a second and realized his arms and legs were quickly getting tired. He made the mistake of looking down and, seeing how high he was, began to hyperventilate. Stewart closed his eyes and focused on slowing down his breathing. He took a few deep breaths and, ignoring the fatigue in his arms, resumed climbing.

Nearing the top, he came upon Raymond, his eyes red from crying.

"What's everybody doing here?" Raymond asked, pointing to Stewart and everyone below on the ground.

"I have to talk to you," replied Stewart as calmly as he could.

"Go back," said Raymond, turning his head away. "I don't want to talk to anybody."

"I need to talk to you," Stewart insisted.

"I don't want to talk to anybody! This is my problem!" bellowed Raymond.

"It's not just your problem. I'm the reason you're up here," explained Stewart.

Raymond shook his head. "No, you're not. I'm the biggest loser in the world. Everyone hates me. I've done a lot of bad things. I've done a lot of bad things to you."

Holding onto a rung with only one hand, Raymond leaned as far forward as possible. Stewart's hands instantly felt sweaty as he watched Raymond tempt fate.

"Don't do that!" yelled Stewart. Surprised by Stewart's reaction, Raymond pulled himself back against the tower and looked down at him.

Raymond's eyes filled with tears. "I'm sorry I mistreated you. I mean it. Forgive me."

Thunderstruck, Stewart's mouth hung open from hearing words he thought he would never hear Raymond utter in a thousand lifetimes.

Stewart cleared his throat. "I'll forgive you if you forgive me."

"What are you talking about?" asked Raymond.

"You know those weird thoughts you've been having at school?" asked Stewart.

Raymond stared at Stewart in disbelief. "How do you know?" he cautiously responded.

"I invented a machine that sends thoughts to people and I put those thoughts in your head. I've been telling you to do all of those crazy things because you've made my life miserable from the first day of middle school and I wanted to get back at you. I've hated you more than anything. I wanted awful things to happen to you. It's all my fault." A flood of tears rushed down Stewart's cheeks as he made this admission to Raymond. He had never envisioned that using the machine could cause a person to have such dangerous thoughts and the feeling of being responsible for Raymond's predicament caused a searing pain throughout his head.

Raymond wiped his eyes with the back of his hand. "I deserve it. I'm a failure, just like my dad."

Stewart pulled the container out of his backpack and showed it to Raymond. "This is the machine I invented. It's done more harm than good." He looked at it one last time before throwing it as far as he could. The boys watched it plummet to the earth. Upon hitting the ground, the container burst open and the brain splattered everywhere.

After a moment, Raymond looked at Stewart.

"Do me a favor and go back down, will you?"

"No," said Stewart firmly. "I'm not going down without you."

"What's the point? Nothing matters." murmured Raymond. "Just...go." Raymond leaned forward from his perch. Stewart reached over and grabbed Raymond by the ankle.

Raymond looked down at Stewart. "What are you doing?"

"I'm not letting you jump." Stewart tightened his grip.

"Let go," Raymond ordered.

"No. I won't." Stewart tightened his grip further.

Raymond shook his leg vigorously in an attempt to free his ankle from Stewart's grasp. Stewart squeezed Raymond's ankle as tightly as he could. Raymond shook his leg again and managed to yank his ankle out of Stewart's grip. The force of Raymond shaking his leg spun Stewart sideways, whose feet slipped off of the rung, leaving him, clinging for dear life with one hand. The momentum from freeing his leg also caused Raymond's feet to slide off the rung as well, though he was able to hold on with both hands. Feeling a tinge of panic he hadn't expected, Raymond pulled his feet back onto the ladder.

Stewart felt his grip quickly weakening and looked up at Raymond.

"Help me," he muttered softly.

Horrified, Raymond squatted as low as he could and reached out for Stewart's free hand.

"Take my hand!" begged Raymond. He leaned forward, trying to catch Stewart's hand as he thrust it upwards.

"I…can't hold on…," gasped Stewart.

As his hand on the rung began to open, Raymond leaned as far as he could and grasped Stewart's free hand. With all of his strength, Raymond pulled Stewart upward so that he was able to put both feet and hands on the rungs. Stewart pulled himself as close to the tower as possible and closed his eyes, grateful to be alive.

Catching his breath, Raymond leaned back and looked towards the horizon.

"It's best if I get it over with. Please. Go away."

His eyes narrowing with unrelenting determination, Stewart looked up at Raymond. "I'm not going anywhere."

The boys remained in the same position for what seemed like an eternity to Stewart. He realized he was running out of time to persuade Raymond to climb down, as his hands and feet were turning numb. Struggling, Stewart pulled himself up a couple of rungs to get as close to Raymond as possible.

"Raymond, would it help if you could just start over? Hit the reset button in your life? Would that make a difference?"

"I don't know," Raymond replied slowly. "Maybe. I guess so."

"Okay," said Stewart. "The first thing you can do is stop being a jerk to everyone at school. Be nice to them and they'll be nice to you. You'll have a lot more friends. Good friends. You just have to try."

Raymond turned his head slowly from side to side, as if he had already received a life sentence. "What's the point of trying? Nothing matters."

"Everything matters!" said Stewart emphatically. "Every moment matters. You've just got to try. You can't give up. Your life can be great if you just try your best. And, you don't have to do this alone. I can help if you want me to."

Raymond looked down at Stewart, who had the most genuine and sincere expression he had ever seen. No one had ever said such encouraging words to him. Maybe Stewart was right. Maybe his life could get better. Maybe it was worth trying. He looked out over the city as he pondered Stewart's suggestions. Maybe there was hope for him. It wouldn't hurt to try. He took a deep breath and slowly exhaled, feeling like the weight of the world was lifting from his shoulders.

"All right, let's get out of here." Raymond looked at Stewart. "I can't believe you made it up this tower."

"I can't either," replied Stewart.

The boys slowly made their way downward. As they neared the bottom, Carl appeared on the crest of the hill on his motorcycle. He parked and walked over to the tower, keeping his distance from Stewart's family, Alex, and Annie. Carl noticed Mr. Pike, moaning on the ground, and wondered what was going on with him.

The boys reached the bottom and climbed over the chain link fence. Carl, clearly not in a good mood, marched up to Raymond and towered over him.

"What the hell do you think you're doing?" bellowed Carl.

"Get away from me! I told you I hate you!" screamed Raymond as he turned to run away from Carl. Carl took a few steps after him and grabbed his arm.

"Knock it off, you hear me?"

Raymond turned to Carl and stuck his face inches from Carl's face.

"I want you to hear ME!" said Raymond, his eyes burning brightly. "I'm not your punching bag. I'm not living with you anymore. I'll live on the street if I have to. You make me sick. You're a pathetic excuse for a dad." Raymond tore himself loose from Carl's grasp. Stunned, Carl watched Raymond storm away from him.

Running after Raymond, Carl grabbed his arm and spun him around. He pulled back his hand, ready to strike Raymond.

"Go ahead. Hit me," said Raymond without emotion. "That's your answer for everything."

Carl looked at Raymond, who simply stared into Carl's eyes. Carl slowly lowered his fist. He shook his head, looked up at the sky and struggled to find the right words.

"I'm sorry," he began.

"I don't believe you!" blurted Raymond.

Carl's face reddened at Raymond's outburst and rather than lash out at him, he took a deep breath and exhaled. "I am! Listen. I know how you feel."

"How can you know how I feel? You don't care about anybody," said Raymond, biting his words.

Carl's features softened and he looked sadly at Raymond. "This is how I felt about my dad," Carl began, his voice a hoarse whisper. "He used to knock me around all of the time. I hated his guts. I told myself I would do better than him. I didn't do better. I did worse. I'm sorry. I'm really sorry."

Raymond looked at his dad's face. For the first time, he saw genuine concern in Carl's eyes.

"We can't go on like this anymore, dad. Something's got to change."

Carl nodded. "I know. You're all I've got." Carl looked away from Raymond for a moment as he wiped his eyes. He put his arm around Raymond's shoulders and they walked away from the tower.

Mr. Pike opened his eyes and sat up, rubbing his head. He jumped to his feet and ran to Stewart.

"Where's the machine?" demanded Mr. Pike.

Stewart pointed at the debris lying on the ground around them. "Right there."

Mr. Pike looked at the pieces of the machine scattered around the base of the tower. His face grew tight in horror at the sight of the debris.

"I'm a dead man," mumbled Mr. Pike. With everyone watching, he ran to his truck and started the engine. Wheels spinning and dirt spraying everywhere, Mr. Pike sped down the road.

Raymond spotted Alex and ran over to him.

"I'm sorry I broke your leg," said Raymond, full of remorse.

Alex nodded. Raymond turned and jogged back to Carl. Annie ran over to Stewart and stopped, not sure what to do next. Stewart hugged her as tightly as he could and looked over to his parents.

"Can we go home now?" asked Stewart. "I'm hungry."

EPILOGUE

COUNTLESS STARS HANG SUSPENDED in the vast darkness of the universe. A lone comet streaks past the stars, making its way to an unknown destination. Planets move along their orbits, faithfully circling their suns.

An object appears across the horizon. As it approaches, the object becomes larger and larger until it is recognizable as a spaceship.

Inside the spaceship is a large window allowing for a spectacular view of the galaxy before them. Beings of a different sort inhabit the spaceship. They have human characteristics, though they are very pale, with pale skin, pale gray eyes, and white hair. Taller than earthlings, they also have broader shoulders and narrower waists.

One of the figures, the obvious commander of the spaceship, sits in a large chair facing the viewing window. A subordinate walks up to him.

"We received a very weak signal carrying a message."

"From where?" asked the commander, instantly focused upon hearing this information.

"Galaxy nineteen."

"Was the message deciphered?"

"Yes, from an unusual language. The translation is: 'This is Starhawk Ranger from Mother Earth. Does anyone read me?' " answered the subordinate.

The commander smiled. "We finally have our first sign of intelligent life. Prepare to change course. Let's find this Starhawk Ranger from Mother Earth."

About the Author

Skinny and fairly tall as a child, Richard was an ideal target for bullies. Unpleasant memories of being bullied inspired *Stewart's Incredible Machine*. Despite these difficult encounters, Richard did well in class and eventually had success as a basketball player on the school teams. Richard graduated from the University of Colorado and has spent his career working as a Certified Public Accountant where he lives in Lakewood, Colorado with his wife and two children.